Entry Label

Please <u>print or type.</u> Make as many copies of form as needed, one for each title submitted. Tape to the inside front cover of <u>each book submitted</u> or to the audio/video package.

LATIN AMERICAN CONSPIRACY
Title

39 BEST FIRST BOOK
Category (number and name)

SABRINA ZACKERY
Contact Person

DELTA PUBLISHING COMPANY
Company

316 CALIFORNIA AVE #134
Address

RENO NV 89509
City, State, Zip

(702) 828-9398
Telephone

Describe in 75 words or fewer (**printed or typed**) the book or tape and the audience for whom it was written or taped.

A SUMMARY OF *LATIN AMERICAN CONSPIRACY*
By John van Geldern

After 18 Latin American countries default $1 trillions of debt, much of the financial
community faces technical bacruptcy and a crisis of confidence. The threat of bank runs and
currency shortfalls leave government leaders searching for a solution.
John Garland's Global Computer Trading Company is already operating an international
computer system that could be expanded into a worldwide monetary system. Such a system of
computerized credits replacing currency would all but eliminate crime for profit and under-the-
table dealings. Those who profit from such transactions will go to any means to stop Garland and
system.

LATIN AMERICAN CONSPIRACY

By

John van Geldern

1994

DELTA PUBLISHING COMPANY

Delta Publishing Company
316 California Avenue, #134
Reno, Nevada 89509

Manufactured in the United States of America
First printing : May 1991

Library of Congress Catalog Card Number 91-71506

Van Geldern, John Bernard, 1926-
  Latin American Conspiracy :
  John Bernard Van Geldern.—
  p. cm.
  ISBN 0-9628923-0-0

  I. Title. Latin American Conspiracy

PS3572.A43   813.54
                                   QBI91-468
Manufactured in the United States of America
First printing : December 1994

987654321

First Edition

ACKNOWLEDGMENTS

There are always more people to whom an author is indebted than can ever be properly acknowledged but there are always those special people without whom one's writings might not have seen the light of day. The writing of this book was stimulated, edited, proofed and babied by these people.

My son Nick and his talented wife, Lew. My friend Larry Young, Betty Brenchly, Geoff and Candice Daigle, Frances Wright, Barbara Renick and finally, Jim Benesch and Shawn Patterson.

To these and the many others too numerous to list here, my deepest thanks for the synergy that helped fuel, correct and improve my story and my writing energy.

JvG

INTRODUCTION
A Word About Money

One of the most powerful instincts buried deeply in each living creature's genetic code is that of survival. The human has adopted many tools for his or her survival perhaps beginning with the club that afforded some protection and provided food.

In these modern times, the club, for the most part, has been replaced with *money*. It is perhaps the singular most important tool we have for survival. In today's world it is used for protection, to acquire shelter and clothing, attract a mate, provide food for the family and self, and provide security and pleasure. Therefore, this writer feels it must be better understood.

Aside from such conventional interpretations of *"money"* being a medium of exchange, the word *"money"* itself evokes powerful emotions and means different things to different people.

To some, *money* represents power, to others, pleasure. To still others, it represents escape and freedom from want. It also may represent security, buy privacy, bring loneliness, impose obligations and even cause pain. Because of the power it represents, *money*, its acquisition or the lack of it, dominates the larger part of every society's waking hours.

Money can be a very emotional thing. Its necessity for survival in a modern society is recognized by everyone yet its philosophical aspect is understood by almost no one. Its political importance is accepted in a love-hate relationship, but without it modern politics could not exist and political power over others would be all but impossible.

In recent history, "paper" money has been universally adopted by world economies and politics as an accepted medium of exchange. Though in and of themselves, the pieces of printed paper we call money have little real value (especially in countries of "runaway" inflation), the average person throughout the world automatically accepts the value printed thereon and is often prone to protect those little pieces of printed paper with their very lives when confronted with any attempt to forcibly relieve them of it.

And yet, it is only by mutual consent that paper money and evidence thereof has any value at all. Without recognition of its value by mutual consent, paper money has little or no intrinsic value other than as paper itself.

Modern day money takes on many forms besides its printed paper currency form and coin. It is also found in electronic wire transfers, magnetic disks and tapes, documents, letters of credit represented to be worth specific amounts of money, notes, bonds, shares of stock and numerous other paper documents represented to be worth specific amounts of "money."

Money, in almost every society, is evidence of wealth. Whether it be ten dollars or $10 million, wealth or equity value is always measured in terms of money.

The "real" or "intrinsic" value of paper money can only be maintained in a modern society when it is backed by precious metals of a given weight such as gold or silver. Such paper money is considered "hard currency" because the owner knows that he or she can always turn in that piece of paper for a specific amount of gold or silver at their pleasure. The United States went off the gold and silver certificate status or so-called hard currency base in 1976.

Thus it is through the use of money that political power has been accumulated, industrial empires built, hedonistic pleasures bought, wars fought and the warring countries peoples often enslaved.

In recent times, the misuse of wealth represented by money, has slowly denigrated paper currency to a point where confidence in all but so called "hard currencies" has eroded to a point that now threatens monetary systems throughout the world.

When accumulated wealth is invested in new ideas, inventions, factories, farms, fishing, mining, forestry products and services, it has always created new jobs, new income and more wealth.

In today's world, where investors buy so-called "junk" bonds in order that others may buy out existing companies, where the buyers sell off the assets in order to help pay off those "junk" bonds and where the side effect is to reduce such a company's size and employment capability, money's value is denigrated.

In countries where misuse and abuse of wealth and borrowed money have caused runaway inflation, printed currency or paper money loses its ability to maintain confidence as a medium of exchange and becomes all but worthless.

This story deals not only with money but what the writer views as inevitable change. The era of powerful computers and so-called information highways providing instant worldwide communications also will provide the potential for a worldwide monetary system and systems of trading goods and services that will soon be beyond the ability of any person, group or government to manipulate.

It will be an era where workers and producers will receive closer to the real value of their output than ever before and consumers will pay closer to the real value of the products they buy than ever before.

Diminishment of one's assets and savings through manipulated inflation will no longer be possible. Collapse of a country's monetary system will no longer be possible.

Power-driven bureaucrats, devious politicians and greed-driven businessmen will no longer be able to control others through the manipulation of the amount of printed currency in circulation at any given time.

Bribery and most, if not all, crimes for profit will become all but impossible to conduct because such a system will not permit the laundering or hiding of *money*. Elections for our political representatives and leaders will be based on seeking out the wisest and most honorable of leaders rather than being swayed to vote for those who can afford the most TV coverage.

This then is the story of the beginning of a new era of change, the politics that bring it about and the characters who must work and fight and love or die in the turmoil that precedes all changes of this order of magnitude.

CHAPTER ONE
FIRST INKLING

London, England
Monday, March 1, 12:15 a.m.

Deep within the stone and glass monolith that is Benchly's Bank world headquarters communications center, an urgently chattering telex machine was interrupting the placid chewing of Gerald McMahon's midnight lunch.

As night communications officer, he was in the middle of his favorite work-a-day pastime when the telex disturbed his mid-shift repast.

"Bloody nuisance," he mused. "That thing seems to know precisely when I'm in the middle of my bloody tea break." He thought for a moment of ignoring it until he had finished his meal, but the non-stop clattering of the machine suggested a matter of far greater importance than just some gold or currency closing price halfway around the world.

Picking up his tea cup he walked over to the still active machine and began to read the folds of paper cascading down the back of the machine.

"Dateline Mexico City:" it read. "After a secret weeklong meeting at the presidential retreat, the finance ministers of eighteen major Latin American countries today issued the following joint statement:

> The government leaders of our individual nations have agreed to form a 'default' committee to work out a solution to the crushing debt load which our countries now face.

Señor Jaimie de la Torres, Mexico's finance minister and the spokesman for the group, declared that their countries owed a total of almost $1 trillion (U.S. Currency) in interest bearing debt to a group of foreign governments through the International Monetary Fund, the Inter-American Bank and most of the world's largest private banks.

The group had determined that it has become virtually

impossible for its individual countries to meet their present foreign debt obligations without totally bankrupting their own countries and people.

Therefore, the finance ministers, acting with full approval of their individual governments, have formed the DEFAULT COMMISSION OF LATIN AMERICAN COUNTRIES (acronym DECOLAC) to jointly seek financial stability and rehabilitation by calling a twenty-year moratorium on all of their foreign debts.

Each of the member countries has, as of this date, declared a freeze on all currency and precious metal movements in and out of their individual countries for an unstated period.

Commerce, trade and trade settlements will flow freely within the eighteen member nations on a conventional basis with the establishment of their own common market.

All commerce with countries outside DECOLAC will be dealt with by commission members as a whole on a straight goods and commodities of equal value barter basis.

Martial law has been declared within the countries of the member nations to enforce the present economic status. END OF MESSAGE."

McMahon swallowed his last bite of lunch with great difficulty and began frantically pushing phone buttons on his console with one hand, trying to reach the bank's chief operations officer while massaging computer keys with the other. The compliant green screen was quietly scrolling figures across its expanse, stopping periodically to print in a country's name and then following the name with ten and twelve-digit currency figures.

Gerald McMahon swallowed hard as he read, "Total Latin Debt Benchly's Bank; 7.31 Billion Pounds Sterling."

CHAPTER TWO
FIRST CONTINGENCY

New York City
March 1, 3:15 a.m.

The 25th floor elevator of one of New York's largest bank was disgorging crowds of men in dress ranging from evening clothes and business suits to sport jackets and overcoats hurriedly pulled over pajamas. They were responding to the same news that had just caused Gerald McMahon in London the worst case of indigestion he had ever experienced.

They crowded into the usually sedate board room, which now resounded with their unnaturally loud, and in some cases hysterical, voices—filling the air with a flurry of unanswered questions.

David Malcolm, the usually controlled chairman of the board, banged loudly on a metal carafe with a glass ashtray until he had gained the attention of those in the room.

Behind him, secretaries from the bank's communications department were bringing in brightly colored folders while technicians labored quietly in the background, stringing cables and hooking up computer screens and consoles.

Malcolm looked over the assembled people and started to speak in a calm, matter-of-fact manner. "I presume you are all aware by now of the eighteen Latin American countries defaults on their collective national debts?" There were nods as he took a telex sheet from a folder. "We have just received a last minute follow-up from our office manager in Mexico City and I quote." He unfolded the sheet and began to read from it.

"Have contacted and spoken to fourteen members of the default commission. They have refused our latest proposal of a zero- interest, twelve-month loan package for purposes of paying interest and rolling over the principal in order to buy a year of grace.

"Señor Jaime de la Torres, Mexico's finance minister, stated that his country has already paid back our original loan in the past eighteen years just in interest payments alone. He emphatically stated 'No more loans.' He further states that they intend to stand in default as stated the same as if an American company had filed under Chapter 11. End of message."

Jerome Bailey, a longtime board member, half rose from his seat in disbelief. "They can't do that can they, David?" The board chairman waved him back to his seat.

"They've already done it, Jerry. Not only that but they are offering us a junk bond they call the 'Latin American Sovereign Bond' that pays no interest for the next ten years, 3 percent interest for the last ten years and is redeemed at the end of twenty years for the amount of the original principal of each loan. They said in effect, 'take it or leave it.'"

Mel Trask, senior partner of one of New York's largest brokerage houses, shook his head incredulously. "Why that's all but worthless Do they really think we're going accept that paper for the hard currency we loaned them?"

David Malcolm ignored the outburst and turned to the computer operator behind him who had quietly been evoking mounds of printouts from his whispering printer. The operator nodded at Malcolm and all eyes turned to the hypnotic green screen as the scrolling lines of numbers suddenly stopped.

The operator quickly tore off the folded paper and handed it to the chairman of the bank. The silence was so sudden that one could hear the hum of the machines as Malcolm began glance reading through the printed figures.

Finally, a stately looking gentleman in evening clothes said, "Well, David, what's the prognosis?"

Malcolm turned slowly back to the board table, never taking his eyes off the figures he was reading, and began to speak. "In this country alone, ninety-two banks have just had over $640 billion in Latin sovereign loans defaulted. This bank alone holds over $80 billion."

There was a shocked hush as the chairman paused and read another part of the financial statement before him. "As of twenty minutes ago we are $28 billion below our stated capital and that does not take into account the run this will trigger on all our demand deposits when news of this gets out. Gentlemen, not only is this bank technically bankrupt, but a great number of our peer banks and correspondent banks along with us."

For a moment those present were too stunned to react. Then suddenly the room erupted in a chaos of sounds. An anemically thin, frightened looking board member named Purdy, a senior partner in one of the country's Big Eight accounting firms, jumped to his feet waving a silver mechanical pencil as if it were a magical wand.

"That's impossible, David, simply impossible. Why if we go down as one of this country's largest bank, the whole damn country goes down. The whole thing is too incredible. We should be on the phone to Washington. We should be on the phone to the President. Surely the government can control this. They can't let this happen. What happened to the bank's contingency plan, what . . . what . . ."

The hysteria in his voice began to infect the others. Bill Stover, a huge, self-made billionaire started rumbling in his streetwise voice, "Hell, we'll send a few bill collectors in F-15s after these dead beats and with a few well-placed bombs you'll see how fast they start thinking about ways to pay off those loans."

Retired General "Dutch" Armand's commanding voice joined in the melee. "After what we proved we can do in the Persian Gulf with Desert Storm, we'll offer them a deal they can't refuse. Either they roll over their debt and play ball or they'll wind up being the biggest smoking hole in the planet."

"Gentlemen, gentlemen!" Malcolm had begun banging on his carafe again, trying to bring order. "We are not here to hold a wake, we are here to implement a contingency plan. You may recall that when a previous administration twisted our arm, we bailed out one of the country's largest auto manufacturers with government-guaranteed debt. You may also recall that it was our lobbyists who prevailed on the President and Congress to bang heads at their board to get them to accept the Fed guaranteed loan which, if you remember, kept us from having a very nasty loan default. Now we simply have a slightly larger problem."

"Now wait a minute, Dave!" It was Mel Trask shaking his finger at the chairman. "Aren't you underplaying the hell out of this situation? I remember a contingency plan that dealt with maybe one or two of these Latin governments defaulting but dammit, we're talking here about half the Third World. You know damn well that when the other half figures out how to play this game they're gonna jump on this bandwagon so fast the damn axle's gonna break."

Malcolm slowly rose to his feet and held up his hands from an already imposing six-foot-two. "We have," he said, pausing for effect, "a contingency plan which we have not had a chance to brief you on. If you will all calm down, I will explain."

He paused again and signaled his functionaries and assistants to leave the room before he continued. After the door closed behind the last one, he continued, "Many of you sitting on this board of directors are also directors on some of the boards of the world's largest multi-national companies and several of the world's largest banks, not to mention many of the wealthiest foundations and trusts in the world.

"Moreover, when you add to this our counterparts throughout the western world you begin to see that we are not without some very imposing clout. In one way or another we as a group control a large part of the world's fuel, energy, transportation, communications, commodities, processed foods, manufactured goods and financial institutions.

"There isn't a government in the Western World, or for that matter in most of the rest of the world, that can function for very long without us."

Mel Trask raised his hand for attention and when David Malcolm nodded he said, "Don't forget our political clout, David."

"Good point Mel, our consortium of companies, banks and politicians throughout the Western World own or control everything worth a damn—which includes these defaulting countries whether they realize it or not. And, whether anyone believes it or not, we have taken preventive measures long ago to ensure us against the loss of these companies either by force or nationalization."

The room full of movers and shakers sat transfixed as if seeing themselves and their power for the first time. Malcolm continued.

"Let's strip away all the layers of paperwork, societal niceties and cosmetics and look at the nitty gritty. That is, in the final analysis, we owe the defaulted debt to ourselves.

"It isn't this 'stated' default I'm even concerned about, there are ways to handle that, what I'm really concerned about is the several trillion dollars of other people's money we hold in demand deposits in our banks and I mean all the Western World's banks when I say 'our' banks.

"There is already a serious loss of confidence in the banking industry, what with the S&L failures, insurance company failures and some of our larger sister banks becoming insolvent. And all of this coming at a time when we are in the middle of a worldwide recession.

"Now with this default thing, what happens when the owners of the money we hold on deposit start to panic and bang on our doors demanding to draw it all out? There isn't enough paper money in circulation or printing presses in the world to cover that kind of a demand.

"We all recognize that banks are 90 percent smoke and mirrors. We lend money to individuals and companies who deposit it back with us until they use it and we lend it out again in a never-ending cycle.

"As long as there are no runs on banks it all works smoothly. But when all our depositors show up at the same time to withdraw all of their money, that's when everything begins to fall apart.

"We have a very delicate balance of business to industry requiring the public only buy, pay for, and use what they need as they need it. If that balance is upset, it all starts to fall in like a house of cards or a Japanese domino extravaganza only much less orderly. And that, my friends, is when we lose control."

The hushed room sat spellbound, hanging on Malcolm's every word. Jerome Bailey broke the spell by asking, "What do we do if that happens, David?"

David Malcolm turned his head to look balefully at Bailey.

"What we do is not let it happen. What we do is stop this default dead in its tracks by shutting down the international currency and bank note exchange on a worldwide basis, turn every fuel tanker and cargo ship carrying cargo for the defaulting countries around, stop all our airlines from flying in and out, shut down all overseas telephone and TELSAT communications in and out of their countries and shut down every damn subsidiary we own in those countries.

"As I said earlier, WE OWN IT ALL, AND GENTLEMEN . . . WE . . . CAN . . . SHUT . . . IT . . . ALL . . . DOWN. But, that is not the real problem, the real problem is to convince the presidents of several major First World countries to declare national bank holidays to avoid bank runs and set up martial laws in all our countries 'til we get a handle on this thing.

"By noon tomorrow, we will be hooked up on a worldwide conference call with our counter-parts all over the world and put into motion our TOTAL CONTROL contingency plan."

Looking around the room, Malcolm's piercing eyes riveted each of them as if hypnotized. He continued, "In front of each of you is a folder with your name on it describing what you need to do. And I expect each of you to do your part on every corporate board you presently sit on."

With that statement, Malcolm handed his computer printouts to his administrative vice president and walked quietly toward the door. At the private door to his suite of offices, he stopped and looked back at the stunned assemblage.

"I presume I have your full support in doing what we all know must be done?"

There were embarrassed glances around the room. Trask started to say something and stopped. Someone cleared his throat nervously while others looked blankly at the unused pads and pencils sitting antiseptically before them. The lack of an alternative was all too obvious.

Malcolm turned on his heel and went through the door, which swung silently and emphatically shut behind him.

CHAPTER THREE
AND ALL THE PRESIDENT'S MEN

Washington, D.C.
March 1, 10:00 a.m.

The snow on the ground was crusted hard from a sub-zero cold and crunched noisily as one official limousine after another pulled up to the North Portico of the White House to discharge their harried looking occupants.

Buck Raymond, the President's chief aide grabbed a bulky stack of file folders from a military aide just inside the portico doors as the deputy secretary of state came through the door stamping his feet.

"What's this crazy business about a total press blackout Buck? Good God, you know you can't keep secrets in Washington. What the hell is going on?"

"Tex" Billings, the disgruntled questioner, was shucking his overcoat with the help of a Marine orderly while juggling the bulky packet of briefing documents just handed him by the President's aide.

As he turned from the completed chore, Buck said, "What if I told you that as of right now you could wipe your behind with all the U.S. dollars there are in the world because they've just become less valuable than toilet paper?"

Billings stopped cold in his tracks and looked for a long moment at the dead serious expression on his friend's face. "That bad huh?"

"Worse." The two men started walking back toward Buck's office adjoining the Oval Office as Buck started to tick off statistics on his fingers.

"First of all, every Third World country and a few Second World countries are thinking seriously about jumping onto this default bandwagon.

"Second, banks from Bangor, Maine, to San Diego, California, are preparing for runs the likes of which will make

1932 seem like a picnic. Third, exporters and shippers are turning back planes, trains and ships full of merchandise to their home ports until the smoke clears, and we need that foreign cash flow for our country's survival, my friend."

The two men had reached the aide's office where other cabinet members and their aides were scanning briefing documents and making comments in hushed tones.

"Finally," Buck continued in a lowered voice, "what are the countries not in jeopardy going to do to take advantage of this situation?"

He turned to the rest and said, "Gentlemen will you all join me in the Situation Room?"

When he had herded everyone into the meeting room, he excused himself and walked over to the connecting door of the Oval Office and knocked quietly and then stepped into the room that housed the seat of power of the greatest nation on earth.

The President was standing at a frost covered window with his back to the room listening to the raspy voice of Jack Brockman, cigar chewing head of the Federal Reserve as he reeled off statistics on the state of money in circulation. "Finally, Mr. President," Brockman continued, "the Fed and the Treasury put together don't have enough paper in circulation or available without an extended press run, to cover even 20 percent of the expected runs on just the major banks in each reserve district.

My personal feeling is that you must get Congress to agree to declaring at least a fourteen-day bank holiday starting tonight."

Everyone waited silently for the President to respond. After a long moment he turned, looking first at his aide and then the tall, imposing figure of Brockman.

"And then what, Brock? There are dozens of things that have to be interlocked with a move like that. Let's not let fear guide our actions. No, I think there might be a better way."

Brockman shrugged his shoulders. "Like what, Mr.

President?"

The president walked over to his desk and picked up a crystal paper holder and looked at it thoughtfully as if devining the future.

"First of all, I have sent the Secretary of State and our trade representatives to Mexico to meet with the Latin-American ministers meeting there to see if we might not iron out some of the problems. The best we can hope for in the near term is to work out a temporary barter system just to keep NAFTA alive."

Brockman asked, "What do you hope to accomplish with that?"

The President sat down, placing his hands on his desk. He leaned back and looked at the men in the room for a long moment before answering. "Nothing right now. The psychological damage has been done, hysteria is growing, and even if we could reverse the DECOLAC committee's decision, it will not solve the immediate situation."

Brockman shook his head in puzzlement. "But you said. . ."

The President held up his hand, "Brock, I said that a total bank holiday may not be the answer."

The President leaned forward. "Perhaps Brock, it might be better if we limit each depositor to a withdrawal of a specific percentage of whatever their total balance is. The percentage could be figured out on the basis of M1 and M2 spread over two weeks.

"That would give Treasury time to run the presses for back-up currency and distribution. It would give us time to talk to the worried citizens of this country explaining what we are doing to solve the problem and hopefully reduce the hysteria. Also that would allow citizens to take care of bare essentials and then, whatever does disappear under the mattress won't cripple the economy. More important, it buys us time to deal with the situation."

As the President mulled over this thought his face broke into a small smile. "In fact," he said, "if we make the amount of each withdrawal small enough, just enough to cover bare essentials, it will actually create a lot of physical shopping activity that will keep everyone busy, in touch with others on the streets and perhaps even boost the economy for a short time."

Turning to his aide, the President asked, "Have you called the networks and arranged for emergency air time before the six o'clock news?"

Buck quickly flipped through his ever-present notebook and read, "Yes sir, the three major networks will all pick it up within five minutes of each other starting at 5:15 p.m.

"The camera crew will be ready at 3:45 p.m. for a run through and Bert and Charlie are working up a script based on our earlier discussion and notes. Also everyone is ready in the Situation Room, Mr. President."

The President briskly walked over to the connecting door to the East Room. In a calm voice he said, "Shall we go gentlemen?"

Brockman marveled at the apparent calm and control of the President. *"Or,"* he mused, *"was it that he didn't understand the seriousness and full extent of the problem?"*

CHAPTER FOUR
THE CHINA FACTOR

Beijing, China
March 2, 1:30 p.m.

The Zhong Nan Hai compound was bustling with activity as various high government officials left their residences within the compound to hurry to a special meeting unexpectedly called by the vice premier at the main conference room on the top floor of the Xin Hua Meng building.

The men hastily gathered in the center conference room, taking their places in the overstuffed chairs of a bygone era around the huge, polished table. The room bespoke of China's ancient history with its pictorial tapestries and, even though it was early afternoon, the room seemed dimly lit by its hanging lanterns. One had the feeling that the twentieth century had been left behind when walking into this room.

The muted conversation quickly subsided as the venerable Chairman entered the room, breathing heavily from the long climb up the stairs of the old building. He took his place at the center of the long conference table and instead of pausing to light his ever-present cigarette, quickly called the meeting to order, a sign to everyone present of the importance of the business at hand.

After the formal protocol of acknowledgments and greetings finally ended, the vice chairman in charge of economic development anxiously made himself heard, totally out of the normal order for this form of meeting. The excitement was barely restrained in his voice.

"A most unique moment in history is at hand Comrade Chairman and our economic intelligence sector has distilled the information relating to this situation.

"The report states that the European and North American governments have been caught completely unaware by the action of the Latin American countries. At present, they are all in a very disoriented state. Comrade Lo Pi has developed three possible scenarios which. . ."

The chairman held up his hand in a manner that stopped the vice premier in midsentence. In the ensuing silence, the Chairman wearily leaned forward and looked around the room at the faces so familiar to him.

He realized that fully half of them expected a direction that could easily escalate into a major confrontation. The thought crossed the chairman's mind that men of this type seemed to be the same everywhere. Despite the fact that they wielded great power and were accorded great responsibility, wisdom and maturity seemed always to be tempered by a first reaction of base instincts requiring aggressive action. He shook his head as if to shake the thought away, remembering his own younger days.

He began quietly, "I am sure that comrade Lo Pi and no doubt, many more of you have all considered various plans. And these many plans would, no doubt, in some form or another, commit this great Republic, its bright young men and its already over strained economic assets, to an action designed to take advantage of the economic problems taking place in the West.

"Does any one of you present here today know with any certainty that such action will not turn against us at a time when we desperately need the economic and technical assistance of those very governments? When we so desperately need to maintain our *Most Favored Nation trade status* for the benefit of China's emergence into the next century. It is time to look at these situations over the very longest term possible.

"No, gentlemen, I am inclined to recognize the virtue inherent in patience at this time and do nothing. I say this because when one carefully analyzes all sides of the situation, I believe that you will see that we can turn this unusual circumstance to our advantage without compromising our country in the least or committing even so much as one yuan to the situation.

"It is imperative my friends, that we put aside our past

mind sets and think in terms of our new position in the world, our rapidly growing and advancing country and our newly developed world trade.

"It is my firm belief that the Western nations will be so preoccupied with their economic survival, so short of funds with which to maintain a military posture, and so limited in the ability to make political demands that, by default, we will not only win large concessions and prominence in places throughout the world that are desirable to us, but we shall also be in a better position to redirect much needed funds from unproductive expenditure to our desperately needed internal economic uses.

"After all, our Ren Men Bi or domestic currency and monetary stability is totally under control and presents no problem. Moreover, we have recently been able to trade our exports for commodities of equal value where currency values have no effect through a new global computerized trading system that recently became available.

"In short comrades, we will do nothing. The economic situation confronting the Western World, after having just come through the costly Persian Gulf situation, will do more for us than any physical, political or military action could hope to do."

The practicality of what the Chairman had just so forcefully and effectively stated had its desired effect on the gathering.

CHAPTER FIVE
*IF YOU JUST DON'T KNOW WHEN
BUT YOU STILL HAVE THAT YEN*

Tokyo, Japan
March 2, 8:00 a.m.

The assembly of chauffeur-driven limousines lined up in parking spaces adjacent to the elevators of the Tokyo Shimbun Building's parking garage was not only unusual in its size but also for the time of day.

The elevator doors were just closing on the last group of businessmen to arrive and the operator turned a special key and punched in the penthouse floor.

Omi Sokuro could not help feeling uneasy about this hastily called, top-level meeting. It was completely out of character for Japanese businessmen, but the invitation sounded so ominous and contained the names of so many commanding figures in the business world, no one had the audacity to question its importance.

At the penthouse, the doors opened and the assemblage was met by a uniformed, gloved, female page and led down the corridor to a door opening on a large, impressive meeting room.

Already seated at the long table were the heads of most of the largest international companies and banks in Japan. The urgency of the meeting was made obvious by the dispensation with the formal protocol normally a part of any business meeting in Japan.

Oshiro Tanaka quickly called the meeting to order when the last man had been seated and the page had silently left the room.

"The reason we are meeting here in the headquarters of the Tokyo Shimbun this morning is that it possesses the world's largest collection of financial data. From this information, I have taken the liberty of having a summary prepared, which you will find in the briefing files before you.

"Please do not take the time to read now. There is time later to digest all the aspects of what we are about to discuss this morning. You may also call the names listed in each folder for an expansion on the information at a later time.

"Most of you probably have heard by now of the bank debt default the countries of Latin America have declared. Though it has significant impact on Japanese business and economics, it is not as devastating as that which will be felt in the United States and the European Common Market.

"The governments of the United States, Canada, Great Britain, France, Germany, Belgium and the Netherlands have asked the Japanese government to join them in a complete boycott of the defaulting countries.

"We have been asked to advise our government as business and banking leaders on the course of action to take. Our council has been examining this situation from many sides throughout the night and we have concluded that it is not to our advantage either as businessmen or as a nation to join this international boycott.

"Let me explain to you why we came to this conclusion and why no one from our government is at this meeting. Our government leaders and diplomats must present the most supportive possible face without taking significant actions until this meeting is concluded and all present have agreed upon our suggested course of action."

Shizu Miyamoto deferentially raised his pencil to gain the Chairman's attention and when the speaker nodded to him he said, "I wish to ask if you have accumulated the statistics on what each of our companies has at jeopardy if we did join the so called boycott and . . . what do we place in jeopardy if we do not."

"An excellent point Shizu and one that is well covered in the folders before you. Upon reading the data contained in those folders you will find that we may stand to lose some foreign inventories and perhaps some bank deposits together with some sovereign loans totaling over one trillion yen. In our present financial state, Japan cannot afford such an additional burden.

"If, however, we do not join in the boycott, we expect to lose nothing and in fact, we should gain a much stronger trade position."

Shizu again raised his pencil for attention and the chairman of the meeting again nodded.

"Thank you for permitting me these rude interruptions, but I am concerned about how we would settle sales and trades without an internationally accepted medium of exchange other than direct barter of our goods and services for some product of equal value from each country."

The chairman nodded, smiling slightly.

"The answer to that question is not fully described in writing in your folders because we do not wish to jeopardize the system we feel will work.

"As you are aware, much of my own company's main income-generating components are its computer division. Perhaps the largest manufacturer of computer components and computers in the world.

"In order to maintain such a position we must, among other things, keep careful track of how our equipment and components are being used in order to identify any important trends.

"An American gentleman has for many years been promoting and developing an international computer barter system that has caused a considerable quantity of our equipment to be purchased and put into use.

"The system is based on an incredibly fast mainframe computer and driven by a unique and complex computer program that incorporates a combination of huge data bases and very advanced, artificial-intelligence software. In fact, the software's code is a form of international language that can communicate in any country's language.

"It is tied into a worldwide network by satellite, phone lines, television sets and phones themselves and incorporates an existing network called "Internet." Our observation in the past forty-eight hours shows it is working far better than we expected.

"It operates totally outside the control of any industry, government or political force at this time and we feel that it should continue so because of its simplicity and great efficiency.

"Our company has been a contributor to its organization and design with both finances and equipment for several years, anticipating the possibility of using it in such an emergency. If the present monetary emergency continues, this particular system could well become a totally independent international monetary system. One that is actually owned by its millions of users as a group, without political or governmental interference.

"This may initially disturb many governments and large multi-national banking institutions, but it is our belief that they and we would be better served under this method of operation.

"We have already seen those benefits in the past forty-eight hours by utilizing the network to settle many of our own foreign trades efficiently.

"Contained in your folders are instructions describing how each of you may utilize this extraordinary system to ensure your successful international trade. And now gentlemen, let me explain how each of you may use this trade settlement system and benefit from its operation . . ."

CHAPTER SIX
TWO BANKERS IN THREE QUARTER TIME

Mexico City
March 2, 11:00 p.m.

Estaban Delgado ("Beni" to his friends) sat patiently in the outer office of Jorge Beltran, presidente de Banco Financiera de Mexico, S.A. and the country's leading financial brain.

As he sat nervously smoking his slim cigarro, his eyes wandered over the many testaments to Jorge's education hanging on the walls of the waiting room. Wharton, master's in business administration, Harvard University, doctorate in economics, Oxford, doctorate in philosophy. From the University of Geneva a doctorate in international finance and banking.

"I see you are reading my commercials Beni." Dr. Beltran had silently entered the thickly carpeted room while Beni was lost in thought over the array of impressive documents.

Beni smiled. "This is the first time I've really read all these things and realize how truly well educated you are my good friend."

Dr. Beltran smiled and shrugged his shoulders. "They are merely official proof that one has finished certain basic training. What they truly mean is that I was well prepared to learn the lessons of the real world and better prepared to understand what those lessons mean."

Placing his arm around his young friend's shoulder Dr. Beltran said, "Come into my office and tell me what I can do for my esteemed brother banker on this day?"

Beni shrugged his shoulders as he walked into the office. "I am concerned Jorge. The default by our country and our neighbors has me very worried. It is no secret that you were called upon as an adviser to the Default Commission. My bank, as well as every other commercial bank in Mexico, has substantial assets in the banks of the countries to whom we are in default. I realize that we, as private banks, are not responsible for calling the default. But what happens, for instance, when the hundred billion pesos worth of U.S. Treasury Certificates we hold mature?"

Dr. Beltran smiled as he gestured for him to sit in a comfortable chair by the desk. "Beni, you know of course that this default may well change the entire world's monetary system. Should that happen, most likely, all currencies world-wide would be replaced by a globally recognized medium of exchange without anyone suffering any loss."

Beni shook his head in consternation. "How can this happen Jorge? How can this situation suddenly make all the currency of the Western World worthless? How can countries and governments and businesses and people function? How can they survive? It's insane, Jorge. One must have a medium of exchange in order to function in an orderly society."

Dr. Beltran sat down on the edge of the desk closest to his friend and, leaning over, put his hand on his shoulder. "Beni *mi compadre,* there will always be a medium of exchange.

"When three or more people gather for the purpose of commerce, they will arrive at a medium of exchange out of necessity. It may be dried corn, a few chickens, a pair of new zapatas, salt, tools, gold, almost anything with an intrinsic value. However, these producers of goods and services will always find an acceptable medium of exchange for themselves."

Beni shook his head. "But . . . but what about the billions upon billions of pesos, of yen, of dollars, of monetary assets?" Beni asked. "How can one just completely wipe out all of that with a proclamation and the stroke of a pen?"

Dr. Beltran walked over to a window looking out on a serene courtyard filled with greenery and birds. It seemed totally removed from the world about which Beni was now so confused.

"First let me say that everything is not always as it appears to be. Nothing is ever carved in stone where politics and money are concerned. I cannot discuss what was revealed to me in confidence, but often moves such as this are taken to get someone's attention.

"Perhaps it is time for a short refresher course in economics *amigo*. What is happening today is not something that has been decided on the spur of the moment. Rather it is the visible manifestation of a long-suffering illness that has slowly spread throughout the Western World's financial community."

Dr. Beltran walked back to his desk as Beni shifted uneasily in his chair.

"You and I both know that wealth is not based on paper or paper money or even gold and silver. Rather it is based on a great number of things. This combination of things is generally accepted to be made up of natural resources, human creativity combined with human labor and the subsequent output from this combination of materials and effort. And all of this must be developed in a manner of harmony and undergirded with good intentions.

"Once this combination produces more than is required to meet the immediate needs of the producers, there develops a need to trade some of that abundance or excess output for those things that the producers of this excess are not able to provide for themselves.

"At the point where one finds that the need to barter those goods and services on a scale larger than a 'me-to-you' basis, the producers of surplus goods and services begin casting about for a medium of exchange in order to affect the trade."

Beni sat transfixed as he followed every word. Dr. Beltran stood up and began to walk slowly back and forth as he continued.

"Once that medium has been determined and used for a time and the users of that medium develop a certain confidence in both the medium of exchange and the system that administers it, the medium of exchange becomes an accepted, unquestioned method of settling trades. As long as nothing gets out of balance, the medium of exchange and the system that administers it remain healthy.

"You and I are in a service industry, the financial services industry. An industry that can only survive and prosper as long as a true value underlies the medium of exchange we administer and house for others.

"In other words, each peso in your bank must represent some farm commodity, wood product, mineral output, energy or fuel output, communications, transportation, food, clothing, housing, labor or service essential to the survival, needs or wants of society.

"However, problems arise when basic values underlying this peso begin to be diminished with an over abundance of non-essential 'convenience' goods or services and a political power that prints too many pesos for the purpose of buying votes with which to keep itself in power.

"When the financial community becomes infected with the disease of greed; the greed to lend 'money' at exorbitant interest rates, the greed to develop income from non-essential services or the greed to make 'money' in the stock or commodities markets of the world by buying and then selling at ever higher prices without there having been a corresponding increase in under-lying value of that which one is selling, the original reason for investing in securities, that is to create new industry and products that create new jobs, is lost. It is at this point when the medium of exchange becomes unbalanced.

"Add to this gross political misuse of a country's assets for personal political gain and suddenly you find that a majority of the wealth-creating labors and natural resources are being misdirected into non-productive areas that only detract from true wealth and value. There is an accumulation of the wealth produced by others in the hands of a few where hoarding or misapplication dissipates its value."

Beni shook his head in disbelief. "Are you saying that to become wealthy or to accumulate wealth is wrong?"

Dr. Beltran smiled and shook his head. "Not at all *mi compadre,* the accumulation of wealth is not bad at all. On the contrary, when done by responsible people who recognize the obligation that goes with wealth, it is healthy for they intelligently reinvest it in things that help to create new and better industries and employ more people, which further helps to maintain the harmonious balance.

"But when accumulated by irresponsible people, the imbalance becomes too much to keep the economic wheel turning harmoniously, parts begin to break and fly off in all directions without control. At that moment, when it becomes apparent what is happening, the survival instinct of the human takes over and forces onto society a new set of values making the old values and medium of exchange obsolete."

Beni sat transfixed at the picture his older and wiser friend was painting. It was difficult for him to fully comprehend what Dr. Beltran was describing but he struggled with the many implications.

Finally, he said, "Does that mean that my bank, your bank, everyone's bank will eventually go out of business? That we stand to lose everything we have worked so hard to build up over these years unless a new medium of exchange or monetary system comes to pass?"

Dr. Beltran shrugged his shoulders and smiled. *"Quien sabe amigo?* However, I have an old friend, an American who has developed a possible alternative to currency driven economies. I think you might find it most interesting."

Dr. Beltran went around his desk to sit down in his comfortable chair. Leaning back, he began to relate to Beni his American friend's plan.

"Many years ago my first job when I finished my schooling, was as a lawyer for the Departamentado de Minerales in the little town of Mazatlan.

"In the course of my work, I met a man the locals called *Juan Barbas* or *El Barbon,* the beard. His real name was John Garland, a very tall man with a big black beard.

"He was a mining engineer in charge of reopening a silver and lead mine up on the Rio Panuco. Since government concessions were involved, he and I had many business dealings and in time we became close friends.

"This man had already become well known in that part of Mexico, not just because of his size and strength but for his compassion for the local people. He had worked with the *Indios* near his mine to help them form *cooperativas* for the purpose of more efficient farming.

"He bought the *cooperativa* a tractor and taught the farmers how to maintain it. He showed them how to build a water wheel that lifted water to their farmland for irrigation, increasing their crops and making them self sufficient."

Beni interrupted Dr. Beltran by holding his hand. Shrugging his shoulders, he said, "But Jorge, I don't understand. What was his motive for all this effort outside his normal mining business?"

Dr. Beltran smiled and shrugged his shoulders. "As far as I can see he had no selfish motive unless it was to develop good relationships with the people of that region so that his mining operation could operate successfully.

"It was his insight, his farsightedness that constantly impressed me. He correctly predicted in those years that the political corruption and misuse of power to nationalize oil and other industries, and that manipulation of the monetary system and borrowing power, would lead to a situation similar to what is happening to us today.

"We spent many hours discussing the dangers of runaway inflation and he convinced me that a controlled barter system could circumvent a bankrupt economy to permit people to survive and prosper. At that time, however, the methods and speed of communications had not yet been developed to support such a system on a grand scale.

"Long after his work in Mazatlan was finished, we remained friends and often visited each other. He on my rancho on La Isla del Mar, and I at his rancho in northwestern Nevada.

"As time went on and the growth of the computer industry and high speed communications became the reality it is today,

Juan Barbas began developing a very workable plan for a worldwide barter system.

"Among other things, it tied together independent commercial banks throughout the hemisphere with a very sophisticated computer system.

"Even then, he foresaw the possibility of an orchestrated Latin American default of debt and how it would bring a large part of the Western World's banks to the brink or ruin.

"Nevertheless, he knew that banks, more than any other business group, could become a part of a well-organized computerized world monetary system, with banks acting as the repository for electronic credits, and transfer of credits between depositors.

"In other words, rendering the same services to their depositors they do now except electronic credits would supplant paper currency and perhaps even checks.

"Not too long ago, he called me to let me know that he had a central computer in place with worldwide communications capability and that he would like me to help organize the banks of Mexico to join the system. It will help us to keep NAFTA alive and it will probably lead to a more intelligent monetary system for all countries. Have patience, *mi amigo,* I feel that when everything is settled, all will work out for the betterment of all."

Beni sat wide-eyed, listening to Dr. Beltran explain a plan that could save his bank and years of hard work.

Washington D.C.
March 2, 4:00 p.m.

Alphonse Courdelet, though best known for his exploits as a Legionnaire and as the first French administrator in Algiers, North Africa, was chosen by his peers to head the powerful International Monetary Fund because of his later experience in international banking, his unflappable practicality and, most of all, his conservative approach to intelligent lending practices. It was hoped he could bring under control what had long been an erratic, open-handed lending practice tied to irrational geopolitical goals and policies.

He had long ago foreseen the possibility of a massive regional debt default and had insisted on funding a study group comprised of the brightest brains in the financial world available to him to devise a solid contingency plan to the envisioned default possibility.

Now he stood at the window of his office awaiting the arrival of Jacques Martine, his hand-picked chairman of that group. In light of what he had just learned of the default by the DECOLAC committee, he needed to be briefed immediately on the contingency plan they had just completed.

As he watched the homeward-bound Washington traffic snaking its way from one traffic light to the next, he began ticking off in his mind the chain of events he knew would be taking place.

First, the financial centers around the world will have suspended all trading for the day to avoid panic selling. Major state banks would be asking their governments to declare some form of bank holiday to protect their assets.

Board rooms of multinational corporations around the world would be filled with people frantically planning production cutbacks, ordering withdrawals of cash from banks around the world and trying desperately to stop the shipment of goods to the defaulting countries.

Military men flanked by their intelligence officers would be rattling sabers and giving doomsday scenarios. And while all this tragic nonsense was taking place, the average man in the street representing 95 percent of the population would still be totally oblivious to what was going on.

Fortunately, thought Courdelet, the disease of hysteria would not infect them for several days, perhaps even a week. Not much time for a remedy, no matter how good, to take effect.

He sighed and shook his head as a polite knock interrupted his thoughts. The massive carved door swung open to reveal the incongruity of his petite secretary holding the heavy door open for the tall, graying man with an obvious military bearing, who entered.

Jacques Martine was followed by two of his commission members and warmly shook hands with his chief. *"Comon se va, Mon Commandant."* He smiled and began introducing the others.

The director waved them to a small comfortable conference table in the corner of the huge office while his secretary efficiently set out cups, saucers, aperitif glasses and a pot of steaming coffee.

While the men arranged themselves Martine passed out the ever-present briefing folders endemic to bureaucratic agencies throughout the world.

Just like the old days when he had served as adjutant to the then General Courdelet in Algeria, Martine thought. They had practical answers for difficult situations in those days too, but General DeGaulle had chosen to ignore them. Martine wondered if times had changed and common sense might now prevail.

He opened his folder and began, "You will notice on the first page *Mon Commandant,* there begins a list of the defaulting countries, the amount of each default and to whom the amounts are owed. On the third page is a list of the assets each country presently has in foreign banks and institutions that lie within our sphere of influence.

"On the sixth page begins a list of trade goods not yet paid for by the consignees but still in ships' holds, on docks or in warehouses again within our sphere of influence.

"Finally, there is a list of each of the defaulting countries' hard assets outside their countries such as real estate, embassy buildings, airline terminals and ships and planes presently on the lending countries' soil.

"The bottom line, as the Americans so aptly put it, is that total assets of the defaulting nations that we can control, represents about $70 billion in replacement value and perhaps 30 percent of that if sold at auction.

"Moreover, the cost of going through the World Court for settlement would take years and eventually be greater than their actual value. The committee's assessment is that attaching those assets would be more trouble than it's worth.

"We have developed the following proposal. The total amount of just the principal and interest payments due this year on the defaulted debt is about $188 billion. The organization presently has available in its SDR account about $180 billion.

"The fund could, in effect, buy the defaulting countries' debts, at a small profit of course, issue notes against each member country's special drawing rights account pro rata to the amounts due banks from each country. Then issue guarantees against those amounts coming due this year. Only the interest would be collectible this year and any principal payments rolled over 'til next year."

Courdelet pursed his lips in thought as he read along with Martine's explanation. Finally, he looked at his old friend and said, "What do you suggest as an alternative way to carry on international and even national trade settlement that might be acceptable to most people?"

Martine placed his folder on the table before him and took a sip of coffee. Carefully placing the cup back in its dainty saucer he leaned forward toward his old friend in a gesture well recognized by Courdelet as the beginning of a plan.

"To begin with, *Mon Commandant,* we evaluated many possibilities. It was most obvious that first and foremost was the need to arrive at a method of trade settlement in which the majority of the international community would have confidence. Since the present problem is printed currency or paper with questionable underlying value, we began to examine various forms of technology already in use by the financial world."

Courdelet's eyes lit up as he began to follow Martine's thinking. "Computers, *n'est pa?*"

Martine smiled and nodded his head. "Yes *Mon Commandant,* computers. I believe it is possible to organize all the present banking and securities firms' computers along with appropriate government computers into an international network using satellites, phone lines and radio communications.

"This would permit governments and industries to settle or trade each other's exports and imports by barter and further, would permit the defaulting countries to trade their products and raw materials directly for the commodities and imports, each needed just for their basic survival.

"This approach would, of course, initially bypass the normal banking community and perhaps cause some financial loss to a number of international trade organizations and companies. However, I believe that this approach would act to head off any massive hysteria, civil uprisings and, in some countries, possibly even anarchy."

As Martine's dissertation unfolded the plan, Courdelet carefully followed the briefing in the statistics contained in the folders he had been given.

When Martine finally finished his presentation, Courdelet leaned back in his chair and, cradling the back of his head in his hands, focused his eyes on the ceiling as if answers were written there.

"If this plan, which I would point out is brilliant, were actually implemented by our organization, every major bank, every multinational corporation and every Western World government would be seeking our scalps or worse."

Martine's commission members looked at each other and finally their chairman in puzzlement. "I don't understand sir. We're talking about a plan that would save half the Western World from financial chaos. Why should anyone be disturbed by that?"

"Because," the IMF chairman began slowly, "it would also undermine much of the extraordinary powers and controls the multinationals, the banks and the politicians of each of these countries now exercise.

"You see, if people were to suddenly become aware of the ease with which they could deal directly with one another and how suddenly inexpensive all these goods and services might become without middlemen, commission agents, sundry wholesalers, government bureaucrats and agencies, it is conceivable the producers of the world might change the way business is done.

"If they were suddenly thrown into such a system of direct computerized trade, our entire economic protocol might be changed—a benefit for many, to be sure, but a sudden and perhaps, nasty shock for others.

"Imagine, if you will, a politician trying to exact a tax from two men who have just traded the repair of one tractor tire for two chickens and one dozen eggs?

"Or how do you suppose a corporate executive could justify $1 million-a-year salary from a financial institution whose services are no longer quite that valuable or necessary?"

"There was a long silence in the room as the men present contemplated the enormity of Courdelet's statement.

"No gentlemen, the plan is excellent but we cannot be openly involved in its initial implementation."

"Why not?" Martine shook his head in puzzlement. "How then can it be implemented on an international scale without us?"

Courdelet looked at his old friend and smiled. "Do you remember the big mining project that was being developed in Algeria by the American company?"

Martine smiled as memories of those days flooded back and said, "John Garland, *n'est pas?*"

"Precisely. Do you know what our engineer friend has been working on for the past six or seven years, Martine?"

"A barter system?"

Courdelet smiled and put down his demitasse. "Not just a barter system, but it is as if he read your contingency plan. It is the most sophisticated system I could ever imagine. In fact, it could be converted from a worldwide barter system to an electronic monetary system within days. Just this morning I received a confidential brief from him outlining the entire operation. It is dazzling in its scope."

Waving toward his desk Courdelet said, "Read it and see how we might incorporate it in your plan in such a way that, at the outset, we are not perceived to be as a part of it. We will however, quietly help it to become a reality."

Martine smiled a broad smile. He loved it when, as one of the actors on his favorite television show said, *a plan comes together.*

CHAPTER EIGHT
THE SMART MONEY MOVES

New York City
March 2, 9:30 a.m.

The traffic on Park Avenue was moving smoothly considering it was the tail end of the morning rush hour. Melvin Trask's limousine was being deftly maneuvered in and out of traffic by his longtime chauffeur as it moved downtown toward the canyons of Wall Street.

Trask had been one of the directors present at the predawn meeting of the Case City Bank where he first learned of the full extent of the Latin American consortium's loan default.

Being a pragmatist, as well as the head of one of the nation's largest brokerage houses, he had immediately begun mapping out what he felt would be an effective series of protective actions as well as some shrewd speculations based on his advanced information.

The smooth-riding limo provided a quiet office in the plush passenger area of the car. A fold-away desk swung out to accommodate a leather-bound note and appointment book.

Meanwhile, his riding companion, the vice president of finance for the brokerage house, was quietly giving orders over the car's mobile phone while information was fed back to him. He was quickly translating the information to a lap top computer. Finally, he placed the phone receiver back in its polished recess and turned to Trask.

"Looks like we're in good shape. Accounting has drawn down cash in every bank in every city where we have an office so we can handle overhead and salaries for at least sixty days. We've cashed out every money market, treasury bond and CD and bought all the gold, platinum and silver any dealer from here to Hong Kong had for sale.

"We tried to buy all thirty-day gold and silver futures being traded anywhere but we ran into a strange thing. The precious metals mines throughout most of the free world had stopped selling their metal futures as if they had some inside information on this default."

Trask interrupted, "We'll look into that later. Right now we're going to need more cash than just our operating expenses Dick. We're going to have a few hysteria settlements at our offices throughout the country I'm sure. Just this morning, the market opened down sixty-seven points on the first insider news."

Dick Simon smiled and waved his hand at his boss. "Covered that starting at 5 a.m. when your phone call got me out of bed.

"I got all our friendly bankers out of bed to OK cash wire transfer requests for all the money traffic would bear in 128 U.S. cities and fourteen overseas offices.

"We also bought a big hunk of short-term currency futures for delivery this a.m. in both London and Hong Kong. It will be flown in by courier plane today. We're still slightly short but we should be out clean by the close of today's business."

Mel knitted his brow as he stared thoughtfully out the car window at the passing traffic and then turned back to Dick.

"Did you ever wonder what would happen if everyone decided that all paper money was worthless and then . . . decided that gold, platinum and silver bars would only be good for door stops?"

Simon shook his head in confusion. "I don't get it Mel. You said that paper money would lose most, if not all, of its value within ninety days. If that's so, what the heck is there to use for money but gold, platinum and silver?"

Trask leaned back in the plush cushions of the limousine and, steepling his long slender fingers, began talking in a lecture-like drone. "History tells us that during the French Revolution, when paper money became worthless, only those things essential to survival like food, clothes, tools, weapons and the like had any real value. They became the money of that time. Gold, it was said, was only accepted by greedy fools and well-fed merchants.

"After World War I, when the German mark became worth less than a bucket of warm spit. Gold was OK, but bratwurst and pumpernickel bread could buy a monarchy.

"No . . . money isn't really essential in an upheaval like the one we're about to see. A barter system based on basic value goods is much more likely to work. Dick, with all the computers sitting around the country, it's only a matter of time before some smart-ass figures out how to bypass the country's monetary system.

"They're already selling everything Sears Roebuck has on television and by computer for a hell of a lot less than what you pay for it in a store. Hell, there are thirty million home computers sitting out there now along with God only knows how many television sets, not to mention the number of phones, all of which could be hooked up into one neat communications network. Before you know it they'll be swapping Mexican chili beans for grease jobs, oil changes and pussy."

Mel paused as he looked out of the limousine's window at the tops of New York's skyscrapers and continued.

"If that comes to pass my friend, we might find that the $6.5 billion in gold and precious metals we bought this morning will make a very shiny headstone for you and me."

The statement left Dick Simon speechless as tiny beads of sweat began to break out on his forehead.

CHAPTER NINE
OPERATION BYPASS

Toiyabe Valley, Nevada
March 2, 2:30 p.m.

Charlie Ross took the steps two at a time as he walked up to the entrance of the mine-shaft elevator building. Pushing through the doors he nodded and smiled at the security guard as he signed in and took his hard hat from its place. The security guard smiled back and said, "The head genius in for the rest of the day?"

"As far as I know, Jerry," and he raced for the mine shaft elevator just as the doors shut. He had never gotten used to the sickening drop of a mine shaft cage.

After passing four working transportation tunnel levels, the cage came to a bouncing stop at the fifth level. Charlie pushed his way out of the elevator and strode quickly around the corner of what looked like a typical mine tunnel only to walk into a modern office corridor and down to an unmarked door.

Sticking his magnetic card in a slot beside the door, he announced his name and the door swung noiselessly inward revealing a large room full of large computer systems hooked up in tandem and glass fronted offices with scores of people moving about.

Charlie moved to the largest of these offices, which was lined with computer terminals and chattering printers. Walking to the largest bank of terminals, he tapped an intent young man hunched over a keyboard with his eyes glued to the screen in front of him. "Well?" Charlie asked.

The husky young man swung around with a grin on his face. "Works like a charm Charlie. In fact, it works exactly like it's supposed to—no glitches, no program hang-ups, one millisecond response."

Charlie took off his coat and threw it on an empty chair and sat down at the terminal just vacated by his assistant. As he began to play the keyboard in front of him, he shot questions at his assistant. "What's the latest news on the reaction to the DECOLAC loan default?"

The young man leaned one hand on the back of Charlie's chair and the other on the computer desk to lean forward and watch the screen that Charlie was manipulating before he answered.

"The idea of a sovereign loan default seems to have spread to Africa and possibly India. Some are beginning to call it a Third World loan default. The President is addressing the nation at 5:15 tonight. No sign of panic yet outside of the banks and multinational corporation board rooms. Only the so-called cognoscenti would understand what the default means at this point anyway.

"There seems to be a news blackout on anything but bare bones announcements of what's happened. To this point, everyone just seems to be reporting it as straight financial news."

Charlie nodded his head and began watching his monitor screen scrolling up lines of information. "Looks like the data base is doing its thing perfectly. I just noticed a line about some sheet steel available for trade and three lines later somebody bought it for a million and half credits from the sale of 70,000 barrels of crude oil." Charlie leaned back from the desk and looked up at his assistant. "How is the communications satellite system working?"

"We've tied in four more satellites so that now we're able to get COMSAT coverage from Alaska to Argentina and from Australia in the west to Moscow in the east. I'd say that right now, 75 percent of the planet can be reached by our phone lines and Satellite link, which includes most of the old globe."

"How many subscribers do we have?"

Charlie's assistant reached over to a keyboard in front of another terminal and started calling up data, reading as it came on the screen.

"As of yesterday at 5:30 p.m. we had 27,400 mainframes,

528,000 mini's and about seventeen million desktop computers give or take a 100,000. And that's Europe, some in Russia, the North and South American continent and the immediate Pacific Rim.

"In Europe we've got a little over twelve million including, believe it or not, 24,000 subscribers from Eastern European countries.

"Then, scattered from Australia to South Pacific, we've got another five and a quarter million ranging from banking houses to an alligator-hide trader in Queensland."

Charlie pursed his lips in thought and leaned back in his chair. "How many are actually active right now?"

Bob turned to his keyboard again and began to punch in numbers as he talked. "You've got to remember Charlie, sub-scribers are only active when they've got something to trade so I'll pull up the number of barter offers and completed swaps in just the last seventy-two hours."

The computer began to respond to his fingered request with a series of columns in which figures and totals began to appear.

"Now this is just the U.S. and Canada beginning 6 a.m. day before yesterday until ten minutes ago, seven million of-fers to trade and 5.2 million completed swaps. But get this, since the default was announced at 7:30 p.m., March 1, Mex-ico City time, that's about eighteen hours ago, over half of that activity took place."

Charlie shook his head. "Betsy here is going to have to handle a hundred times that a day and maybe a thousand times that when the crap really hits the fan.

"Bobby Boy, how many dollar transactions alone do you figure take place every day just in business buys and sells? Not homemakers, not households or schools or organizations or government agencies, just between business people at the wholesale level?"

Bob shrugged his shoulders. "I don't know, twenty million?"

"More like 200 million, but that's not the important thing.

The real question is, can Betsy handle the traffic?"

"You're the genius who designed the software and put together this hot shot hardware, you tell me."

Charlie smiled as he answered. "Betsy's heart is based on the best mainframe *Cray* puts out. Theoretically, the system can make and take transactions at a billionth of a second. We have a fifty Tetrabytes of RAM partitioned into ten gigabyte in-out response sectors. The software is able to bypass non-essential or unrelated information on our memory banks through its artificial intelligence and parallel computing capability and zero in on where the matching buy/sell swaps are located. It is supposed to be able to do that in one ten-millionth of a second. Our only hang up is with phone line transmission. If the other party has a 9,600 or better baud rate phone modem, super. If it's an old fashioned 300 baud rate transmit and receive system the information has to sit in the buffer and wait 'til it can be transmitted.

"Actually, the way Betsy is set up she should be able to handle a million transactions every ten seconds. We've got 5.5 Tetrabytes of memory on line using the new laser disks for storage and we can triple or quadruple that if necessary.

"Of course, with these new disks and our program, after a trade is settled and both sides indicate delivery, the information is automatically archived and memory freed up for a new transaction with the credits either way being recorded in a central accounting system."

Bob slapped the arms of his chair for emphasis. "But that's not where the weakness will show up. It's getting people educated to use the system instead of looking to paper as a medium of exchange. At least 150 million people in this country alone are going to have to learn about Operation Bypass and then learn to trust it. That's not going to happen overnight, especially when you can't advertise it."

Charlie Ross heaved his gangly frame from his chair and walked over to the window looking out over the banks of computers. Brushing a lock of hair out of his eyes, he stuck his hands in his pocket and rocked back on his heels as he mulled over an answer. Finally, he turned around to face his young assistant.

"Bobby Boy," he finally said, "I have an undying faith in the survival instincts, awareness and understanding of Big John. He's seldom been wrong about things like this and there's something else that's kinda spooky about our boss man. I can't really explain it but it's as if he's tuned into the universe and not just the six o'clock news.

"He seems to pick up messages and directions no one else does and he is uncannily right about nine times out of ten. And the time he's wrong, he's not really wrong, it's just his timing is off a couple of heart beats.

"Not only did this system work just as he envisioned it, and not only did he convince thousands of businessmen around the world to help put up the money for it, the subscribers picked up on it just as he figured they would. I guarantee you that people all over the world will learn about it and begin tapping into it as fast as necessity dictates, just like he said it would happen.

"Speaking of the boss, it's about time for his call to be zinging in here."

The two men sat down at their respective monitors and began to clear lines and tap in instructions to the modems. As if on cue, John Garland, president of Delta Mining Company and the creative architect of this computer concept, began signing in on the screen from his motor home atop Pine Ridge overlooking the Truckee Meadows and the city of Reno, Nevada.

CHAPTER TEN
THIS IS YOUR PRESIDENT SPEAKING,
YOU HAVE NOTHING TO FEAR BUT FEAR ITSELF

Washington D.C.
March 2, 5:15 p.m.

Technicians were scurrying around making last-minute lighting adjustments to properly focus on the desk in the East Room of the White House. A man with a cordless head set was quietly speaking into his mike and then gave a hand signal to a Secret Service man standing by the door. The man opened the door and said, "Thirty seconds, Mr. President."

The President entered the room showing no signs of concern and purposefully strode over to the desk with a sheaf of papers. He sat down and carefully arranged the papers on his desk while a make-up man removed a protective cloth from his collar and moved away. This newly elected young President had a remarkable intellect and an uncanny ability to absorb and prioritize details and develop conclusions for action not seen in Washington for a long time.

Off camera an announcer droned into his microphone, "And now ladies and gentlemen, the President of the United States." The red light on the close-up camera came on and the President began speaking.

"Good evening fellow Americans. I have asked the networks for this time to talk to you tonight concerning a very important matter and to discuss with you the measures that I feel must be taken in order to head off problems that might otherwise arise.

"As you are by now aware, our Latin American neighbors have banded together and announced a joint default on all the foreign loans their countries have made over the past years.

"They have stated that the action was taken to allow their countries an opportunity to redirect their assets to the development of their own natural resources and industries so that, at some near future time, they can repay these debts and stabilize their own countries.

"Now a move of this proportion is bound to affect a large number of banking institutions in our country and elsewhere throughout the world. But it is something I believe we can handle if we all are willing to work together.

"This is a time when we must pull together to reinforce our confidence in our banking system and not let others sway us into unwarranted actions that might jeopardize our country and our monetary system.

"I am speaking to you tonight to assure you that your government, the United States Treasury and the Federal Reserve banks stand behind every affected bank in this country.

"As President Roosevelt so aptly put it at another time of pending economic chaos, 'There is nothing to fear but fear itself.' And *that* is what I would like to point out to you tonight. Only fear can make us irrational and cause problems. If we keep our heads and follow the parameters I will set down, we will successfully handle this unforeseen disruption.

"Furthermore, when the smoke clears, we will continue to be the greatest nation with the most productive economy on earth and be stronger for it.

"To ensure this, there are certain basic protective steps we must all take and every one of us must be prepared to adhere strictly to the rules I am going to spell out tonight.

"Let me stress that these rules are only temporary and will remain in effect just long enough to ensure that our government agencies have the time to take the actions necessary to ensure stability in our economic and monetary system.

"First, I am issuing an order tonight to all banks in the United States that no one will be permitted to withdraw more than 5 percent of the total balances of their checking or savings accounts during any given banking week. In accounts where balances are small, less than 500 dollars, larger withdrawals will be permitted. In order for this to properly take effect, I have issued an emergency order to close all banks for the next two days while the temporary emergency regulations are distributed and explained.

"Furthermore, I have directed the SEC to suspend all trading in the stock and commodities markets for the rest of the week until the monetary system has had time to put its controls and plans into effect."

CHAPTER ELEVEN
THE BAIT IS A LADY

New York City
March 3, 11:15 a.m.

The door of the private elevator to the executive suite of the Case City Bank slid open silently, allowing Lorelei Young to step out and stride purposefully toward the receptionist's desk.

The starkly simple but elegant tailoring of her business suit did nothing to hide her blond sexy attractiveness as a woman. The men who passed her on their way to the just-vacated elevator invariably turned to look at her as if drawn by some invisible magnetic force.

If she was aware of this reaction, she either paid no attention to it or was too preoccupied to notice.

The receptionist got up from her chair and said, "Miss Young, David Malcolm is expecting you. Please follow me."

The art work, the paintings, the interior decor through which they passed on the way to Malcolm's office bespoke of incredible wealth and power.

The receptionist opened the door to the outer office of David Malcolm's retreat and politely handed Lorelei off to Malcolm's secretary whose voice was barely audible when she spoke. "This way Ms. Young, Mr. Malcolm is expecting you," and opened the door to Malcolm's office for her.

The elegantly attired chairman rose from his seat as they entered and quickly came around to greet her.

"Lorelei, so good to see you again. You're incredibly beautiful as ever."

Lorelei smiled as she extended her hand. "And David, you're as full of blarney as ever. But thank you for the compliment."

David led the way to a comfortably furnished drawing room area overlooking the skyline of New York. There he beckoned her to one of the plush love seats while he seated himself in a chair across from her which had beside it an end table piled high with folders.

Lorelei wasted no time on pleasantries. "When you called me yesterday, both the President and the Secretary had just phoned to tell me that I was being assigned to assist you in a matter of national importance. To my knowledge, no assistant secretary of Commerce has ever been commanded in that manner. So coming here was, in effect, an order and not the result of your charm."

Malcolm looked at Lorelei with a frown as he answered. "Lori, this is truly a national emergency."

Lori's hand brushed her long, blond hair back from her forehead. "I suppose that explains why the chairman of the most powerful bank in this country can somehow convince the President to get me on a plane to New York on a moment's notice. How exactly do you expect me to help in this situation?"

David looked at this strikingly beautiful, incredibly intelligent woman for a long moment as he carefully organized his thoughts. Leaning forward, he said, "Lori, it's worse than all the wars and dangers this country has ever faced rolled into one. The fallout from this situation could well bring down many financial communities throughout the civilized world."

He allowed the severity of that statement to sink in before proceeding. "If controls are not put in place immediately and hysteria headed off at the pass, anarchy is the next step. And I mean *worldwide* anarchy."

Lori shook her head in disbelief. "You really believe it's that bad?"

Malcolm nodded his head sagely. "Yes, I do. Furthermore, I know that various government agencies, the Federal Reserve and the President's office have contingency plans in an event such as this, just as we and every other multinational corporation have. But, being a multinational bank, we often have lines of information in the financial and industrial world that federal agencies do not have. So we learn of certain situations even before the feds do."

Lori looked at Malcolm quizzically as she answered. "Exactly how does that make me essential to the problem at hand?"

Malcolm looked at Lori thoughtfully and drew a breath. "Your computer skills are well known especially in light of your reorganization of the Commerce Department's computer systems. We need that kind of knowledge, coupled with your analytical mind, to help us locate and understand something that may either be very helpful or very dangerous to us."

Lori swung her head to throw her long blond hair back over her shoulders as she asked, "And just what is it that you perceive to be so potentially dangerous?"

Malcolm picked up a folder from the stack beside him and said, "Recently we became aware of a computer network set up in such a manner as to be able act as an electronic monetary system. It may well be able to circumvent this situation and put organized civilization firmly back in control before anarchy takes root."

Lori leaned back in her seat and looked thoughtfully at the ceiling as she gathered her thoughts for a response. "Are you saying that there may be a computer system already in operation that could take the place of our present monetary system?"

Malcolm opened the file on his lap and turned to a specific page as he continued. "Here is what we know, Lori. Since DECOLAC was publicly announced, our analysts have been monitoring all financial markets to spot anything unusual that might either be helpful or warn us of a potentially serious problem.

"Yesterday morning there was a significant fall off in some of the market trades and settlements of our largest multinational customers. That is something no company in international trade can do without for even a day, default or not.

"Coupled with this, we became aware of a lack of long-term futures being traded by producers of precious metals and other commodities.

"It's almost as if there were an underground market already set up to bypass conventional monetary systems based on advance insider information of the Default Committee's plans."

Lori was intrigued by what she was hearing. There had only been a hint of this in the intelligence material she had been given in the past twenty-four hours.

"What do you attribute this global marketing operation to?" she asked Malcolm.

"That's the puzzle," Malcolm answered. "It is not a politically grounded or motivated situation. Not one contact in any of the countries we have talked to has any idea of what is happening even though, they too noted the situation when we described our findings.

"There is only one possibility to explain that situation. We have been observing various computer barter systems for some time now for a number of business reasons including the possibility of acquiring one of the more successful ones just to keep our finger on the pulse of things.

"One of the most vocal evangelists for barter systems is a man named John Garland. He's an internationally known mining engineer and mine operator. He is also a self-taught computer whiz with widespread international contacts.

"Apparently he has, for many years, been preaching the idea that a worldwide computer network could be set up that could, in any monetary emergency, act as a well-ordered electronic monetary system, taking the place of failed national currencies or conventional systems.

"In theory, this setup would, in the beginning, provide an inexpensive, free market medium of exchange in the form of a computer-oriented international barter system." Malcolm paused to invite her answer.

Lorelei looked thoughtfully out over the Manhattan skyline for a moment as she evaluated Malcolm's remarks. Finally, she said, "Sounds feasible to me."

Malcolm smiled tightly and said, "Feasible only if it is in the right hands and under proper control."

Lori laughed. "By *'right hands'* I assume you mean your bankers' consortium and the controls of our Federal Reserve and Treasury policies."

Malcolm laughed. "It's not that bad Lori, but I feel it is necessary to keeping an orderly financial system alive in this chaotic world."

She sat forward and rested her chin between her hands as she fixed her piercing eyes on Malcolm. "And just what is it you think I can do?"

"Go to Nevada where the founder and his base system are located. Meet this man, John Garland, and ask him if he would show his computer operation to you. Evaluate what you see and give us an insight as to its viability."

Lori smiled as she shook her head. "What makes you think this man is just going to lift the hood of his baby and let me poke around in its innards?"

"Well," Malcolm began, "first of all, you'll be there representing the President of the United States and our government and he certainly recognizes the needs involved. Second, you have a way about you that few men can resist. Not only are you the under secretary of Commerce, but you are a beautiful woman. Finally, you are the only one I know with the computer knowledge who is intelligent enough to understand and evaluate what you see, hear and learn there."

Lori stood up and walked to the window, her back to Malcolm. "And if this mining man, computer whiz has, in fact, organized an intelligent plan, what then?"

"Learn all about it. How it operates, if it works, why it works. Then report back to the secretary, the President and to me about what you have learned ."

She turned from the window and looked at Malcolm.

"And if it works and if it is a viable alternative to a failing currency as a medium of exchange, what then?"

Malcolm looked at her and shook his head. "I don't know yet, but it is something we must get a handle on. Either it is an answer for this and other countries or . . ." Malcolm paused as he looked at Lori and shrugged his shoulders.

Lori looked at him impatiently and said, "Or what?"

Malcolm shifted uncomfortably in his chair as he answered, "Or it could subvert whatever intelligent action we hope to take. As a good bureaucrat I am sure you can understand that."

She shook her head. "Sometimes I wonder if I did the right thing making government my career."

Malcolm laughed. "What in the world are you talking about? Every senator and congressman I know thinks you are the most brilliant and productive bureaucrat in Washington.

"It's only a matter of time before you get appointed as the director of one of Washington's key agencies."

She cocked her head and looked at David Malcolm with a slight smile on her face, "You're pouring on an awful lot of soft soap, Mr. Banker."

He stood up, reached down and scooped up the folders on the end table beside his chair and held them out to her.

"Here is all the background on John Garland we have, including pictures and stories about his various projects from trade journals and newspaper articles."

Lori took the file folders and put them into her shoulder strap briefcase and said, "You bankers seem to have more sources than the FBI. Where did you get all this stuff? And by the way, where do I find this man?"

"He operates a mine and engineering business located in Toiyabe Canyon a several-hour drive east of Reno."

She thought for a moment. "And you think he'll just invite me into his office and tell me the whole story."

"Apparently so," Malcolm answered. "He's always been very open about the entire operation, which is probably why everyone missed it. He is a real evangelist for his cause and he'll talk about it to anyone who'll listen."

"You're sure?"

"Look Lori, first of all you are an incredibly beautiful woman. Second, your importance in our government is well known and anyone would be flattered by the fact that you are interested in their pet project. And third, your understanding of computers has to be an irresistible combination for a man as intelligent as Garland apparently is."

Lori asked, "How old is he? I may pledge allegiance to my flag but that does not include such cute things as bed hopping no matter how dangerous you think the emergency may be."

"Garland is probably in his late fifties or early sixties and the man is said to be a total gentleman of the old school. I doubt very much that he would be prone to chasing you around the sage brush. No matter how sexy you look."

Lori gathered up her things and headed for the door. Her mind already clicking along on the travel arrangements she'd need, the kinds of questions she should be asking and a strange feeling that the man she was going to meet might well have the right idea.

Malcolm's highly efficient staff worked like a well-oiled machine. When Lori left the elevator to go to the main lobby entrance in quest of the bank's limo that had brought her from the airport earlier, she saw Malcolm's limousine brazenly parked in the 'no parking' area in front of the bank and the smiling chauffeur holding the car door open for her.

Her luggage was still in the trunk from her ride in from La Guardia earlier. As she walked to the car, the chauffeur held out an envelope for her.

"Your tickets to Reno, ma'am. Mr. Malcolm had them sent down for you. Your flight leaves in 45 minutes from La Guardia to Reno non-stop on Intercontinental Air."

As she settled in the back seat and opened the envelope, she thought to herself, *I must make a note to reimburse the bank for this ticket. No conflict of interest or favoritism for me, David, old boy.*

She looked at the chauffeur in the rear view mirror and said, "Excuse me but what is your name please?"

"Charles, ma'am," he answered, glancing at her in the mirror quickly.

"Charles, I don't understand, I've taken flight 1726 many times before and it always stops in Denver before flying on to Reno and San Francisco. This ticket says it's a non-stop flight to Reno."

"Yes ma'am, the bank is the majority shareholder and they had all Denver passengers put on a special flight to Denver."

"I'll be damned!" she muttered under her breath.

"Yes ma'am," answered Charles.

Then she pulled out another smaller envelope from a pocket in the ticket folder. The note inside was from David Malcolm and it read, "I've taken the liberty of arranging for a rental car for you in Reno. The keys will be at the desk of the car rental agency along with a map showing the shortest route to Toiyabe Canyon. Before leaving, there is a suite booked for you at the Reno Hilton." It was signed 'David.'

"I'll be damned!" she said again.

"Yes ma'am," Charles answered again.

CHAPTER TWELVE
FLYING CAN BE DISTURBING
TO YOUR SERENITY AND LIFESTYLE

Somewhere over the Rockies
March 3, 2:20 p.m.

The plane hummed along so smoothly that Lori thought perhaps Malcolm's bank owned stock in the weather and the skies as well.

Though she had been thoroughly briefed on the Global Trading system by her assistant in Washington, she had been reading the material in the briefing folder Malcolm had given her and relating it to the material she had read about this concept in her office the day before.

From some of the papers that John Garland had published over the years she concluded that she'd be dealing with an impressive intellect.

The news articles about him were all based on his work and focused on his projects rather than him. *A very private man,* she thought. *Not a glory hound. Interesting,* she mused.

She read several dissertations he had written about the value of organizing and operating a worldwide electronic monetary system based on credits for intrinsic or real value rather than paper money. *It all made practical sense,* she thought. *Especially in the situation now facing the world's commerce.*

She put down the outline she had been reading and gazed out of the window at the brilliant blue skies dotted with wisps of clouds. *But would it be able to handle the massive amount of daily transactions that would now suddenly flood the main computer banks of such a system?*

She thought about her own long hours of work at Commerce. The heartbreak of struggling with the department's massive antiquated computer banks, working to write new software and install modern computer hardware in order to process the enormous amount of data they gathered every day

Page 59

in a more intelligent and efficient manner.

There were so many breakdowns, so many mistakes and program rewriting and tinkering. Yet, somehow she muddled through and made it work. It made the monthly and quarterly Commerce Department figures much more accurate and generated incredible reports and forecasts never before possible and made them all instantaneously available.

She smiled as she thought about how that success had boosted her career up the bureaucratic ladder several dozen rungs overnight and then brought her the prized assistant secretary of Commerce post.

That had been something she had not expected nor had it been her goal. Her only interest had been to make that department more honest, more responsive and its reports far more reliable.

It's funny, even corny, she thought, *but I actually did it for my country, just like the men in uniform always say.*

She turned back to the thick folder and began to read again, glance reading what was not pertinent but filing away key sentences in her mind for later reference and reading all the important material in depth.

Finally she opened the section marked "personal information." There were pictures of Garland as a sailor in the World War II Navy. And later pictures of him with his children when they were young, usually at some mining site in the mountains.

As she leafed through the pictures she thought, *He is a handsome man in a rugged sort of way. Not 'pretty boy' handsome but rather he seems to have the look of a man who would automatically engender confidence when you dealt with him.*

Most of the pictures showed him in open-collar work clothes one would wear in rugged mining country. No evidence of an attempt to pose or posture, always just natural. She liked that.

One picture showed him at the wedding of one of his daughters, dressed in a dinner jacket. Lori glanced back at the other pictures and then back to the wedding scene. It struck her that when he was dressed up he was quite a handsome man. He looked as if he'd fit in anywhere.

She judged from the people around him, that he was tall. Quickly leafing to the back page of statistics she saw that he was well over six feet. She thought of her own height and how it sometimes made her feel uncomfortable in a room full of short men.

The captain's voice came over the intercom to interrupt her musing.

"Ladies and gentlemen, we will be landing at the Reno Cannon International Airport in twenty minutes. Please fasten your seat belts and give the flight attendants your cups and trays as they pass down the aisle.

"The weather is clear and sunny, temperature in Reno is a pleasant 55 degrees. I might remind you to set your watches back three hours, Reno time is now exactly 2:35 p.m.

As he droned on, Lori's mind turned to planning her itinerary. The in-flight phone service had permitted her to verify that John Garland was at the Delta mining office and that he would have time to see her the next day.

She was tired so she thought about staying at the hotel and resting overnight before the long drive to Toiyabe Canyon.

The plane touched down almost without a bump. *Another thing Malcolm probably controls,* she thought.

CHAPTER THIRTEEN
THE LADY MEETS A SWEET SWEDE

Reno, Nevada
March 3, 2:55 p.m.

The plane had rolled to a stop at the unloading ramp and people were unbuckling their seat belts and standing up to get their belongings from the overhead luggage compartments.

Lori struggled to get her carry-on bag out of the compartment as other passengers squeezed by her, all trying to get to the door first. In the middle of her struggle, she felt a gentle touch on her shoulder.

Looking over her shoulder she saw the biggest, roughest, toughest-looking man she had ever seen, his weather-beaten face softly smiling at her.

"You Miss Lorelei Young, ma'am?" She suddenly noticed that the man's bulk had stopped all traffic past her as he spoke to her. He had apparently come onto the plane without any problem.

"Don't tell me you work for David Malcolm or his bank or his airline or his whatever?"

The man smiled a warm, friendly smile. "No ma'am, I work for John Garland and he told me to meet you and help you with your luggage." With that, he lifted out the heavy bag with one hand as if it were a bag of donuts and swung it deftly over her. Looking back at her, he smiled again and said, "Just follow me, ma'am."

Lori was flabbergasted, she had made no mention over the in-flight phone of how she was traveling, when she would arrive in Reno or anything else. She shook her head and followed the friendly giant.

When they got into the airport she caught up with him and he turned and lifted his hat to her. "My name's Swede Hanson, Miss Young. Big John asked me to make sure you had no problems and to get you up to Toiyabe Canyon safe and sound."

She had to take long strides to keep up with her escort while she tried to explain her planned itinerary to him. "Mr. Hanson," she said somewhat breathlessly, "I had planned to stay at the Hilton tonight and get a good night's rest and drive down in the morning."

"No need for that Miss Young. We got the company chopper just on the other side of the airport about a five minute drive in my pickup. You don't mind ridin' in a pickup do ya? Anyways, it's just about thirty minutes from here by chopper and a lot more comfortable than drivin' a hunnert and some odd miles over jack rabbit 'n' snake country.

"The wife's got one of the company lodge's guest rooms all set for ya. Take a nice hot bath, a little nap an' you'll be all set for a fine dinner with the boss. It ain't as fancy as the Hilton but I get a feelin' you'll like it a lot better."

Lori quickly got the impression that this was her itinerary no matter what. They went through the automatic doors and walked up to a new but dusty pickup truck parked in a 'no parking' zone with an airport policeman standing by the cab.

As they walked up the policeman smiled and said, "Hi Swede, figured this was your truck when I came up." He opened the door for Lori.

"Hi Dan, been out to your claims lately?" The Swede swung her heavy bag into the back of the pickup while she carried her briefcase into the cab with her.

"Naw, been too cold. Figure on goin' up in May and do my assessment work."

"Stop by the equipment yard when ya go and let me know what you'll need, Dan. You just take care of the fuel and be careful with the equipment." Swede waved at the cop as he put the truck in gear.

"Thanks Swede. See ya in May."

Swede pulled out into the traffic stream as smoothly as the limousine had in New York and turned onto Terminal Way heading north around the airport perimeter to the private air terminal on the other side.

Looking up at her oversized escort, Lori felt small sitting beside him. "Everybody out here in mining Mr. Hanson?"

The Swede smiled. "No ma'am, just them that has rocks in their head and gold fever in their blood."

She looked at him quizzically. "Tell me, how did you know what flight I would be on and when I would arrive?"

"I dunno, it's just that Big John's got friends all over that tell him anything they think he might want ta know or might be helpful to him."

Lori looked out over the town's skyline a moment and then said, "I suppose that by 'Big John' you mean Mr. Garland?"

"Yes ma'am."

"Is he bigger than you?"

"No ma'am, ain't too many people bigger than me. It's just that Big John is big in lotsa other ways, not just tall big. I reckon he's nearly tall as me and he's tougher than a boot nail. But that ain't the reason folks call him 'Big John.' It's more for stuff like he's got real big kindness, and he's done big things. I mean stuff that means a lot to a lot of people."

"Does everyone around here call him 'Big John'?"

"It's just kind of a nickname I guess. I known him and worked for him goin' on thirty years an' I always called him Big John unless there was big shot business folks around an' then I showed respect and all and called him 'Mr. Garland.' He kinda smiles every time I call him that."

He stopped talking as they swung off the street into the parking area beside a hanger and office. The Swede swung Lori's bag out of the back of the pickup and headed for the office door.

Lori grabbed her briefcase off the seat and ran to catch up with the big man.

Inside the office was a young man in Levi's tearing off some weather reports from a fax machine. He looked up at the two and said, "Ready to go Swede?"

"All set, Carl. This here's Miss Young. She's with the government and she come to talk to the boss."

Carl looked appreciatively at Lori and said, "The government's taste is getting better all the time. Come on, let's crank up the bird. Weather looks perfect and you'll be able to see some beautiful desert shadows this afternoon."

Chapter Fourteen
Congress Is As Congress Does
Whether We Like It Or Not

Senate Office Building, Washington, D.C.
March 3, 4:40 p.m.

Jim Ketchall, the highly respected majority leader of the Senate, was carefully rereading a thick document on his desk before him. His brow was knitted as he made margin notes and highlighted certain sentences with a yellow, felt-tipped pen, a habit left over from his days as a federal appeals court judge.

A light tap on his door interrupted his concentration and he looked up as his senior aide came in with a folder and a note pad.

The senator looked quizzically at his aide. "What's the prognosis, Tom? Will we get it out of committee for a debate and a vote?"

"It was touch and go with our friends from North Carolina and Wyoming. As usual, they both felt it was some kind of 'commie plot' to destroy our country's financial system. But we struck a deal."

The senator looked pained. "What kind of a deal?"

"I convinced the good senator from the south that the only way he can hope to get the tobacco subsidy extended is to go along with you on this vote. And the senator from Wyoming didn't want to take a chance that his state's biggest military base might be closed."

Senator Ketchall leaned back in his chair and rubbed his patrician brow.

"I guess I can live with that. More and more people are giving up cigarettes every day and the base in Wyoming is actually phasing itself out of business.

"What I've been trying to do is reword this outline of how Garland's electronic barter system works in such a way that it will generate the least amount of negative debate when it gets to the floor.

"It's so damn simple and so practical that the bank lobbyists are going to be afraid of it. Especially when they get through reading the analysis we're having done on the theory of its operation by the National Science Foundation, Treasury and Commerce departments."

Tom sat down in one of the chairs in front the senator's desk and leaned with his chin on his fists and said, "I don't get it? If it's so practical and simple, why should anyone be afraid of it."

The senator smiled. "Because Tom, it might work and work without their being able to get pudgy, well-fed fingers on the control switch in some way. And perhaps because their supporters in the banking and finance industry will be afraid of losing the ability to charge usurious interest rates on things like credit cards and consumer loans, that's why."

Tom raised his head as if the light had just gone on and said, "Oh! Is that all? What about all the gentlemen who count on big-time taxes to support heavy spending in their districts or for their supporting PAC's whose industries, like the ones that supply the defense department all its military hardware? Like for instance eighty dollar hammers and $400 toilet seats?"

The senator got up, walked over to the window and looked out at the cold night scene before him and then turned to look at Tom. "And let's not forget all those who don't want to lose the ability to get a little spending cash in unmarked bills that won't show up on someone's computer.

"This system will be stepping on the toes of a lot of vested interests. But it will do more for ethics in government than all the bills we can write and pass. Yessir, I do love this plan. This Garland fella really came up with a blockbuster when he dreamed this up."

Tom nodded his head in agreement. "Yup, he sure did."

The senator walked over to his desk and picked up the thick outline he had been working on, and, leafing through the last few pages, made a few penciled notations on the borders and handed it to his aide.

"Get Mindy and the two of you go off to your personal computer and rewrite this thing by tomorrow morning with the changes I've suggested. I especially want you to highlight the part explaining how the federal, state and local governments will still be able to collect their taxes from within the system.

"When you print it out, make only fourteen copies and then erase the whole thing from your computer's memory. Don't let anyone see any of it and get it back here by 9 a.m. tomorrow."

Tom took the papers from the senator and said, "Done."

The senator knitted his brow as he continued. "I will be setting up a meeting with the chairmen and members of the banking and finance committees of both houses and spring it on them as soon as we take our committee vote and go to the floor with it.

"With the state of affairs and the limited time in which we have to arrive at some kind of answer, this barter system is the only thing I've seen that might get us out of this mess. And, by God, I'm going see that it's approved and passed for the good of the country as a whole and to hell with the lobbyists, the PACs and some of our esteemed colleagues who can't seem to get re-elected on their own merits."

Tom got up smiling and said, "Way to go boss" and, manuscript under his arm, headed for the door to do the senator's bidding.

CHAPTER FIFTEEN
IF YOU WANT TO KEEP A SECRET, DON'T WHISPER

Mayflower Hotel, Washington D.C.
March 3, 8:40 p.m.

The suite was one of the most opulent in the venerable old hotel as was befitting the wealth and power of the men present this wintry night.

David Malcolm was pouring a drink for a man whose bearing suggested he was a military man though he was dressed in expensive, well-cut civilian clothes. David looked up and said, "Say when, General."

The general smiled and said, "Three fingers is plenty Dave. Want to keep my brain on the alert tonight."

Standing nearby, a small group was heatedly discussing the default. Among them Congressman Garvin, chairman of the House Armed Services Committee; George Murdoch, assistant director of the CIA; and Corbin Esterbrook, chairman of Brighton Industries, one of the nation's largest defense contractors.

A knock on the door brought an Army orderly from a pantry off the main entrance to open the door. He recognized the colonel leading the contingent of late arrivals and stood aside as he saluted smartly.

The colonel led the group into the entry area where they shed coats and hats, handed them to the orderly and entered the drawing room.

After the handshakes and greetings were over and drinks were served to the newcomers, David Malcolm invited them to sit down on the semicircle of sofas and overstuffed chairs.

When the assemblage had settled down, David put down his glass on the bar and walked over to a fireplace around which the seats and couches were arranged.

"I presume that everyone here arrived via the private elevator from the basement garage."

There were several nods and murmurs of assent.

"Good, our meeting here tonight must remain our business and our business alone. For lack of a better title, I would like to call this a cross briefing so each of us can advise the rest of what we presently know and or have reason to believe concerning this so called 'barter system' that seems to be the leading contender to replace our nation's monetary system by osmosis."

There were nods of assent and murmured agreements from the assemblage before Malcolm continued.

"Let me begin by telling you that, at the President's direction, one of this government's brightest and most computer-knowledgeable people is on her way to observe and evaluate the system and its founder, John Garland, the architect of what some are calling 'Operation Bypass.'

"She is Lorelei Young whom I think most of you know is our assistant secretary of Commerce. My people in Nevada tell me she was met at the plane this afternoon by one of Garland's employees and taken by his company helicopter to the headquarters.

"As soon as she gets as much information as possible on this system and its location, she will be reporting to the President, the Secretary and, of course, myself.

"In the meantime, we have learned some interesting things about this man and his barter system. It seems that he has been working on this concept for well over ten years."

Congressman Garvin interrupted Malcolm's dissertation with a raised glass and asked, "I know that the leaders of the House and Senate have directed the Treasury and the National Science Foundation to drop everything and study the feasibility of Mr. Garland's system and all other possible alternatives, but what makes you think this particular barter system has so much going for it?"

Malcolm rocked back on his heels and closed his eyes for a moment before answering. "Well Congressman, it seems that Garland has, over time, sold the concept to banks, corporations, bureaucrats and some of our leading senators and congressmen. He has even convinced a few heads of state of some of the world's largest countries. It is my understanding that Russia, China, and South Africa have wholeheartedly embraced the concept.

"Of course, for them it is obviously a way to get around embargoes on certain goods and services and bypass the need for hard currency for trade.

"Perhaps equally as important is that ALL of the DECOLAC countries banks are tying in to this computer network and are therefore able to conduct business as usual regardless of the boycott that went into effect yesterday at noon.

"I might add that their 'business as usual' is at better prices to them than before they began utilizing the system.

"To say the least, we are being severely limited as to the amount of muscle we can bring to bear on these defaulting nations."

Corbin Esterbrook asked, "What about our many friends in Congress, Dave? God knows we've raised enough money for their war chests"

Malcolm arched his eyebrows as he answered, "Now that you ask Corbin, I'm told that Garland has some powerful allies in Congress who believe this system is a viable alternative to the nation's present monetary system. I'm told they believe it could be utilized to head off economic hysteria and restore confidence in the monetary system."

Corbin wrinkled his brow. "Strange that I've never heard of it before."

Malcolm shrugged his shoulders as he continued, "In fact, at this very moment, there is a move afoot to introduce a bill to adopt the system as an electronic monetary system and make it unlawful to interfere with its operation in any way."

Senator Tim Fourchette, one of the Senate's staunchest conservatives and a late arrival, raised his glass to Dave Malcolm to catch his attention.

"Dave, excuse my interruption but I have some information that probably impacts this very situation."

Malcolm nodded, acquiescing the floor to the senator.

"I received a call from Senate Majority Leader Jim Ketchall just before I left my office to come to this meeting. He advised me that there was going to be a committee meeting tomorrow morning at 10:30 to present a proposed Senate bill on this very matter and, in light of the urgency of the situation, move for a committee vote to bring it to the floor for debate and a vote by the full Senate. It's the fastest such action since the World War II War Powers Act."

Malcolm looked shocked. "Does the President know about this, Tim?"

The senator shrugged his shoulders. "I don't know, Dave. But whether he does or not, my aide told me that a group of representatives in the House is pushing a similar version of this proposed bill in their committee starting tomorrow morning."

Malcolm's growing anger was becoming evident. "Dammit George, surely the CIA has had some advance warning on this. Don't tell me that the agency didn't even have an inkling of this barter system operation and its intent?"

George Murdoch shook his head in assent. "Sure we did, Dave. As a matter of fact, less than six weeks ago, we received a letter with a very well prepared political and financial analysis warning us of the possibility of a Latin American bank loan default, its possible effect on the major First World nations' economies and a detailed description of how a computer barter system could be converted to an electronic monetary system to head off problems."

"Who was the author of that and why wasn't I notified?"

"The author was John Garland and he stated that it was of the utmost importance that we bring it to the attention of the President.

"We actually did that in the usual Monday-morning intelligence briefing where it gets lost among all the exciting things like the situation in Yugoslavia, how we're doing in Somalia and how can we solve the health care problem."

Malcolm shook his head in disbelief. "I can't understand why we weren't clued into this."

Murdoch looked at Malcolm quizzically. "You were, Dave. At the same time that the President received his briefing, we sent you a copy of the pertinent information through the usual channels. In fact, your number one financial analyst briefed you on what were discussing here today."

Malcolm shifted uncomfortably and, almost as if he were talking to himself, said, "How could I have possibly missed something as important as this? I must really have been preoccupied that day."

"Don't feel bad, Dave. One of our best financial and political analysts has been bugging us for many months about Garland's approach and ideas, until it took on the character of 'Chicken Little' telling everyone the sky is falling in.

"Then one day he took a leave of absence to go into psychotherapy. When that happened, we just wrote his views off as a 'nut-bag' paranoia.

"Like the President, and like us and everyone else, until the DECOLAC situation actually happened, you and we and they didn't pay any attention to all this."

Malcolm's face flushed a deep red and he fought to control the tic in his eye and the emotions boiling through his frame. He kept shaking his head from side to side as if he were saying *no, no, no.*

"Do you gentlemen realize that fully a third of our banks' profits are realized from the interest we charge on credit cards.

"That another 20 percent comes from our consumer loan divisions where that same percentage rate prevails and it's likely that a large part of that income goes down the toilet with this infernal electronic monetary system!

"It will literally control what we are able to charge and what we can do. There will no longer be any way for any of us in business and industry to quietly own other divisions or pump payments from one division to another to Jack up our profits for a reasonable return on our investments in shares of stock.

"Why, that system could control every damn one of us. You, Senator, will have a hell of a time raising PAC money for your re-election." Whirling, pointing a finger at Corbin Esterbrook, Malcolm said, "And your Brighton Industries, Corbin, will never again get a contract for tanks that don't work or planes that can't stay in repair long enough to make a bomb run."

Corbin Esterbrook shook his head. "I can't believe this guy and his system can be that powerful. We've got some damn strong political and military alliances, Dave."

Malcolm shook his head. "Listen my friends, this damn system, if it is adopted, is going to control you, me, all of us. We won't be able to sneeze without that damn central computer knowing how many credits we charged or spent.

"As I see it gentlemen, we either have to gain control of that system, learn how to set up our own competitive barter system or put that damn thing out of business.

"Before we can even begin, we have to locate the central unit and we have to know how it works. If we know how it works, we may be able to get a competitive operation up and running. We know ours will be sanctioned by the President and many of our friends in Congress. That should put Garland's operation out of business.

"Alternatively, if we know where it's located and all else fails, we'll still be able to physically put it out of business."

Corbin Esterbrook again interrupted and said, "Dave, this may sound foolish, but have you ever thought of making him an offer he can't refuse?"

"Corbin, the man is strange. He has no personal or business debts or even short-term, supplier-due bills. He has an eight figure net worth as near as we can determine and worse, he has no interest in money at all where this system of his is concerned.

"In the last twenty-four hours we've made him offers in figures that are obscene even for me. He hasn't even responded to our phone calls, FAXs or personal envoys."

With that, Malcolm turned impatiently from Corbin to General Mathewson.

"General, since I called you about this, what have you found out?"

The general turned to the late arriving colonel as he answered. "After you called Dave, I talked to Colonel Burns here who is in charge of the most sophisticated signal tracking equipment in the world. He controls everything from a worldwide group of ground-sited identification and tracking stations tied into several military satellites, to a wing of tracking aircraft, all of whom monitor and identify signals twenty-four hours a day on a worldwide basis. Colonel, what do you have to report so far?"

The colonel visibly straightened his shoulders as attention focused on him and he pulled a notebook from his inside jacket pocket to read from notes.

"First of all sir, we picked up numerous signals from private satellites like COMSAT and from domestic and overseas phone lines, all of which were making barter trades in the manner you described.

The incoming signals indicating a desire to make a trade along with the reply signals indicating the value of the trade in credits. They seemed to be routed to different pick-up and reply points every fifteen minutes."

David Malcolm interrupted the colonel momentarily, "What do you mean by 'different pickup and reply points' Colonel?"

"Well, sir," the colonel continued, "whenever there is major financial information traffic or trade traffic, like currency futures, the points of origin and response are always the same.

"We always know that certain banks in New York, Brussels, London, Amsterdam, Paris, Zurich, Rome, Tokyo and Hong Kong are consistently the senders and receivers on the information exchange.

"I can tell you their phone numbers, their street addresses, the location of their communications boards, computers, satellite dishes and satellite addresses and the like. They never change.

"But in this case, though a great number of the offers to trade emanate from the same source such as Krupp Steel in Germany or Royal Dutch Shell in Amsterdam, the central computer receiving the information and responding, is coming from a different location every fifteen minutes.

"One time it will emanate from SATCOM and when we get a fix on it to track where it's going to or from, it will suddenly switch to a French satellite or from a London dish to an American dish in New York or maybe Canada. A couple of times it even originated inside Russia.

"It never stays on the air from one single location more than fifteen minutes and so far we have identified over thirty-five such locations but it never misses a beat. It's as if there are thirty-five different main frames running in tandem that switch off in less than a hundredth of a millisecond."

Malcolm was speechless for a moment. "What are you telling us Colonel? That with all your incredible capability you can't pin point where this damn thing is located?"

"Well sir, at least not yet. When we finally pick it up from a new point it will usually have been broadcasting trades for a few minutes. Then we need to start scanning different radio, microwave dish, satellite dish and phone company emanations to try to pick up how it is being routed.

"By the time we get that far, the emanation will have switched and we have to start all over again.

"We've even tried just monitoring one source like COM-SAT, that we know is used periodically, in order to be able to identify its transmissions the minute they come on the air to give us more time. But damned if they don't change transmission character through some kind of computer cryptography so it takes us a while to figure out what we are monitoring."

Corbin Esterbrook tilted his head as he calmly looked at the bedazzled group. "Looks like this man and his system ought to be training the CIA and a few other people around here."

The blood in George Murdock's face rose to give him a flushed look. "That's unfair Corbin, we already know all those tricks. That's why we use them ourselves. It's kept others from picking up more than they have when we transmit covert information."

The colonel interrupted them, "Don't worry sir, we will eventually track their transmissions to their central broadcast site, it's only a matter of time."

"How much time, Colonel?" asked Malcolm. "Days? Weeks? Months? We need to know now. Gentlemen, it is time we develop a workable contingency plan that will protect our interests one way or the other."

CHAPTER SIXTEEN
TWO PEOPLE OF DIFFERENT MINDS
BUT KINDRED SPIRITS

Toiyabe Canyon, Nevada
March 3, 7:30 p.m.

Lori was pleasantly surprised at the charm and beauty of the little mining town nestled in the fan of Toiyabe Canyon.

The elevation of the area had brought them into the timber and greenery of the snow-covered mountain range and the community was surprisingly large with evergreen trees lining the streets and comfortable-looking houses, stores and businesses set back from the well laid out streets.

The 'room' as Swede Hanson had called it was in fact a very comfortable, well furnished apartment in the company lodge at the upper end of Toiyabe Canyon's main street. It had a fireplace in the sitting room, a luxurious bath and shower and a large, comfortable bedroom. It was a far cry from the rustic cabin she had envisioned.

Swede's wife turned out to be an attractive, soft-spoken woman of middle age who made her feel quite at ease as if they had known each other for years. *In fact,* Lori mused afterward, *it was almost as if I were coming to visit a favorite aunt.*

After a bath and a short nap, Lori dressed casually, as Mrs. Hanson had suggested, and walked down to the main hall of the lodge where a roaring fire was being stoked by the Swede.

"How about a nice cup of hot coffee, Miss Young?" the Swede asked her.

"Thank you very much. One sugar and a bit of cream please."

The cup and saucer were almost lost in his huge hand as he held it out to her with the grace of an accomplished butler.

"I have business to take care of Miss Young, you just make yerself at home and Mr. Garland will be here in a few minutes."

She smiled and thanked him. After he left, Lori walked

over to the window looking westward and down over the community that spread out and down the canyon floor below.

In the twilight, it looked like a picture postcard scene painted by someone who had enjoyed living in a small, comfortable rural community.

She stood lost in thoughts looking over the quiet, peaceful scene as lights went on in windows throughout the picturesque little town.

John Garland had quietly entered the lodge hall from a door on the far side from where Lori stood at the window.

He stood quietly for a moment, struck by the grace and beauty of the woman at the window.

Lori sensed his presence behind her and turned to find the man whose pictures she had seen earlier standing just inside the door smiling.

"Good evening, Miss Young. I'm John Garland and I am delighted to meet you. I have heard and read so much about you."

He walked across the room extending his hand to her.

Lori stepped forward somewhat puzzled and took his hand. "Thank you, Mr. Garland. And frankly, I am flattered that a man like you knows anything about me."

"Miss Young, any businessman who stays current with news about Washington is well aware of the computer magic you worked at the Department of Commerce. All of us anxiously await your department's reports in order to know what is going on in our economic world."

Despite the obvious flattery, Lori instinctively felt very comfortable with this man. She sensed that he meant every word he said and there was no ulterior motive for his praise. She smiled graciously and said, "Please call me Lori. And, if I may, I'll call you John."

John nodded his head and said, "Please do. Come let's sit down in the dining room."

He took her arm and they walked into a warm, comfortable dining room that had several tables, not unlike a hotel lodge.

One of the tables by a large bay window overlooking the moonlit snow-covered mountain, was set for two.

As they sat down Mrs. Hanson came bustling in with a plate of vegetable hors d'oeuvres and a tureen of steaming soup.

"I'm so glad you came in just now. I didn't want the soup getting cold. It's your favorite Mr. G and it's just right and here is a nice salad. I know you'll like this soup, too, Lori. You fit." And with that she whirled around and went out calling over her shoulder. "I'll be back with some hot rolls in a minute."

John laughed, "I see you've made a hit with 'Tante Alice.' If she says you fit, feel flattered because to her, most people don't. That is quite a compliment."

John's laugh was infectious and Lori laughed with him as she said, "Oh really, how does she mean 'I fit'?"

"It means," he said, "that she has adopted you into her own private family. You have impressed her as someone who fits her version of family."

Lori asked, "Are you one of her family?"

"Oh, she adopted me about twenty-five years ago, after she was convinced that I was not trying to lead her husband astray. That took five years from the time Swede went to work for me. You must be special because it only took her a couple of hours to decide about you."

They laughed and Lori said, "You called her 'Tante Alice.' That's German for 'aunt,' isn't it?"

"Yes, she is originally from Germany. Shortly after she and her family arrived, her father came west with the family to set up a machine shop catering to the mining industry. That is how she met Swede here in Nevada. After a five-year whirlwind courtship . . ."

Lori's laughter interrupted John and she repeated, "A five-year, whirlwind courtship? I always thought a whirlwind courtship referred to a few days or a few weeks."

"Not to stolid Germans and careful Swedes," and they both laughed at the shared joke.

John looked at Lori with a frown on his face. "Tell me what brought you to this unknown corner of the world, Lori."

Lori smiled as she answered, "When the President commands, the troops respond. I sincerely believe that he and many people in and out of government want to know whether or not your system might be an answer to the present problem. And since I'm the resident computer hacker, here I am."

John nodded thoughtfully before answering, "I'm delighted and flattered."

They talked animatedly throughout dinner about their work, their political philosophies, the recent books they had read (often the same), the conditions of the world, the possible effects of the default and the possible benefits of the changes it might bring about.

They were amazed at the commonality of their thinking. Though each held their own strong personal beliefs and ideas, they were obviously both on the same wave length.

After dinner they went into the lodge hall and sat before the fire with their coffee. At Lori's insistence, John began to tell her his views and feelings on the present situation and how it might affect the world at large.

As he talked, he detailed, point by point, the history of the loans made to the defaulting nations. Warming to the subject, he got up to walk back and forth — more comfortable thinking on his feet — inviting questions, discussing reasons and filling in a total picture.

"Let us look back at the beginning of these sovereign loans and take Mexico as an example. After the revolution, Mexico nationalized the railroads, minerals, communications, much of the banking and the oil industry.

"Mexico's ruling party, the PRI had been in power most of that time with signs of becoming even stronger. The new constitution afforded the government all mineral rights, and anyone who mined there had to pay a royalty to the government. They also owned the railroads, the major banking institutions and most utilities, thereby controlling the major sources of income."

Lori interjected, "I knew Mexico had become quite nationalized but I had no idea it was that wide spread."

"On the surface, all those nationalized assets suggested they had the assets to indemnify any loan they wished to make. With all that potential income and equity value, they were considered 'good' for it.

"But there was trouble in Mexico City, to paraphrase *The Music Man.* The PRI, in order to continue its political power as a one party system, had many political favors to repay. They also had many hungry peasants to whom a tiny plot of redistributed land was not economically feasible and provided almost no security or even survival.

"In order to keep the peace and keep themselves in power, it became necessary to create many 'make-work' jobs in bureaucratized, government-owned industries such as Pemex, the state owned oil company.

"The once-profitable oil fields became burdened with four men doing the work one used to do more efficiently. The railroads spent money on hiring people who did little or no work, spent almost no money on modernizing and only did minimal maintenance.

"Multiply what I've just told you by Brazil, Argentina, Venezuela and most of the other Latin countries and you begin to see the immensity of the problem."

Lori looked at John thoughtfully. "Certainly that must have been obvious to the various lending agencies and banks who had representatives in those countries?"

John shrugged his shoulders. "Apparently not. No one in the lending banks and nations even chose to do minimal due diligence before making these high-interest sovereign loans.

"You must understand that most of the investigators were bureaucrats from this and other countries who were there dealing with bureaucrats from those countries.

"There are, of course, dedicated, hard working bureaucrats like yourself. But there are also those who slowly, almost as if by osmosis, come to adopt a sort of bureaucratic personae or mindset. Their subconscious drive seems to focus on perpetuating themselves and their agencies rather than actually solve problems they are assigned to solve."

Lori shook her head slightly. "I'm afraid I don't completely agree with that. I know many, many totally dedicated people in my agency who work as if they had to make a profit or accomplish the goals set before them."

"I'm sure that's quite true, Lori, especially since your agency is more business-oriented and your own leadership qualities are more those of private industry. Unfortunately, history seems to tell us that in the past, every great civilization was usually brought to its knees not by wars or famines but by weight its own ever-growing, ever-costlier bureaucracies."

Lori's first reaction was an instinctive rise in blood pressure and an argumentative gorge rising in her throat.

John saw it coming and smiled at her. Holding up his hand he said, "Please, I am just discoursing, not indicting our great government. I just wish to draw a parallel between this perceived political condition and a virus. If the virus continues to grow and multiply unchecked, not reined in by a responsible, elected government answerable to its constituents, it eventually destroys its host body. From the Roman empire to today's India, this disease has eventually brought great nations to a grinding halt and finally to their knees. Fortunately for us, when our citizens have had enough, they rise up and hold their elected representatives responsible, from the President down. But at that particular time in space, the status quo was in charge and the virus was still growing unchecked.

"Oh there were a few hard-nosed businessmen at the International Monetary Fund who kept trying to alert the lenders to the problem, but greed seemed to create a film over the lenders' eyes and interfered with their hearing.

"Meantime, down in Mexico and other Latin countries, buying re-election with borrowed dollars became a way of life. And soon even the interest payments on the ever-growing debt burden became almost impossible to meet out of the ever-shrinking cash flow.

"As Latin Americans elected more responsible, sophisticated officials who were fully aware of the situation and the need to correct it, it had unfortunately already passed the point of no return.

"Wise, well-intentioned presidents and their cabinets were unable to overcome the inertia of an embedded bureaucracy that had taken control of their countries."

Lori smiled. "Sounds like Washington trying to deal with the deficit and the recession."

John shook his head. "Worse, Lori, much worse because in many of those Latin countries, all this tended to spawn an inflationary spiral that soon became runaway and the politically well-connected people in those countries soon were investing the loaned billions back in New York, London, Paris, Geneva and other safe havens instead of investing it in industries and developments that would have given them progress and almost full employment in their own countries.

"Eventually these governments found themselves running in place just to pay the interest payments on the massive debt each year while they 'rolled over' their loans to buy time.

"Then, like hundreds of poorly managed, high-flying companies in our country during and since the '80s, bankruptcy became the only hope of survival.

"Filing for Chapter 11 to seek protection from your creditors became a corporate way of life and survival in the U.S.

"The Latin American countries and their leaders saw this and recognized that it was the only way out of their own predicament. Taking a page from us, they declared their version of bankruptcy and sought protection from their creditors."

Lori listened with rapt attention as John reduced a complicated political and financial situation to the few descriptive thoughts.

She finally said, "You know John, our own government is responsible for a large part of those loans. I remember how various agencies from the State Department to our own agency fully encouraged this situation.

"The bankers were given tacit verbal assurance that they would somehow be covered in the event of a problem and then I suppose greed did the rest."

John nodded approvingly at her level of awareness and understanding of the situation.

"Yes, most assuredly, they are to a great degree responsible for this mess. I have been trying to alert key people in government to this situation for some time now, mostly to little or no avail."

Lori looked thoughtfully at the flames in the fireplace and asked, "Do you know why I'm really here?"

John looked at her before answering, "I can guess. You're obviously one of the few persons in Washington with the brains and competence to seek out and understand the essential information on how this computerized monetary system might operate."

Lori smiled and said, "That's very flattering, but I'm sure there are many others in Washington capable of that."

John shrugged. "Perhaps, but I'm sure that not all of them are as charming, fascinating and beautiful. There aren't many men, including me, who could resist your interest in their project and no doubt, those who sent you recognized that."

Lori shook her had and laughed. "I have had more people tell me that in the last twenty-four hours than in the past five years. However, I was personally very interested in your operation and how it might help relieve the present situation."

John nodded. "Thank you for your interest, but I'm sure there are a lot of concerned, uncomfortable people both in and out of government who desperately want to know how this system might affect them. From the ethically concerned to the selfishly interested, you are no doubt, one of the few people who can give them the information they feel they need to have in order to make an informed decision whatever their goal may be."

Lori looked at her hands for a moment before answering. "The President himself called me. Then the Secretary of Commerce. At first I was flattered. They assigned me to assist David Malcolm, chairman and CEO of Case City Bank, to find out all I could about your system and how they worked and, at least in the President and Secretary's case, if it actually could present an immediate solution."

Lori stopped for a moment, gazing toward the darkness beyond the window lost in thought and then turned back to John and smiled. "Thinking about this assignment on the way out here, I began to wonder whether I would be helping to solve the problem we all face or creating more problems.

"Before leaving, I had my assistant do a thorough research on all the department knew about your proposal.

"After reading our information, it struck me that you had always been completely open and above board about what you felt was coming, what you perceived as some of the problems that might result and how you proposed to solve them with the computerized monetary system.

"I didn't mention this to Malcolm when I saw him in New York this morning, nor did I reveal my personal assessment. He, however, gave me an insight into his own thinking and I believe he perceives you as a serious threat to his enormous financial power and form of banking."

John laughed. "Yes I know, I have friends who work for his bank and who have been giving me a preview of what they feel I can expect from him.

"He may feel that his bank will lose a large part of some very profitable business if an electronic monetary system comes to pass. He probably feels that it would severely limit his method of banking unless he and his friends can control it."

Lori looked shocked. "It sounds like you have an espionage network of your own."

"Not really, Lori, these are truly just friends I have made over the years. Men and women who know me well enough to recognize that I have no ulterior motives in what I do and know that I would never misuse their information or abuse their trust. They really care about what they perceive as a practical answer and a just cause and simply want to help in any way they can."

"And what do you mean by a 'just cause' John?"

"The 'just cause,' Miss Lori," he said smiling at her, "is to protect the American public and the innocents and helpless of the world from financial chaos, from possible anarchy and, as a result of the onset of that, possible dictatorial powers and controls.

"The 'just cause' is to make an orderly transition from a chaotic and potentially dangerous monetary situation, to one that is sound, orderly and completely beyond political or private manipulation."

Lori looked at John quizzically. "I don't quite understand how it can be set up so that it would be beyond political or private control. Isn't that the danger inherent in such a system?"

"Yes Lori, it would normally be a danger, but what I have set up in this instance is a Trust organization acting as the managers of the system and the ownership of the system is vested in perpetuity with its millions of users. It is people-owned, people-managed and people-directed just like a federal credit union. It literally belongs to its depositors."

Lori leaned back and shook her head in amazement. "Yes, I suppose that sort of system can be equated with being a just cause. It would certainly eliminate political or bank control over the value of money. I mean, no one person or group of people would ever be able to create either inflation or deflation at will in order to try to control the economy."

John smiled again. "You are beginning to understand the real value of this system and after I've had a chance to show you how the system operates and introduce you to some of the most dedicated and intelligent young people you will ever meet, I'll leave it for you to decide whether or not this approach to monetary stability is 'just' and a 'cause' worth working for."

He held out his hand to her and helped her up from the couch. "And now I think it's time for us to get some rest. Long years of habit cause me to awaken at 5 a.m. to plan my day, and both of us will have a busy day ahead.

"I hope your accommodations are comfortable and that you have everything you need."

She smiled. "Hilton couldn't have done better. I'll see you in the morning. And John . . . thank you for a most enjoyable dinner and sharing your insights with me."

With that she headed for the stairs to her quarters while John watched her admiringly. *She truly was an exciting and beautiful woman in every way possible,* he thought as he reluctantly turned to go to his quarters.

CHAPTER SEVENTEEN
JUST BECAUSE THERE'S A CAUSE
IS NO CAUSE TO GET EXCITED, OR IS THERE?

Toiyabe Canyon, Nevada
March 4, 7:00 a.m.

The big band sounds of Glenn Miller were emanating from the lodge kitchen as Lori walked into the dining room. The door to the kitchen was open so she walked to it and looked in.

Standing at the range moving in rhythm to the music was John Garland wielding a spatula with one hand and stirring a spoon in another pot with his other and looking very professional.

Lori smiled at the scene before she spoke. "Do you do windows, too?"

John turned and smiled at her. "One of my hobbies, Lori. I love gourmet grits on occasion and Germans never seem to be able to get the hang of cooking them. Come on in and join me in a Southern-style, cholesterol breakfast."

Lori laughed as he motioned to two chairs and place settings at the kitchen table. He poured her some of his strong, black coffee and chicory and brought it to the table.

"This stuff'll give you a jump start but I recommend a little cream and sugar with it, it's pretty strong. Us old New Orleans boys like French Market coffee in the morning. Clears out the cobwebs. Can you put up with music from the Glenn Miller era?"

"Believe it or not, I love it. My mother had all the greats, Glenn Miller, Bunny Berrigan, Benny Goodman, Tommy and Jimmy Dorsey and the best Dixieland records ever recorded. I grew up with it. I also like some pop and a pretty good smattering of classical."

John deftly spooned grits, eggs and sausage onto two plates and brought them to the table.

"Here you are, ma'am. Just what the doctor ordered to give you lots of fat and cholesterol."

They both laughed and sat down to eat a hearty breakfast. John noticed that she had as healthy an appetite as he did and that she apparently had a real taste for some of his favorite cooking.

Lori looked up at him and said, "Mmmm, these grits are delicious. How in the world do you make something so bland taste so good?"

"I'll give you my secret recipe. I cook the grits in beef or chicken bullion instead of plain water, add a touch of seasoned spike and when they're done, I stir in some butter and grated cheddar cheese until it's melted and well dispersed, sprinkle it with green onion tops and the rest is history."

They both laughed again and it was obvious they truly enjoyed each other's company.

When they had finished, John pushed his chair back and looked at her. "May I ask you a personal question, Lori?"

"How personal?"

"Well, young people generally don't like the things I like or behave the way you do. You don't look old enough to like the '40s bands or eat like a trencherman. Just how old are you?"

Lori laughed appreciatively. "How old do you have to be to like good music and good food?"

"You know what I mean. Most young people today listen to obscene noises they call music or bands made up totally of percussion instruments and strident, off key voices. People well into their thirties often act like brainless, thoughtless human tumors with all the taste of a . . . a . . . lunch wagon pie."

She laughed again and shook her head. "My, my, John, what an opinion you have of our younger generation for a man with such deep philosophical views!

"I must say I'm flattered being placed in the category of the young. Mentally and physically I do feel quite young but in truth I'm almost fifty but I'm not going to tell you how almost."

John shook his head. "That's incredible, you barely look thirty. Yet, you have a mind and demeanor that bespeaks of wisdom that comes with age."

Lori smiled and quietly said, "Flattery will get you every-where, my dear man."

He answered just as quietly, "I certainly hope so." With that he got up and began carrying the dishes to the sink with her help.

When they had finished he said, "Tante Alice will get these. She doesn't mind my cooking in her kitchen but she gets madder than hell if I do anything else. Says men don't know how to wash a dish clean. Well, it's time to go and visit 'the cause.' Shall we?"

Lori waved him on ahead and said, "Lead on, McDuff."

John laughed. "See what I mean, you even use phrases from another era."

They walked out of the lodge and into the sunshine, head-ing up the hill toward the mine and mill buildings, talking ani-matedly as they went.

As they entered the hoist building, the guard handed John a hard hat with 'Big John' stenciled on the front.

Reaching for a hat marked 'visitor,' the guard said, "Here's one for you little lady, the band is adjustable. You have to wear one of these whenever you get around this place."

Lori adjusted the band and put it on her head at a cocky angle. Looking at John she said, "You think I'd make *Vogue* in this hat?"

He tilted his head as he looked at her and said, "You'd be the most beautiful cover they ever had."

Then, changing the subject he said, "Now, this lift cage you're about to enter drops pretty fast and first-timers have a tendency to get a little queasy when they're not used to it. Just hang on to me and don't worry, it stops slowly and reliably."

She looked at him and asked, "Are you giving me a cook's tour of the mine before we go to the computer operations department?"

"Both," he said. "Just hang on."

When the cage dropped in its breath-taking descent, Lori

found herself gripping John's arm tightly in spite of her resolve not to appear frightened.

The cage slowed gently and came to a stop at a tunnel entrance marked 'Third Level—Working Face 500 Feet.' The gate lifted as they stopped and a hard-hatted worker carrying a tool box stepped onto the lift with them.

"Hi boss, howzit?" he asked.

"Couldn't be better, Harry. Got fixit troubles below?"

"No big deal, just a frozen air valve on a stoping drill. Nothing I can't fix in ten minutes."

The cage began its high-speed descent again and then slowed once more to its amazingly gentle stop at the fourth level. The gate went up and the worker got off waving as he left and John pulled the gate back down.

Once more the cage floor dropped out from under them and just as quickly as it began, it gently slowed and stopped at the fifth level of the underground mine.

John smiled down at Lori. "This is it Lori, ladies lingerie, housewares and computers, all out."

She smiled weakly at him, glad to be able to get off the cage lift, and walked down the tunnel with him. As they turned into a side corridor she was startled to see it suddenly become a modern office hallway, with office doors leading off of it at various intervals.

John led them to an unmarked door, pulled a magnetic card out of his wallet, placed it in a slot beside the door and announced his name.

The door swung open silently to reveal an incredible computer operation spread out in what appeared to be a cavernous office space. They walked to a glass-front door through which Lori could see several people sitting at computer terminals, while others were scanning printouts and entering data into other terminals on another wall.

John opened the door for her and they entered Charlie Ross's domain. Charlie was, as usual, hunched over his keyboard intently watching the terminal before him.

John tapped him gently on the shoulder and said, "Charlie, I'd like you to meet someone when you have a moment."

Charlie turned and glanced at John and then did a double take as he saw Lori. Pursing his lips as if to whistle he finally said, "You should have warned me boss, I would have slipped into something more becoming."

They all laughed at his irreverence, then in a more serious tone, John said, "Charlie, I want you to meet Lorelei Young, under secretary of the Department of Commerce."

As Lori extended her hand to the wide-eyed Charlie, he said, "The Lorelei Young of computer fame?"

"The very same Charlie. And Lori, this is Charlie Ross of Operation Bypass fame."

They shook hands and there was a sincere look of admiration in Charlie's eyes as he shook his head. "I've read so much about your programming wizardry with that creaky old COMDEP, Miss Young."

She looked pleased. "It sounds like you're an old Washington hand yourself. Only Washington insiders tend to call it COMDEP."

"That's where Big John found me. Sitting at a computer in Washington D.C. at the Bureau of Mines, hacking away at a new program that was supposed to help find likely mining areas. He made me an offer I couldn't refuse and here I am, half a mile underground wondering what the heck I'm doing here."

Lori smiled as she looked around. "It doesn't look like you're wondering too much. This place looks like the most up-to-date computer operation I've ever seen."

Charlie beamed with pride. "Well I did get a few things up and running. Seems like it's all working like it's supposed to."

"Lori," John broke in, "Charlie is the genius who made this complex system a reality, in fact, far more. Its capability exceeds our wildest dreams and makes this whole operation worth being called a 'cause.' A system that could well keep the world from economic chaos and change the way we do business. Off hand I'd say you two have a lot in common."

Turning to Charlie Ross, John explained that Lori was here to see how it worked, why it worked and if it was worth considering as a replacement for the present monetary system. "And I don't want you to hold back any information even if you think she's spying on us," he said with a smile.

Turning to Lori, John said, "I want you to ask all the questions you want, see whatever you wish to see and observe as much of the operation here as you like. Charlie will be at your disposal and take you on a guided tour. He will hold nothing back. While you're doing that, I have to go to my office to take care of some of my morning tasks. When you've finished your inspection and testing, Charlie will bring you to my office and we can all go to lunch and talk further."

With a wave of his hand, he headed back out of the door.

The Senate, Washington D.C.
March 4, 9:45 a.m.

Tom bustled into the committee meeting room with an arm load of documents leading a small army of assistants carrying charts, easels, graphs and various other tools of persuasion.

Jim Ketchall was already in the room speaking quietly with a group of his committee members, planning the proceedings with his usual attention to detail. When he saw Tom, he excused himself and went to his chair in the center of the dias.

"Well sir, here it is," he said as he plunked down the pile of folders. "And I must say I am impressed with the care and thought that went into this plan. That guy Garland seems to be one hell of a planner."

The senator nodded his head. "He put in a lot of time and effort developing this system and it was all based on his perception of this DECOLAC situation coming to pass. The man has a tremendous insight into the economics of this globe. But more importantly, he's trying to do something about it."

"I'll say," Tom interjected enthusiastically. "From what I read last night, he's called every shot so far including what the reaction of different people would be. No wonder some of our legislators are spooked. They must think he can read their minds. What do you want me to do now?"

The senator removed a sheaf of papers from his ever-present portfolio and handed them to Tom.

"I want you to trot this over to the House office building and give one copy of this, together with a copy of the outline you just brought in, to Bill Rivers, chairman of the House Banking and Finance Committee and the other copy of each to the two Dans. We need all the friends and help we can get in the House on this before the House and Senate conferees get together on this thing."

Tom smiled. "You mean 'if' you can get it out of committee and 'if' it is passed by the Senate."

Jim Ketchall slowly stopped thumbing through his papers and looked at his aide for a long moment.

"You've read this whole thing Tom, can you think of even one sensible argument that would hold enough water to keep that from happening?"

"No, Senator, not sensible. But I can see some very frightened senators trying to filibuster this thing into the ground to keep it from happening."

The senator shook his head negatively. "One of the benefits of having been a judge and a constitutional lawyer for as many years as I was, is that you really learn the rules of procedure and how to use them. It's a piece of cake."

They both laughed and Tom took the material he was to deliver and hurried off to do the senator's bidding.

The committee room was slowly filling up with committee members, staffers, stenographic reporters, one or two witnesses called to testify in the matter before them and the usual gaggle of people representing the news media.

Promptly at 10:30 a.m., Senator Ketchall gaveled the committee to order.

"I call the Senate Banking and Finance Committee to order this morning for what may well be one of the most important and historically significant meetings ever held by this committee.

"All of us are fully aware of the DECOLAC situation and the worldwide monetary confusion it has fostered.

"It is not that the default declared by our Latin American neighbors is, in and of itself, so devastating but rather that a clear-cut plan of action for handling such a situation on a global basis was never fully adopted by the major political and economic powers.

"That is not to say, however, that such a plan does not exist. Such a plan was, in fact, developed and presented to most of the world's major governments as long as three years ago."

Senator Derwin interrupted the chairman. "I don't recall being advised about such a contingency plan, Mr. Chairman."

Senator Ketchall looked at Senator Derwin and shrugged his shoulders. "Unfortunately, most governments to whom it was presented, like our own, paid little or no attention to it—not recognizing the plan for its value or writing it off as unnecessary because of what some considered an improbable happening.

"Because most of the world's economies are so totally dependent on the use of paper currency and fiat monies, we are immediately faced with the need to arrive at an acceptable alternative in order to stave off bank runs, make payments, trade settlements and purchases of all kinds and restore confidence in our monetary system. The alternative we choose must be one that can be put into operation within the next few critical weeks.

"What you will be reading and hearing about today, is such a plan. It is not just capable of being in operation within the required period of time, but is actually in operation on a worldwide basis at this very moment as a type of computerized marketplace or a combination marketplace and barter system.

"For this or any other plan to be successful in heading off the crippling of much of the world's economies, of mass hysteria and perhaps even of anarchy, there must be an immediate decision and acceptance by our government and other governments of whatever practical alternative is available to us."

Senator Cox interrupted the chairman's dissertation. "I find it hard to believe that in just these few days, this DECOLAC incident has brought us to a situation as serious as you describe Mr. Chairman."

Ketchall replied, "I know that within this body there are some who simply cannot believe that this situation is as volatile as it really is. Let me assure you IT... IS... MUCH... WORSE.

"Before convening this committee hearing, I took great pains to read all the reports about the fallout from DECOLAC and talk to as many of our best-informed people as possible.

Page 101

"I can, in good conscience, tell you that the situation is potentially far more dangerous than any of us can even conceive.

"There must be action taken immediately to put in place and fully support a practical, working monetary system and medium of exchange to replace one based on what has, for all intents and purposes, become one based on worthless paper currency.

"There will be no time for long-winded studies. There will be no time to play political power games. There is only time for men of good conscience to recognize the severity of what we face, recognize the immediacy of the situation and make a decision for the survival of our nation.

"We will be hearing today from the Chairman of the Federal Reserve, the Secretary of the Treasury, the Secretary of Commerce, the Association of Independent Bankers, the assistant director of the Central Intelligence Agency, the head of the U.S. Chamber of Commerce and head of the economic development branch of the State Department.

"By satellite, you will also hear from and be able to question the developer of the Global Computer Trading Company, Mr. John Garland. His company presently functions as an electronic international trade settlement medium or what some might call a computerized bartering system. It is that system, I am convinced, that can provide a workable alternative to our present monetary system within the shortest possible time.

"And now ladies and gentlemen, we are about to discuss the making of a decision that could affect our very survival as a nation and a civilized society. It could, in fact, be the most important decision each of you has ever had to face.

"I sincerely hope you will all honor my request to limit all bickering and procedural gimmickry and utilize every ounce of your intellectual capacities to conclude this hearing with a decision for survival. Thank you."

The force and sincerity of the senator's statement was so powerful that it was a long time before anyone in the room spoke.

CHAPTER NINETEEN
THE COMMITTEE QUESTIONS,
THE MAN ANSWERS

Toiyabe Canyon, Nevada
March 4, 12:00 noon

Charlie led the way from the computer nerve center to the mine shaft cage lift as he and Lori talked about the various unique aspects of the computer system.

"What's fascinating to me is the microcomputer system you're working on now," Lori was saying, not even aware that they were stepping back on the lift cage to begin the high-speed ascent.

Charlie shut the lift cage while he spoke. "Well, since the advent of RISC chips, Power chips, the new Intel Pentium micro processor chips and others, we borrowed a page from the research conducted at MIT where they developed this approach for their research in artificial intelligence. We decided to set up 200 central processing units based on those chips on a sort of information pipeline or parallel computing system, all of them operating in tandem and directly accessing thirty-two bytes of memory at a time. Each CPU has a gigabyte of RAM and feeds into a ten-gigabyte, fast-access memory bank. When finished, it will be able to process over a billion transactions a second.

"Now we are trying to emulate what the big Cray does on this new setup and if it works without any glitches during this test period, we'll be able to set up over a hundred processing centers around the world for the price of one of those big Crays."

Lori was so engrossed in what Charlie was saying, she was hardly aware of the lift cage going up at its high G-speed. As Charlie opened the lift at the top, Lori automatically removed her hard hat and absently handed it to the guard who had his hand out.

"That's incredible Charlie, that means you'll be able to set up many decentralized processing units in every major country of the world all hooked up in a worldwide network with total backup for each unit.

"If anything happened to one, a backup unit would immediately come on-line without missing a beat. It would literally guarantee continuous, uninterrupted operation on a worldwide basis."

Charlie nodded. "That's the plan. In the meantime, we still have seven mainframes scattered around the world, all working in tandem and all acting as backup for each other. What you just saw down there is just the control operation where it all started and where we do our R&D."

As they talked, Charlie led the way toward the Mine administrative office.

Taking the steps two at a time, he held the door open for Lori. They walked to the end of the hall where Charlie knocked gently on an unmarked door.

John's unmistakable voice answered, "Come in."

Charlie ushered Lori into a large comfortable office with windows on two sides overlooking the valley below. One wall was all shelves filled with books and memorabilia of mining ventures past. A corner beside John's desk was a computer center with several printers and two computers, a video camera on a tripod and several hutches above the corner computer desks filled with files, books and other computer related materials with a large TV screen to one side.

Behind John's desk was a sophisticated short-wave radio with various types of radio telephone equipment and a world map on the wall showing time zones and radio call letters for specific areas.

They sat down on comfortable chairs across the desk from John waiting for him to finish his phone conversation.

When he hung up he swiveled around facing them.

"It seems you're just in time to watch the first satellite dish, long distance appearance before Senator Ketchall's

Banking and Finance Committee."

Lori was shocked, "You mean you are going to appear before the Senate committee from here?"

"That's what that video camera and this lapel microphone are for."

She looked around the room and then back to John. "Where are the lights, the camera man, the sound man and all the usual hoopla attendant to a live broadcast?"

John smiled broadly. "I'm a do-it-yourselfer, Lori. All that stuff is unnecessary for this sort of thing. I ran a taped test to get a good sound and lighting reading. With that high-tech, low-light camera and hi-fi sound system, it comes out just fine.

"Back in the Senate hearing room, Tom Ballard, Senator Ketchall's aide, checked the video and sound reception there while I checked his return signal here during the committee's lunch break. They are three hours ahead of us you know.

"I'm confident I can understand the questions they ask while seeing the questioner's facial expression on that screen and they'll be able to hear my answers and visually read my face back there."

Lori shook her head in wonderment. "The unions are going to hate you John. No makeup man, no light technician, no director, no camera man, no sound man. Shame on you."

John laughed heartily. "This won't take more than twenty or thirty minutes because they have already been fully briefed by Senator Ketchall. I'm sure that most of the questions will be from those committee members making a last gasp effort to find some kind of loophole through which to jump."

The telephone rang and John punched a speaker button and answered, "Garland here."

"This is Tom in Washington, Mr. Garland. If you will activate your sound system, camera and satellite unit with the same settings we had before, the Senator will introduce you in five minutes."

"OK, Tom," and John flipped some switches on a console on the credenza behind him. "How's that, Tom?"

"Just a minute…OK…That's great on my monitor. As soon as the chairman introduces you, I'll switch you on to the big screen."

In the background they could hear Senator Ketchall talking to the assemblage in the committee room.

"And now, let me introduce Mr. Garland, the founder and developer of Global Computer Trading Corporation and the computer system that I feel could be utilized to stave off a possible monetary breakdown. Mr. Garland are you there?"

The muffled whisper of Tom, the Senator's aide came over the speaker in John's office, "You're on, Mr. Garland."

John looked at the camera, relaxed and at ease as he answered.

"Yes, Senator, I am here and thank you for allowing me to appear in this unusual fashion."

"Mr. Garland, I have already briefed the committee on the essence of how your system operates and now, as is their right and duty, they would like to ask you some questions beyond what we have discussed."

"Fine, Senator."

Senator Ketchall turned from the camera and said, "Senator Borders, you have the floor."

There was a pause and the picture on the screen in John's office cut from Senator Ketchall to Albert Borders, senator from Iowa.

"Mr. Garland, I am impressed with the care and thought that obviously went into your computer system. However, I am concerned about how some very basic national needs would be met."

"Thank you Senator. I'll do my best to address your concerns."

Senator Borders continued, "I'm sure you are well aware that our states and the federal infrastructures are in dire shape. They cannot do without the cash flow generated by state and local taxes even for a few months. My question is, how will the federal government and the states be able to continue to collect taxes under the present laws utilizing your system?"

Well out of camera range but from a vantage that let them see both the screen and John speaking to the camera beside the screen, Lori and Charlie sat raptly watching the proceedings as John responded.

"Senator, I am sure there hasn't been enough time for you to do more than glance through the material I sent to the committee but when you have the opportunity, please turn to the chapter entitled, *"How Governments Collect 'Pay as Generated' Taxes."*

What that chapter explains is that the personal, business and corporate taxes, in the form of credits accumulated in the computer archives by the sale of goods and services or by payments of wages to employees, are transferred to the appropriate taxing entities at the completion of each transaction, instead of on a monthly or quarterly basis as is done now by forms and paperwork."

Senator Borders interrupted John and said, "I'm trying to understand how that is able to take place, Mr. Garland."

"Well, sir, the computer programs have been so structured that they incorporate the appropriate taxing formulas, whether by withholding or by quarterly business reports and payments and the correct amounts are transferred to the appropriate agency, be it the IRS, state or local government, all in minutes instead of four or more weeks after the end of a given quarter.

"Obviously the computer system is able to eliminate the float periods. This gives the various taxing agencies the benefit of the funds immediately, thus increasing the dollar value of the taxes by the amount of earned interest from the time of each transaction.

"Moreover, there is little room or ability to manipulate money that rightfully belongs to the taxing entities through the use of creative accounting procedures or other manners. That in itself should increase the real value of collected taxes by another 6 to 8 percent per annum."

Senator Borders looked impressed as he nodded his head

slowly and thoughtfully in agreement.

"If that works out to be correct, Mr. Garland, that would go a long way towards eliminating this country's present deficit."

"Yes Senator, among other things, it would permit drastically reducing the size of such agencies as the IRS, Health, Education and Welfare and others because tax collection would no longer be the problem it is now and disbursement by these agencies would become much simpler, quicker and more reliable.

"Moreover, if the Congress would pass some simple formula amendments on corporate taxation, businesses would pay a withholding tax just as individuals do now and then file for tax rebates just as individuals do, at the end of the year.

"If such legislation were enacted, it would permit all tax rates to be substantially reduced while yielding significantly more revenues for all the taxing agencies. Furthermore, the government would have the benefit of holding the withheld amounts in interest bearing accounts until rebate time, which, by our calculations, would all but eliminate the federal deficit within two years and leave us with a substantial surplus by the third year."

Senator Borders smiled as he responded. "If all that is true Mr. Garland, you will have given Congress the best present ever. Allowing Congress to reduce taxes while eliminating the deficit at the same time would probably eliminate the need for us to campaign for re-election for a long time. Sounds almost too good to be true."

"There is another benefit I haven't mentioned yet. Profit-related criminal activities would be greatly reduced because the ability to generate secret monetary transactions would no longer be possible on any sort of a substantial basis. There would no longer be currency with which to conduct such business or where the proceeds could be laundered or hidden. It is reasonable to assume that this would substantially reduce misdirected wealth while substantially reducing the cost of law enforcement."

Senator Borders looked at the ceiling pondering a thought

and then turned back to the camera as he addressed John again. "There is another point that bothers me with your proposed system, Mr. Garland."

John looked at the camera in his Nevada office as he asked, "And what would that be, Senator?"

The senator rocked back in his chair before he answered. "Well, sir, there are many situations I can think of, emergency car repairs in remote areas or travel in foreign countries where payment for goods or services by electronic credits or even by check or credit card, would either be impractical or completely impossible."

John steepled his fingers as he answered. "Yes Senator, you are quite right and my proposal recommends some 'coin of the realm' for those kinds of small purchases, emergencies or travel requirements where electronic credits might be unavailable or impractical. When you have an opportunity, please turn to Chapter 16 of my outline and read the section titled *"Coins for Emergency Purchases."*

In it, I suggest that each country that embraces the use of this system, also mint coins in values ranging from one dollar to fifty dollars. The larger denominations ranging from twenty to fifty dollar values might be gold and silver metal alloys of certain size and weight with intrinsic metal values less than pure metals thus allowing each country to profit from the 'seigniorage' involved in minting such coins. The circulation would be limited and though some criminal activity might be based on this type of money, it would be significantly less than the grand scale seen today."

Borders shook his head in disbelief. "That is truly incredible, Mr. Garland. It boggles the mind."

John smiled at the screen as he answered. "Well this form of monetary system really isn't that unique. Every time you access an ATM with your debit card or your credit card is swiped through an electronic reader to allow the merchant to be paid and the payment to be recorded on your account, you are dealing with an electronic monetary system. Banks and corporations have long been employing electronic money accounting, payment and transfers for many years with their computer accounting and collection systems.

"What a multinational electronic monetary system does, based on an accurate computer system of credits and an absolutely accurate record of every transaction, is eliminate the ability to put off tax payments or manipulate books and records to avoid tax payments and eliminate the ability to do things such as sell illegal drugs, fence stolen goods, launder money and the like. Moreover, it does it all in the blink of an eye with only a handful of people."

Senator Borders was quietly thoughtful for a moment and then looking at his camera which, from its positioning, was the same as looking directly at John, he said, "Thank you, Mr. Garland. I appreciate your forthright answers and I will indeed read the chapter on taxation with great interest."

The camera returned to Senator Ketchall who was recognizing another unseen questioner.

"Mistah Chairman, I would like to ask Mistah Garland a few questions."

Senator Ketchall looked to his left and acknowledged the person speaking off camera.

"The Senator from Alabama is recognized."

The camera switched to the graying, and somewhat overweight 'Billy' Roberts, senator from Alabama. He smiled and nodded to the camera positioned beside the screen in which John Garland's upper torso was visible and in his inimitable southern drawl he said, "How de do, Mistah Garland. This heah type of appearance is kinda unusual but Ah reckon there ain't much time to do moah. Ah'd sure appreciate ya'll explainin' a couple of thangs to me."

"Please go ahead, Senator Roberts."

"Well," the senator continued, "Ah seem to recollect when you wuz explaining the way the computer would collect an' pay taxes that you used the phrase 'based on an accurate computer system of credits and an absolutely accurate record of every transaction.' Is that correct?"

John smiled at the screen and camera beside it. "The Senator has an excellent memory. Yes, that is correct."

The senator returned the smile and said. "When a man ain't too smart, 'bout the only thang he can count on is a good memory. What I'm a' gettin at suh, is, how do we know, how does anyone know that your computer system is absolutely accurate and there ain't anyone that kin fudge a little bit heah an theah if the right amount of money was ta be paid. Yew know whut ah mean, Mr. Garland?"

"Yes, Senator, I certainly do know what you mean. To answer your question in several parts, first of all, all transactions entered into our system are 'locked in' on both the original memory bank and all the backup memory banks, even if those entries were wrong.

"That simply means that when the computer programs were written, they were made tamper proof in that area so that no one could get into the transaction memory banks to change anything without disrupting the whole system which would, of course, alert everyone tied into the system.

"To correct a wrong entry, the information would have to be entered using a special audit code and with an explanation of why a correcting entry was being made and by password code, who was making it. Such an action alerts the system's independent auditors to investigate the correcting entries to their satisfaction."

The senator nodded sagely as he mulled over the answer. "How kin that be verified, Mistah Garland?"

"The government or any other questioning agency, group or company, is welcome to have computer software experts of their choice examine, test, audit and evaluate the program we use to verify its invulnerability."

"OK, that sounds reasonable. Now whut wuz the second part of your answer?"

John picked up his copy of the brief he had sent to Senator Ketchall and held it toward the camera as he answered.

"On page ten of your copy of this brief Senator, you will find a chapter entitled *'System Safeguards.'* In the first few chapters, you will find a description of the administrative structure of this system.

"Among other things, it is owned by a trust I set up for its ownership and the trust in turn, is owned by its many users, much like a federal credit union. Then the trust was registered in all countries that have agencies and laws under which that can be done.

"This trust details the precise limits on service charges both by Global Computer Trading Corporation and by any service agency such as a bank or other business that would be authorized to provide access to the system for its use.

"To ensure that this would be carried out in perpetuity, we set certain parameters for the choosing of persons from each participating country to act as trustees of Global Computer Trading and its system."

The senator interrupted John at that point. "In othah words Mistah Garland, yew don't own that company or system, is that correct?"

"Yes, Senator, that is correct."

The senator shook his head negatively. "Yew mean ta sit theah an' tell me ya'll went to all the trouble and expense of financin' and settin' up that theah company and them computers and yew ain't gonna see no return from all that?"

"No Senator. I don't mean to tell you that. I have a contract with the Global Computer Trading Corporation Trust that sets aside a certain amount of its income for repayment to me of all audited capital outlays with acceptable interest.

"I further have a consulting agreement for myself and my staff that pays us a reasonable fee to continue to manage and guide its operation, expansion and growth."

"Well, suh," the senator answered, "that does make me feel a bit more comforted. I do have suspicions of people who claim to be a'doin' somethin' fer nothin.' An' it does sound like you set it up pretty good, long as this ole world don't get involved in some majah war. I do have one more question."

"Yessir."

"Whut's the cost to them that uses it? Ah mean, how much does this heah outfit charge for say, sellin' a thousand bales of cotton to some furrin country?"

John smiled as he recognized the wily Senator's homey approach. "The user fees are based on a precise sliding scale, Senator. Since the cost of entering and archiving a transaction is the same whether it's for one dollar or $10,000 unless the transaction is extremely complex.

"It's based on an accurate time motion study. The cost of data entry, archiving, recalling and printed confirmation are all based on time costs and line or broadcast costs. It would be difficult to break down each activity cost here, but I can tell you that the average cost based on a $100 transaction entry is two cents or one five thousandth of the amount of the transaction.

"You'll find an accurate breakdown and description beginning on page sixty-three of the brief."

The senator looked pleasantly surprised "Well I'll be dogged, that don't sound unreasonable atall. No suh, that's downright reasonable. I reckon my monthly bank account checkin' charges comes to more than that. An' you say a part of that goes to the bank with the computer system doin' the transaction for the customer ?"

"Yes sir. One half to be exact. Our research indicates that because of the elimination of clerical work, this amount would be more profitable to each participating bank or access agency than what they are able to generate in income from such a transaction at present."

"Well, Ah'll be dogged!" After a long pause and some obvious cerebral research the senator finally said, "I guess I ain't got no more questions fer ya'll, Mistah Garland."

John smiled. "Thank you, Senator."

The screen changed to show Senator Ketchall's face on the screen. It was a masked poker face but there were smile crinkles at the corner of his eyes and mouth trying their best to behave.

"There were several other requests to question you, Mr. Garland, but those requests have now been withdrawn. On behalf of the committee, I wish to thank you for your time and expense in making yourself available to this committee and for having developed what I believe is an excellent standby monetary system while we try to clear up this Latin American loan default situation. If the committee has any further questions, my staff will contact you. Good-bye, Mr. Garland."

The screen went blank and John flipped some switches on the console behind him turning off the lights, sound and camera.

Lori let out a whoop and Charlie slapped his thigh in glee. "Did you see that, John? Senator Ketchall knew he had 'em."

"Oh yes!" chimed in Lori. "He almost broke up when you headed off old Billy Bob. That old man may sound like a country bumpkin but he has one of the sharpest minds in the Senate and knows every trick in the book. He also knows when to quit while he's ahead." Lori was so tickled she could hardly contain herself. "Oh John, I know this is going to the full senate for vote right away, 'by doggies,'" she parroted.

They all laughed and John got up from behind the desk and took them both by their hands as if they were children and led them to the door.

"Come on kids, time to build up our energy, this is only the beginning. I have a feeling our victory today will not sit very well with a great many people."

Turning to Lori as they walked down the hall, John asked "By the way, Lori, when are you expected to report back?"

"Oh my gosh, I had completely forgotten about that. I better call the minute we get back to the lodge."

They pushed out into the bright sunshine reflecting off of the snow-covered mountain sides and walked down the road to the lodge.

Lori turned to John as they walked. "What shall I tell

them, John?"

John looked down at her concerned face and smiled.

"The truth, beautiful lady, the truth and whatever you wish to tell them about what you have learned here today."

"But I don't want to do anything that might jeopardize this operation."

John smiled again as he said, "Then you have decided that there is a 'just cause' here?"

Lori stopped and crossed her arms and looked thoughtfully at John. "You knew all along what I would decide, didn't you?"

He shook his head. "No, I only felt I knew the kind of a human being you were and that left little room for doubt."

With that, he took her arm and turning together, continued on toward the lodge.

CHAPTER TWENTY
PERSPECTIVE PEAK
A MOUNTAIN WITH AN INNER VIEW

Toiyabe Canyon, Nevada
March 4, 4:00 p.m.

Lunch had been a happy affair with Lori, Charlie and John discussing the day's events. The only air of disappointment was over the fact that Lori's phone call had resulted in her being directed to return to Washington to make a personal report to the President and the Secretary of Commerce the following morning at the White House.

The latest flight out was 6:30 p.m. Reno time, arriving at midnight Washington time. Lori was in her quarters at the lodge packing her bags with a feeling of sadness.

The trip to this remote mining community and these fascinating and dedicated people had filled her with a sense of excitement and dedication she hadn't felt in years. Being in the presence of John Garland had awakened strange and disturbing feelings that had lain dormant for most of her career-seeking life.

This man, she thought, *is different from any man I have ever met. He seems to be an anomaly in this day and age. Intelligent, dedicated, honest and yet warm and human. And,* she thought, *very, very sexy.*

Zipping up her oversized carry-on bag with a feeling of sadness she thought, *I better quit thinking about him while I'm ahead.*

The phone on the bedside stand rang and she put the bag on the floor and picked up the receiver. "Hello?"

"This is John, Lori. I have prepared some material that should help you make your report to the President and relieve you of any possible guilt feelings about answering any questions."

"You think of everything, don't you?" she answered.

"If that were only true. No, this is only a summary of all the things you already know and some you may have guessed. I want you to feel perfectly free to reveal any of it without qualms."

"But you know that Malcolm will be at that briefing and he may have some very unpleasant ulterior motives."

"Lori, there are undoubtedly many people who will resist this idea. If it's an idea whose time has come, nothing anyone can do will stop it.

Your plane doesn't leave for two and a half hours. The copter will leave here at exactly 5:45, which will get you there in twenty-two minutes with plenty of time for check-in. In the meantime, when you're all packed, walk across the balcony from your quarters to where my study is and I will fill you in on some things I feel you should be aware of."

"I'm packed now, John. I'll be there in a couple of minutes."

After she hung up, she shook her head as if to clear out thoughts. She felt a strange excitement over this man. Stopping at her open briefcase, she picked up her portfolio and walked out of her apartment and down the balcony to John's study.

She tapped lightly at the door to John's quarters and he immediately opened the door and stood aside for her to enter.

The room was a comfortable combination of sitting room and study with the ever-present computer occupying one corner beside a radio communications setup.

John had a thick file in his hand and motioned her to a comfortable couch before a fireplace. He said, "Sit down, Lori, and let's go over some of things I feel are pertinent."

After she had settled herself, John looked at her for a long moment and smiled. "Before going into all this data, I just wanted to say that your presence here has been the most delightful thing that has happened to me in a long time."

Lori shifted with embarrassment, as a slight flush came to her face. And yet, she experienced pleasure from his statement.

"For me too, John. I can't recall when I have been more re-laxed and at the same time, more fascinated by everything I've seen and learned."

John looked away to the dancing flames in the fireplace. "There is so much more to understand about this computer system than just a way of providing an alternate monetary system.

"There is, in fact, a reason so many call it a 'cause.' You've only had two days of exposure to it and no real time to think about it so I've taken the liberty of preparing a sort of 'think' piece for you and it's in this file folder marked 'confidential.'"

Lori threw her head back to swing her long blond hair from her eyes and said, "In other words, you don't want me to relate what is in that folder to anyone."

John turned to Lori with a look of intensity on his face.

"That doesn't mean you can't eventually tell everyone about the thoughts I've put down. It's only to say that at the outset, it may not be such a good idea to share them with some people. People who are already afraid of how this proposed system might affect their vested interests."

Lori nodded her head in understanding.

John continued, "No matter what personal feelings you or I or anyone may have concerning this proposed monetary sys-tem, it is much more than just a complex computer system or electronic barter system.

"Perhaps a short preamble describing my feelings about the 'whys' and 'wherefores' are in order."

Lori smiled and said, "You mean there's more?"

John nodded. "Much more. More than I can really under-stand or articulate, but let me just explain a personal view. From what I have been able to glean from these many years of living and observing, here are some basics. Basic number one is that all living species on this planet have a built in survival instinct. Buried in our individual genetic codes are instincts to gather food, provide shelter and protection from the elements. And procreate to ensure survival of our specific species. To employ violence to protect ourselves, our mates and our young when confronted with danger from without."

John stopped and looked at the ceiling to gather and organize his thoughts as Lori watched intently. Finally, he looked at her and began again.

"Humans as a species have a more developed brain and with our advanced abilities to reason, envision, learn, expand, plan and organize we became more complex as a species even though we still retain the so-called primordial instincts.

"As humans, our survival instincts manifest themselves in many different ways. For instance, as a child, if we touched a hot stove and were shocked by the pain our survival instinct imprinted in our mental memory banks a sort of protective paranoia that acted to warn us about touching hot stoves.

"As we developed as a species our survival tools became more civilized, more sophisticated and took on different forms. We farmed, gathered in crops, worked and traded our labors for food, shelter and clothing. As barter was replaced by mediums of exchange such as money, we began to acquire money with which to ensure our survival and money became one of our main tools of survival.

"One of the most powerful manifestations of the survival instinct is revealed in various levels of greed, arrogance, vanity, what we call dignity, self respect and, of course, violence. These are all various manifestations of the survival instinct. As human kind developed and became more and more sophisticated, our survival instincts, and the manifestations thereof, also evolved.

"We began to acquire more money than we actually needed to survive from day to day and began saving for the proverbial 'rainy day.'

"We developed monetary systems and industries to better organize the way we provided for our survival and the survival of our young. Greed often became a pronounced and exaggerated survival drive and many of our specie were driven to acquire far more than was required for their survival. In many cases, this acquisition of physical and paper wealth was at the expense of less clever people and to their detriment.

"In some cases, better *mousetrap* products, natural resources and laws made it possible to acquire such excess without it having been the actual goal of the acquirer. My own case for instance. I found a gold-bearing formation, staked claims, developed a very profitable mine and as a by product, developed substantial 'wealth' far beyond my needs and those of my family and loved ones. In my case, I shared profits with my employees and tried to be intelligently charitable."

Lori shook her head in amazement at John's profound views. "When did you first come to these conclusions, John?"

John smiled at Lori and said, "Many years ago. As my wealth grew I began to realize that with it came an obligation to use it wisely. Giving it away as charity to momentarily feed and clothe poor and hungry would not solve their long-term problems and more often than not, exacerbate their problem by trapping them into seeking charity rather than developing their own abilities to survive self sufficiently."

Lori smiled and said, "You mean you stopped giving to charity?"

John shook his head. "No, I continued to help those less fortunate than I but I also began to think of how I might utilize my growing wealth to make the playing field for all people a more level one.

"I began to recognize how the greed aspect of our survival instincts in some of the members of our species moved them to acquire thousands and in some cases, millions of times more assets than they might ever need for even a comfortable survival. Further, that political power for personal gain, all sorts of crime and crooked business were all acting to divert a large part of our natural and developed wealth into the hands of a few and was reducing the ability of the many less educated, less clever, less violent and less greed-driven members of our species to provide even subsistence level survival for themselves.

"It was at this time that I also became fascinated with the powers of the computer and began to ponder the weaknesses of our various monetary systems that permitted such unbridled misuse of our natural and developed wealth."

Lori interrupted. "That almost sounds like you don't believe in a society based on free market economics."

"No, Lori, to the contrary. I strongly believe in the economics of a free market society as long as the playing field is level. A playing field, if you will, where the weakest, poorest, most uneducated and unskilled members of our society have, at the very least, an equal chance to provide a reasonably comfortable life for themselves by stint of their own honest labors.

"However, it seemed to me that using a medium of exchange that lent itself to manipulation, diversion and irrational acquisition by the clever few to the detriment of a large part of our society was badly skewed and badly lacking.

"It was also during this period of intellectual search that I became aware of the conditions in Latin America that have now manifested themselves. It was then I began thinking about how our monetary system might be changed in some way to eliminate the huge illegal, immoral diversions of our wealth."

Lori sat forward with her elbows on her knees and her chin cupped in her hands as she listened intently. She was deeply moved by this man's quiet description of his innermost thoughts and as he paused, she said, "How did you come to this computerized monetary system idea?"

John took a deep breath and looked at Lori thoughtfully for a long moment before he spoke. "Let's begin with what might be called the 'human confidence factor.' In recent times even the most tuned out of our society must have become aware of the extraordinary happenings all around them.

"The election of leaders to our country's highest offices who pushed through legislation that removed the many barriers that men of great wisdom had erected to protect the many trusting, unsophisticated citizens among us. It was done under the guise of 'less government control.'

"The unfortunate result was unrestricted abuse of the thrifty person's savings resulting in the massive savings and loan industry failures. At last count the bail-out of that debacle is expected to cost our citizens well over $500 billion.

"The outrageous pork barrel legislation that venal politicians passed to favor the few of their constituents to ensure their re-election at the expense of the many.

"Sting operations by the FBI in state capitols all over the country revealed incredible amounts of bribery and other unlawful activities by our state legislators.

"The greatest number of federal judges ever impeached in one decade for criminal acts and unethical conduct in office. Things that would never have taken place just twenty years ago."

Lori interjected, "And let's not forget people elected to the highest offices in the land, accused of blatantly selling their influence for cash."

John nodded. "And let me add to that the outrageous misuse of capital through the financial manipulations of junk bonds. The massive indictments and convictions of some of the largest financial houses and their executives of massive, crooked, insider dealings.

"The indictments and convictions of some of the largest defense contractors in collusion with government officials. And all throughout the world, uprisings of oppressed peoples overthrowing inept, socialistic state governments and bureaucracies to seek democracy and freedom. Lori, the whole world is experiencing one of the worst confidence crises in history.

"People everywhere have the uncomfortable feeling that they can no longer trust anyone in government, that institutions that have always been above reproach can no longer be trusted and that they are totally helpless to do anything to change that. Recent elections have shown the extent of that following and the desperate desire for change—change for the better.

"And now, if the monetary systems of the world's major countries go down, there will be nothing left to believe in because it will have wiped out every penny that billions around the world have worked so hard to save and accumulate in one form or another for their modest hopes of survival.

Individuals feel that they no longer have control over the fruits of their labor because individuals, financial institutions political parties, and governments, individually and in concert with each other, often manipulate the medium of exchange for their own benefit through the various so-called monetary systems."

Lori leaned forward and said, "You know John, in the back of my mind I have always felt that there was something radically wrong with our monetary system. I have read enough and know enough about how our Federal Reserve system operates to realize it can be manipulated to create inflation or reduce it at will. I just never spent enough time to delve into it to really understand it."

John nodded. "You were on the right track and eventually, you would have arrived at the obvious conclusion. Though most fed chairmen and the appointed board of governors have been honorable people trying to do a difficult job, often they too have been manipulated. Most citizens simply aren't aware that the Federal Reserve System is not controlled by the government but is independent, often influenced by private banking institutions. And all too often, its manipulation is designed to serve devious individuals more than benefit the citizens.

"Which brings us to this computer system we call 'Operation Bypass.' Because of the way I have set it up with the ownership held by the individual depositors and their elected management, its operation is beyond manipulation or bribery and beyond any external political control. It imposes a discipline of honesty and ethics on all who use it.

"The uniqueness of the system does not lie in the fact that it can accurately and reliably make several million transactions a minute or that it can accurately record and archive each such transaction.

"Rather, it is in the fact that it cannot operate unless every data entry is totally honest, because the program instantly compares the entry with other data and any dishonest entry is immediately recognized.

"Further, it does not lend itself to secret or covert transactions such as arms smuggling, illegal drugs, money laundering, blackmail, loan sharking or bribery as do paper currency, precious metals or other monetary assets. Every transaction that takes place within this system is always a known and recorded transaction that simply cannot be hidden from appropriate auditors.

"If you think about that for a minute you begin to see what an effect that might have on crime of any kind for profit. It makes those kinds of criminal activities all but impossible."

Lori joined in excitedly, "Of course, I didn't even think about that aspect. Why that's a fantastic benefit. In fact, why would a robber kill someone for their car or jewels if they couldn't sell it in an untraceable manner?"

John smiled. "Like the man said in 'My Fair Lady,' *'By George, you've got it, I think you've got it.'* But, there's more. Aside from helping to re-establish trust and confidence in systems and humans operating within those systems, it has another very powerful and meaningful benefit. That is to bring all the peoples of the world who use it, closer together.

"Do you realize Lori, that this system transcends all barriers, all borders, all languages and lets people everywhere communicate openly with each other. "What a powerful impetus for world peace and better understanding, for honesty and trust.

"This computerized monetary system can be an extraordinary way of bringing about world cooperation in everything from saving rain forests to eliminating poverty and everything in between.

"The most important of these however, is the rebirth of trust, of confidence, of belief in one another's honesty.

"Can you imagine a nation where politicians can no longer be bought because every single financial dealing is now recorded and traceable, where defense contractors couldn't possibly get away with over-charging the government because the General Accounting Office would have the benefit of pulling out reports of all government spending on a daily basis if they chose to do so?"

Lori drew a deep breath and slowly shook her head as if to clear it. "The concept and its possibilities are overwhelming. My mind is reeling from the endless possibilities. It's almost as if suddenly people everywhere will begin to regain control over their lives. The overwhelming feeling of powerlessness and frustration will slowly begin to dissipate."

John smiled at her with a fondness and warmth in his eyes and said, "Think on these things on your way back to Washington and when you get there, you will know exactly what to say."

Lori sat stunned by the powerful concepts that had been unfolded for her. After a long moment she spoke.

"I'm embarrassed to say that I was so preoccupied with the hardware and the software, the nuts and bolts of this system, that I didn't stop to examine the moral and philosophical aspects."

John smiled at her. "Don't be embarrassed, Lori. Remember, I have had well over ten years to ponder all these things. You probably would have been able to do it in half the time."

Looking at his watch, John said, "Come with me for a few minutes, I want to share another perspective with you before you leave."

Taking her hand he pulled Lori off the couch. Her touch felt warm and her hand trembled slightly in his grip, causing him to look at her. Her eyes were slightly moist and she quickly looked away as they walked out to a Jeep parked by the lodge entrance and climbed in. John cranked the Jeep up and pulled out.

As the Jeep headed up a well-worn trail John pointed to the crest above them. "That's Perspective Peak" he said.

Lori asked "Where does this peak get its name, is that an anglicized version of an old Indian name?"

A smile crossed John's face. "No, it's an old mining engineer's name given to it when I first came up here with the Swede over twenty-five years ago."

As the Jeep pulled up over a ridge and onto a flat area on the very top of the mountain, Lori was confronted by the incredible panorama of northwestern Nevada. She could see for miles in every direction.

John parked the Jeep facing west toward the setting sun and looked out over the dramatic scene quietly.

Lori turned from the breathtaking view to look at John's weather-beaten face with its lines now etched more deeply by the setting sun.

"You know John, you have created something here that could well prove to be one of the most important happenings in recent history."

John looked over at Lori for a moment before he spoke.

"Lori, we humans seem to be born with the tendency to exaggerate our importance. We often think that what we do individually and collectively, are the only things that matter in this world.

"The author of Ecclesiastics in the Old Testament had an exceptional insight on this aspect when he wrote, 'Vanity . . . vanity, all is vanity.' Whether it is greed for money, power, lust for another human or the desire for universal recognition, the trap is always the ego or vanity. It clouds one's perception, understanding, awareness and most of all, perspective.

"When I find myself caught up in that state of mind, I am moved to come up here to put things back into perspective. What I see, hear and sense up here is the enormity of the universe.

"From this vantage point you can see the mighty Sierras over there spreading north and south out of view. Battle Mountain to the northeast of us looming up out of the desert. Huge, seemingly empty, peaceful deserts that were once great seas of water teeming with life . . . and the spirit of man striving to tune in to all this creation.

"Then I ponder the incredible order of all this. Our sun, just the right distance from our globe to bring us warmth without frying us. Just the right amount of heat to evaporate the water from the sea into clouds. Just enough temperature changes and gravity to let the clouds turn back to water over our land and drop gently as snow and rainfall, in amounts just enough to water the growth of our plant and animal life, and then return to the sea from whence it came.

"I look at all this immense creation and its incredible orderliness and I have to say to myself, 'John, you're not nearly as smart as the one who did all this, so let's recognize exactly where we fit in all this.'"

The powerful thoughts spoken in his quiet way and the immense panorama surrounding them evoked the feeling of insignificance and the sense of closeness to this fascinating man. It had an unsettling effect on Lori who found herself unable to control her emotions any longer as tears welled up in her eyes.

John turned to her with a feeling of great gentleness and understanding. He put his arm around her shoulder and pulled her gently to his chest. Tilting her head up, he gently wiped her tear-filled eyes and held her for a moment.

"This place," he said quietly, "has brought tears to my eyes many times, beautiful lady. It has done much to keep me in tune with reality. I wanted to share it with you . . ."

After a moment, John looked at his watch and said, "I must regretfully say that it is time for us to get to the copter pad."

Putting the Jeep in gear, he turned back down the trail they had come up on. They rode to the lodge in silence, each wrapped in their own thoughts. John was trying to sort out his feelings for the exciting woman beside him while trying to evaluate the importance of the project to which he had devoted the last ten years of his life.

Lori was fighting the mixed emotion of a lifetime of discipline and loyalty to her job and country and now trying to understand the feeling that made her want to throw it all out the window just to be with this one man.

John broke the silence. "We'll stop and pick up your luggage at the lodge and then I'm going with you to the airport to see you off."

As they pulled up to the lodge Lori said, "I know how busy you are and there is no need for you to do that. I'm a big girl you know." She felt as if she wanted to bite her tongue the minute she said it.

"I'm not that busy and besides, I have a selfish motive."

Lori looked at him questioningly, "Oh, what is that?"

John smiled at her. "I want a few more minutes with you before you leave."

The chopper ride was uneventful though it was starkly beautiful over the desert at that time of the evening. Both of them sat lost in thought as Carl expertly flew the chopper to the helipad nearest the airport terminal.

The Reno Flying Service jitney took them to the terminal shuttle where Lori quickly picked up her return ticket and they went up the concourse to the airline boarding area.

After she had gotten her seat assignment and boarding pass they went to a corner of the lounge by the window overlooking the airfield.

"We still have a few minutes 'til boarding time," John said looking at his watch. He looked down at Lori with his gentle smile and said, "I guess that right now it might be considered legitimate if I were to kiss you goodbye. Wouldn't you say?"

She smiled back and said, "It would be awfully bad manners if you didn't."

He put his arm around her waist and pulled her to him and said, "This is about the only place I could trust myself to do this," and he bent down and kissed her lips with a passion that surprised even him.

She felt her whole body trembling with emotion as she pulled his head down to her lips.

The passengers were being called to board when they finally and reluctantly let go of each other.

Picking up her bag and carrying it to the boarding gate,

John said, "I sure hate seeing you leave."

"Don't worry," Lori said quite firmly. "I will be back."

"Call me and let me know what the President's response was."

"I will." She turned and started up the boarding ramp and then stopped, turned back and blew him a kiss before continuing.

John stood at the window for a moment, feeling emotionally and physically drained.

He watched as the plane taxied out to the runway and took off. When it was out of sight, he experienced a sudden feeling of emptiness.

CHAPTER TWENTY-ONE

NOTHING TO FEAR EXCEPT FEAR ITSELF
WHICH SELDOM APPLIES TO THE WEALTHY

The Mayflower Hotel, Washington, D.C.
March 4th, 9:30 p.m.

David Malcolm was standing behind the desk in the drawing room of his suite, talking on the phone while Mel Trask
and his ever-present financial vice president, Dick Simon,
were going over some notes they had brought with them.

They had all flown down from New York that afternoon to
prepare for their meeting with the President and to hear Lorelei
Young's anxiously awaited report.

Malcolm was on the phone with Lt. Colonel Burns about
his findings on the source from which the constant flow of
trades and settlements was emanating.

"So you've finally pinpointed the source?"

"Four sources to be exact Mr. Malcolm."

Annoyed, Malcolm fought to control his response. "What
do you mean 'four sources,' Colonel?"

"Sir, there is an office in New York on the 14th floor of a
building across the street from your own building. The sign on
the door says Global Computer Trading Corporation.

"It contains a computerized, automated switchboard with a
bank of forty incoming phone lines and a dedicated, untap-
pable, fiber-optic line up to the roof of the building where it
connects to a satellite dish.

"There are three employees there who handle minor paperwork answering global inquiries about the system and its
operation.

"Then there is a similar office located in downtown Min-
neapolis, in a building next door to one of the largest grain
trading operations in the U.S.

"There is another one in downtown Toronto, next door to
your Canadian banking division and one in Zurich, in the same

office building where your Zurich branch is located. They all have essentially the same setup as the office in New York.

"It was the location of those offices that made it so hard to track down. The electronic communications traffic from your foreign currency operations and the grain operations masked the trading company signals."

David curtly cut into the colonel's G.I. description. "So where is the main computer located?"

The colonel's discomfort could be sensed over the phone line. "Well sir, there's the rub. The computerized switchboard in each office picks up an incoming call from the different phone lines at random.

"It never stays on one line more than ninety seconds, which is too short a time period for us to place a trace and the signals never broadcast up to the satellite dish for more than fifteen minutes at a time before they switch to one of the other four offices at random.

"Right now we're trying to set up a line reader tap. That's a non-physical phone tap, to see if we can do a number read-out on the incoming call with some new equipment that's just been developed. I should have some numbers to check out by this time tomorrow."

Malcolm almost shouted at him. "Well, call me tomorrow when you have some of those numbers." He slammed down the receiver with such force that everyone in the room looked at him. "That damn Garland and his system are beginning to get under my skin."

Mel Trask stood up and walked over to Malcolm.

"Look Dave, this guy is not deviously trying to put us out of business. In fact, he's been trying to tell us about it and tie us into it for years and we've been ignoring him.

From what I've been reading and hearing, every bank in the country can tap into that system and make almost twice as much money as they now do servicing checking and savings accounts."

Dave Malcolm looked at Trask balefully. "Mel, you know

as well as I do that is not where we make our money. We make our money using other people's money to lend out at higher interest rates than we pay for its use. We make our money off of float, off of credit cards and other types of consumer loans where we make 18–21 percent off that damn float! With this new system, there will be significantly less float with the speed at which this system is supposed to work. It will also be damn hard to pay depositors 3, 4 or 5 percent interest and lend it out to someone else at 18 percent. If we don't get control of that damn system or put it out of business, we're out of business!"

Mel Trask looked at Dave Malcolm for a moment. "I understand all of that Dave, but just answer me this. If you put this guy or his system out of business, what exactly do you propose to do to put off mass hysteria when the banks re-open without enough currency to cover withdrawals on demand deposits? You think you'll have a business left at all without it?"

Malcolm thought about Trask's statement for a moment. "I know, I know. We've got to come up with something and I'm counting on Lori Young to tell us enough about that operation so we'll be able to make some decisions and plans."

"What decisions? What plans Dave?" Dick Simon asked.

"Plan A," Malcolm said, "Can we copy it and put one up like it overnight in competition? If not, Plan B. Can we locate this operation and somehow take control of it and operate it under our management? And finally; Plan C. If none of the above, can we put it out of business and put forward our own plan in its place based on government paper guarantees?"

Dick Simon shook his head negatively. "The only thing that makes any sense to me is to somehow get control of the already up and running system on a friendly basis so we can control how it's going to work for us.

The only way we can do that is if Congress doesn't pass a bill protecting the system the way it's presently set up and requiring its operating procedures and operating costs to remain in place for whoever operates it."

Mel Trask nodded his head in agreement and said, "From what I hear, the Senate bill got out of committee yesterday and has a 60-40 chance of winning a full Senate approval. The House has almost an identical bill expected to get out of committee and go to the floor today. If the House approves it, which they're expected to do, they will be able to override a Presidential veto just as easy if the President is even disposed to veto it. Then the whole game is over. I'd be willing to bet that this Garland guy even wrote both bills for the people who introduced them."

Dick Simon interjected, "From what I hear Mel, he did meet with the Senate and House majority leaders some time ago and made some recommendations on how to approach the situation."

Mel Trask nodded in agreement. "No doubt Dick, and from where I sit, it's do or die right now because five or six days from now will be too late. I tell you this guy Garland had this figured out to the minute. He's been lobbying Congress on this thing for almost four years non-stop while we were asleep at the wheel.

"He's laid out a precise plan of action which, I grudgingly have to admit, will work like a charm except guys like us won't be able to generate the kind of profits we're used to seeing.

"And maybe toughest of all, he's already gotten a number of the world's major governments and I don't know how many international companies tied into the plan and they're using it on a daily basis. If you think you're gonna put that out of business, Dave, old buddy, you have badly underestimated Mr. Garland."

David Malcolm looked at Dick Simon and Mel Trask for a long time before answering. Finally, with a faraway look in his eye, Malcolm said, almost to himself "I wonder how good the son-of-a-bitch is at dodging a .357 magnum bullet?"

CHAPTER TWENTY-TWO
THE PRESIDENT LISTENS TO A LADY
WHILE THE SHARKS CIRCLE

The White House, Washington D.C.
March 5, 9:00 a.m.

The President sat intently listening to Dave Malcolm as he described how, with the help of government guarantees and so-called scrip, the banking community might handle the present crisis.

The President nodded sagely and finally said, "Dave, scrip is all we have now. Paper money that, for all intents and purposes, would be worthless in a massive bank run.

"First of all, we both know that there isn't time to educate the business community, the corner grocery and the hardware store, to accept a piece of paper called 'scrip' instead of a piece of paper called money that they're used to dealing with now.

"Second, we couldn't print up enough paper scrip any quicker than paper money to accommodate the kind of bank runs we are going to see when the banking restrictions are lifted.

"I appreciate your advice. I appreciate your financial help during the campaign and even now. I also appreciate your situation, but frankly Dave, we are in the worst situation this nation has ever faced. It's worse than 1929, worse than 1932, it's worse than World War II."

Malcolm leaned forward in his seat and said, "Mr. President, I'm sure our bank and the banking community could get a handle on this thing if you would just empower us to act in the country's behalf."

The President shook his head. "I appreciate what you're saying but my advisers have done an in-depth analysis of this situation. Thanks to you and other businessmen who have loaned me your talented people, I have been supported by the best staff of advisers any President has ever had. All my

Page 135

appointees are the top brains in the U.S. Their staffs and advisers are the best that can be found, many on loan from industries like yours.

"Based on their analysis, and almost to a man, they are all in accord on several points. First, this situation is the worst this nation has faced, in fact the entire world has faced in modern times. Moreover, none of the usual quick fixes will work in this case. There isn't time, there isn't capability.

"All agree that we need some sort of vehicle to provide an alternate monetary system that is available immediately, that has some sort of track record to prove its workability, and, to some degree, would be acceptable not only to our citizenry but also to the international community.

"At this time, I am really not sure of what that might be other than this computer barter system we've all been hearing about and on which Miss Young is about to report. Frankly I'm not at all comfortable with what boils down to a choice of one. Unfortunately, it's the only choice available at the moment that meets all the requirements.

"As you know, at your suggestion I asked George Calder, the Secretary of Commerce, to direct Assistant Secretary Young to investigate the viability of the system developed by Global Computer Trading Company.

"Since that time, Senator Ketchall and Congressman Kord have both visited me and given me very enthusiastic reports on that system and what they feel it might accomplish.

"Yesterday, Senator Ketchall sent me a videotape of the proceedings of his committee and, frankly, I was impressed by what I heard and saw. The Chairman of the Federal Reserve also feels that it can be plugged into our monetary system effectively as do the heads of both the Office of Management and Budget and the Congressional Budget Office—providing it has certain controls and reliability.

"Finally, I have asked several of the 'Big Eight' accounting firms to evaluate the situation with an eye toward incorporating Global's setup into the monetary system and so far their reports have all been positive.

"In a few moments we'll hear Miss Young's report on her first-hand look and evaluation. Now, that is where we stand at the moment unless you have something extraordinary I haven't heard about yet?" The President stopped with a questioning look at David Malcolm.

Dave shook his head negatively and then shrugging his shoulders said, "Mr. President, it's just that I feel this system needs to be under some kind of joint control of the banks and the Federal Reserve. We need to work together to see that every industry and every depositor is protected and I feel that means we must know how it operates and how to manage it. If the Senate and House bills, as presently structured, pass, it is my personal opinion that they will be writing an obituary for the American business community."

The President looked thoughtfully at Malcolm for a moment before answering. "As I said Dave, I appreciate your feelings and concerns, but right now, let's just hear what Miss Young has to report when she arrives, shall we?"

* * *

Lori inspired the usual amount of head swiveling and appreciative glances as she walked into the White House. This was her fifth visit and she was still awed by the power it represented. It still commanded her respect as did the office of the President—whoever he might be.

Buck Raymond met Lori in the hall and took her coat before the orderly had the opportunity.

"I'm Buck Raymond, Miss Young, I believe we met a couple of months ago at the British Embassy when the Ambassador was hosting a trade group bash."

"Oh yes, I remember. Our department was there to help sell the British on buying our over-priced goods."

Buck smiled. "Correct, and about the only thing any of the Brits wanted to bid on was you."

Lori smiled back. "And I wasn't for sale."

They had reached the door to the Oval Office and Buck knocked deferentially and then opened the door, standing aside for Lori to enter.

The President and the men inside rose to their feet as Lori entered and Buck closed the door behind them.

Buck quickly walked around to Lori's left and said, "Mr. President and gentlemen, may I introduce Lorelei Young."

The President smiled and said, "We've met before, good to see you again Miss Young. I believe you know Mr. Malcolm and this is Mel Trask and Richard Simon of Trask, Hench Securities and of course you know George. Mr. Brockman, Chairman of the Federal Reserve will be joining us shortly but asked that we go ahead without him."

Lori nodded to the men present and sat down in the chair offered by Buck Raymond. Opening her portfolio she removed a file and her seldom-worn glasses.

As she opened the file she looked up at the President and smiled.

"Mr. President, I spent the day before yesterday evening and all day yesterday at the Delta Mining Company offices with Mr. Garland and his Global Computer Trading Company staff.

"Until yesterday, I felt I had an excellent knowledge of computers and computer programming. I was introduced to the most advanced, most incredible computer operation and system I have ever seen or even heard about.

"This system incorporates approaches that I thought were only in the research and development stages until now. Its capability, its capacity and its obvious reliability are undoubtedly the most advanced in the world today."

David Malcolm interrupted Lori. "You mean you were invited in to see and observe the main system? Where the thing is actually located?"

Lori turned to look at David as she answered him. "It's one of seven fully operational, duplicate nerve centers scattered around the world but it's where the creators of the system do their on-going research and development." Then she looked back to the President as she continued.

"The programmers, technicians and staff are the best I've run across anywhere and its operation is flawless. I spent at least two hours trying to throw that system every curve I know. Everything from so-called 'virus' programs to codes that would have tied any other computer up in knots for days. It didn't react to or accept even one.

"To say I was impressed, would be a gross understatement. I sat watching the system handling over 100,000 business transactions a minute. The operations manager told me the system was capable of handling over 100 million such transactions and save them to memory every minute of the day."

The President sat transfixed as he listened and finally interrupted. "You mean this computer system can handle all that without making even one mistake?"

Lori shook her head in assent. "Probably even more Mr. President. Its capacity and capability is incredible. Mr. Ross, the operations manager, showed me records that indicated over twenty million businesses and government agencies in fifty-five countries including the U.S. were using that system just yesterday.

"Of course, that is because of the default situation and the present confusion in the business world."

She turned to Dave Malcolm for a moment and said, "In fact, while I was sitting there I saw a number of business settlements take place between several of your bank's foreign divisions and some German and Swiss companies."

David Malcolm was visibly shocked when he heard that and Lori secretly gloated at his reaction.

"I'm going to have to talk to our foreign operations manager about that," Malcolm responded. "I certainly knew nothing about it nor did I authorize that kind of activity."

Lori interrupted Malcolm's tirade. "Mr. Malcolm, these were all transactions you would have lost instead of being able to complete them and profit from them."

The President shook his head in amazement and then asked Lori, "Do you actually believe this system could temporarily act as a reliable monetary system in place of our present system Miss Young?"

"Mr. President, to answer that question, let me point out that I have spent twenty years of my life studying computers and computer software, writing software programs, organizing and reorganizing computer hardware systems and developing systems that work for our government.

"As you are well aware, I was able to reorganize the Commerce Department system with new hardware and software so that we can now develop important financial data in a matter of a week instead of the previous two to three months. I thought I was well versed in the state of the art. Global's system can do all of this and more in minutes, literally, perhaps, even seconds."

The President shook his head in amazement. "That's impressive Miss Young. It sounds like they have developed a computer approach that far out paces anything I have ever heard or read about. What I don't understand is how they are able to interconnect so quickly throughout the entire planet."

Lori pulled out a sheaf of statistics from her briefcase to check some figures before answering. "Well, aside from being able to connect computer to computer via modems and phone lines which is certainly impressive, there is *Internet*. I know your own office and staff use it regularly to stay in touch with the country's voters."

She glanced at her notes before continuing. "At last count they had over twelve million computers networked throughout the world with over 100,000 more a month signing on. I think it would be safe to say that for every computer sign on you are adding at least ten more persons to Internet alone."

Just then the intercom buzzed and the President depressed the talk button and said, "Yes?"

A muted voice on the intercom said, "Mr. Brockman has

just entered by the North Portico, sir. Shall we send him right in?"

"By all means. Thank you." The President turned back to the assembled group and said, "Let me have some coffee sent in while we bring Brockman up to speed here. By the way, he will be making a summary report on the state of our currency in float and in printing process, and I expect all of you to maintain the strictest confidentiality about what you may hear."

They all nodded. Just then there was a knock and Jack Brockman was ushered in. After coffee had been served and Mr. Brockman had made his report about the impossibility of the currency situation, he reached into his briefcase and pulled out a sheet of paper.

"Just before I left New York this morning the head of my emergency team gave me this report." He paused and looked at the others in the room and then looked questioningly at the President.

"It's OK, Jack, they will maintain our confidentiality." The President added, "I believe that everyone present understands that violating this confidentiality in any way is subject to prosecution under federal law."

Brockman continued, "Well sir, we are getting the first major reactions and feedback to the banking restrictions you imposed day before yesterday. The demand for currency on bank withdrawals, even though everyone's aware of the restrictions, is frightening.

"I just heard a radio newscast reporting from some rural communities where armed citizens were threatening the town banker's life if he didn't give them all the money they have on deposit immediately.

"Not only that, but Treasury's printing presses can't keep up with the currency demand for just the permissible withdrawals. We have tried every public relations trick in the book to convince people to pay for their purchases by check or credit card regardless of how small the amount. In some areas we have even gone to the extent of guaranteeing checks being tendered to small merchants for goods and services.

"No good. Everyone wants currency to stash in the mattress. The confusion that's building is frightening. It's just a matter of time before riots break out and the news media showing pictures of all that will exacerbate that situation a hundredfold."

"In other words Jack," the President answered, "we need a decision on some kind of an alternate plan and we need it now."

Jack Brockman nodded his head affirmatively.

The President directed his attention back to Lori. "Miss Young, I read a transcript and saw a video of the Senate committee's hearing yesterday on the bill that would approve the use and protection of this Global Computer Trading Company's arrangement as an interim monetary system. I'm still not quite clear on how the government would collect and spend its taxes using this system."

Lori pulled some sheets of paper and small graphs from her portfolio and passed them to the President. "If you will follow what I explain by looking at the tables and graphs when I ask, you may have a better understanding.

"First of all sir, I was given some statistical data that the Global people had prepared some time ago on that subject. Being scientifically trained, I have a natural skepticism for data with which I'm unfamiliar. Therefore, before I present data upon which a reasoned decision might be based, I want to satisfy myself that those projections were reasonable.

"When I got back from Nevada last night, I went to my office and ran all their numbers back through my own spread sheet data base to see if they held up."

Dave Malcolm leaned forward in some hope as he said, "And what did you find Lori?"

His face fell when Lori said, "If anything, they were overly conservative. I should have expected that after seeing how dedicated and straightforward the people at Global were.

"Here is some data that I'd like to present to you. On the

first graph you will see a breakdown of last year's taxable transactions. They are divided into taxable personal income, taxable business and corporate income and permits and user fees. You will note that the total is almost a trillion dollars in transactions. These figures come from DEPCOMM's computers and not Global's.

"What is interesting here is that, using the IRS's present methods of tax collection and by using a mean average of an 18 percent tax rate, which levels out the top rates of 32 percent and the bottom rates of 5 percent and plugs in the major tax deductions and even the low income reverse tax payments, the government did not collect over 55 percent of the taxes legitimately due it. Historical data from the IRS shows that 30 percent of that will never be collected for one reason or another."

The President shook his head and said, "I had no idea it was that bad."

Lori continued. "If I wanted to go into detail, it's worse than that. The present ponderous tax forms, the incredible paperwork, the enormous burden placed on an understaffed IRS at tax time even though that agency is huge, all take its toll. We are still trying to collect taxes over two years old every year.

"But that is not my point, I'm just bringing this up to show a contrast. Using the figure of a mean average tax of just 8 percent per year as opposed to 18 percent for personal income and 5 percent on all business income, and plugging in the same data using the proposed Global system of taxation, which is detailed on page two and graph II let me describe the difference.

"First of all, Global proposes a standard withholding tax law for all personal and business income. The withholding tax of 8 percent on personal income across the board and 5 percent on business profits."

The President looked surprised. "Isn't that a rather drastic cut Miss Young? I mean by that, we have difficulties now trying to keep our infrastructure intact while still trying to reduce the deficit."

Lori looked up at the ceiling for a moment and then looked back at the President. "Let me explain that, Mr. President, by saying that tax withholding deductions on personal income are made at the time of the transactions. For instance, when a person is paid, the withholding tax, in the form of computer credits, is deducted from the individual's income credits and immediately credited to the Treasury account.

"No paperwork, no waiting 'til the end of the month or quarter only to find the withholding company paying the wages might have gone bankrupt taking with it the money withheld. No possible loss to the Treasury. It goes without saying that these credits can also be put to work for an additional two to three months at some modest interest, further increasing the value of that collected tax.

"The same takes place for business, only here the 5 percent deduction is based on an estimated profit for each transaction. At wholesale level, that profit ratio is arbitrarily set at 10 percent. The tax withheld is 5 percent of that 10 percent.

"If the transaction is a retail one, the profit ratio is arbitrarily set at 20 percent and that portion is subjected to a 5 percent withholding tax.

"If, at the end of the year, the manufacturer so taxed, can show that his profit was less than 10 percent or the retailer can prove his net was less than 20 percent, they are both due a tax refund. If their profit ratio was greater, that is their good fortune.

"Finally, it must be obvious that the tax collection agency, the IRS, can be drastically reduced in size and budget, saving hundreds of millions of dollars per year."

Mel Trask and Dick Simon shook their heads in admiration. Jack Brockman was transfixed by the dissertation. Dave Malcolm shifted uncomfortably as he slowly saw all his arguments go down the drain. And the President intently followed Lori's presentation on the spread sheets and graphs before him.

Lori continued, "On personal income, the same approach is utilized. Data by the individual showing that they were entitled to certain tax deductions, is fed into a local computer terminal that feeds into the Global system. If the data appears correct, and remember, this computer can search its archives in a split second to verify the veracity of a deductible expense for both business and personal, it allows the deduction and credits the refund back to the filer of the tax return.

"Now look at the spread sheet and graph that summarizes the total collected taxes after deductions and incorporates the additional use of the float of those funds, to use a term Mr. Malcolm is very familiar with. The federal government will have collected and generated over four times as much revenue as it does now at probably one third or less the cost."

"That's almost unbelievable Miss Young. Why that means we could wipe out the deficit in . . . in . . ."

Lori interjected, "Two years, Mr. President, and have a sizable surplus at the end of the third year."

The President sat pondering these statements and said, "But it's still not quite clear to me how this system can operate on a national basis.

"This system you're describing is a computer system. For it to be completely functional, I would assume there would have to be millions of computer terminals available everywhere. Every little town will have to have an awful lot of these computer terminals that can all communicate with this Global outfit's system. Am I not correct?"

Lori nodded affirmatively. "Yes sir, you are correct to a point."

"Well isn't that going to take a lot of time—time we don't have—to install terminals in every little hamlet that can communicate with Global?"

"Sir," Lori continued, "let me first point out that for all intents and purposes, this country is already on an electronic, computerized monetary system with hundreds of millions of credit cards, ATM cards and other debit cards and even electronic checks.

"Global's software program is unique, it has been written to recognize and translate all computer languages digitally transmitted to it. That means any computer or computer terminal anywhere, any touch tone phone all can communicate with Global's computer with complete understanding.

"But that is not all. The program is so designed that it has what is known as a front end.

"Every bank, almost every retail store down to the corner convenience store, almost every service station that is part of a chain, almost every post office, every government office, every police and sheriff's department, almost every fire department, almost every school, millions of offices and millions of homes in this country all have computers and telephones that communicate with each other over phone lines."

The President leaned forward intently. "And just how do we arrange for the permission to utilize all these computers?"

"With the right legislation," she continued, "every available computer terminal anywhere in this country, would be authorized to communicate with Global's mainframes. It wouldn't take much to fill in the gaps with additional terminals. Global already has a program that sends to any terminal screen, what is called a 'user friendly' menu.

"The user simply picks out from the menu on the screen, either with a cursor key, a mouse or a light pencil, what sort of information he or she wishes to transmit.

"A second menu then appears with a sort of 'check the box that fits your situation' questionnaire that allows for extra comment. The user then types in the information, whether on a computer or a touch tone phone. In the case of a phone, the computer provides voice menus so the user can respond, and the computer deciphers the information and appropriately handles it whether it's a farmer selling 10,000 chickens to a poultry processor, a steel company selling a thousand sheets of steel, or a grocery store ringing up a bag of groceries.

"All the computer needs to know is the buyer and seller's

federal ID or social security number and it makes all the appropriate transfers of credits, or we can call them dollars if you wish, from the buyer to the seller, or the employer to the employee, all in a split second. It's almost the way it's done now.

"When a person is paid salary, in credits of course, the payer's account is credited and the payee's account is debited with an appropriate amount deducted for withholding taxes and social security and just as quickly that amount is debited to the Treasury 'withheld taxes' account."

The President and the assemblage present sat stunned by Lori's presentation. Finally the President shook his head and said, "That sounds incredible, Miss Young."

Lori interrupted. "That is not all, Mr. President. Any touch tone telephone can also access the system. The Global people have developed what is known as a 'front end' program that responds to a telephone and allows the caller to key in their account number and then key in the type of transaction, payee and amount."

The President sat for a moment, flabbergasted by what he had just been told. "That would mean that at this moment, anyone, anywhere except perhaps in the middle of a desert or a sea where there are no pay phones and if they have no cellular or portable phone, could access that system right now."

Lori nodded her head and smiled. "Yes, Mr. President, that system is fully operational right now."

Finally, the President stood up. "Miss Young, I, we all, are deeply grateful for your thoughtful evaluation and excellent presentation and description.

"I feel confident that you've given us what we need to know. I am going to discuss this with all our agency and department heads as well as Congress and I feel there is enough information here for us to make a reasoned decision.

"Please don't take what I am about to say as a personal affront to your capability or your loyalty, but as President of a country faced with a deadly problem, it is incumbent upon me to make sure that what you have described here today, works as you say it does. Do you know if Mr. Garland will make his system available to anyone. May I send him to test and evaluate it?"

"Mr. President, I was told that the Global system is composed of at least seven duplicate systems, strategically placed throughout the world as backup to one another. A sort of insurance against disruption or interruption.

"One of these systems is located just a few minutes drive from here and Mr. Garland assured me that we are free to send anyone we wish to examine and evaluate it at your convenience."

David Malcolm stood up suddenly, his excitement obvious. Before the President could continue, he interrupted him.

"I believe it would be in the nation's interest to have a computer fluent representative of this country's largest bank as a part of that evaluation team, sir."

The President looked at Malcolm for a moment before answering. "I don't see why not." Then looking at Jack Brockman he said, "How about the Fed, Jack? You certainly need to have someone determine how the Federal Reserve would plug into this."

Brockman nodded. "We certainly do and I might suggest that the DP manager for Treasury and the IRS sit in. Maybe Mel Trask here might bring one of his people in to see how the brokerages can plug into this and at least one of the 'Big Eight' accounting firms as well."

The President nodded and looked at Buck Raymond, his ever present assistant. "Buck, will you handle the details?"

"Yes sir, Mr. President. Miss Young, can you give me a number where I can reach Mr. Garland to set all this up?"

Lori dug into her portfolio and pulled out John's Global business card and handed it to Buck Raymond. "If he's not at this number they can patch you through to him wherever he is."

Washington D.C.
March 5, 10:45 a.m.

The limousine turned out of the White House drive and onto Pennsylvania Avenue toward Georgetown. Mel Trask was staring moodily out of the window as David Malcolm finished his conversation on the car phone. Hanging up the phone, Malcolm turned to Trask and Dick Simon who was sitting on the jump seat.

"It's time we call in some debts gentlemen. My secretary is preparing a list of everyone on the Hill who owes us and calling all of my associates to whom political favors are owed. I also took the liberty of having her call your secretary Mel and coordinate with her so we don't duplicate."

Mel Trask nodded without looking at David Malcolm and then turned to face him.

"You know Dave, I've been thinking. What about throwing in with this guy Garland? You know, let's call him and schmooze him about how the nation's biggest bank and its biggest stock brokerage firm can put an international network of money savvy people at his disposal along with several million computer terminals all over the world?"

Dave Malcolm yelled, "Are you crazy Mel? That guy would walk all over us . . . he'd . . . he'd try to turn us into some kind of damned charitable operation. We'd be nuts to even consider it."

Mel held up his hand to cool off his friend. "I think you're missing the point, Dave. I don't mean that we are *really* going to give him the ranch. I just mean that it's a way for us to get on the inside of his operation so we can find the weak spots, the chinks in the armor so we can work up some kind of a takeover that would be acceptable to Congress and the Prez."

David Malcolm shook his head. "No, no Mel, this guy is too sharp for that kind of stuff. No, we're going to have to try my way first. We're going to call in all our favors from every congressman, senator, agency director and department secretary and anyone else we can think of and see if we can dump these bills before they become law."

Mel Trask challenged him. "And if that doesn't work?"

"Look Mel, I've got all the brains at the bank and a team of the top computer experts in every university that has ever received a grant from our bank working on our own version right now. The bank has some of the biggest and best computers anywhere in the world. I've been sending that team tapes of everything that we've learned about that system from day one.

"This afternoon, after I speak further with Lori, they're going to have everything she's learned. They've got a blank check and orders to work around the clock to either duplicate that system or come up with a better one within the next seventy-two hours."

The limousine pulled into the garage entrance of the Mayflower Hotel and up to the private elevator that accessed the floor of David Malcolm's suite as Mel asked, "And just suppose they *can* duplicate Garland's system or come up with a better one? How do you get Congress and the President to accept your operation in place of his and . . how do you take over that network he's already got set up?"

David looked at Mel and held his finger to his mouth as the chauffeur opened the door for them. "I'll explain when we get upstairs."

The private elevator whisked them up to the penthouse floor where the door opened silently onto the hall that served only the two suites.

Once inside, David shucked his coat and headed for the phone. He called down for messages. Then checked with his secretary on her progress.

"Good, good. Fax that list to me right away and, Carol,

please call my wife and tell her I have to remain in Washington at least another night."

Turning to Mel and Dick Simon, David said, "Let's have some lunch sent up, I'm starving. Carl is on duty and he knows us all and our favorite dishes. Let's just let him order for us, shall we?"

The two men nodded and David called the maitre d' and gave him instructions.

Dick Simon went to the bar and mixed them each a drink. Drinks in hand, they settled down on the couch and chairs facing each other.

David swirled his drink around in his glass and took a big swig. Looking at Mel Trask and Dick Simon in turn he began to explain his thinking.

"*If* we can't get the bills killed and . . . *if* we can't get the President to pull off a veto, I'm told that our people are very close to a system that works almost as well as Global's.

"They've tied in all the international communications lines the bank has including our own Telstar and Comsat links plus a few I doubt that Garland has access to.

"All he has to do is stumble, maybe miss eight hours of operation or maybe have some of his trades go astray and we will jump in with press releases, phone calls, visits and arm twisting wherever possible, to get Congress, Treasury and the Fed to recommend that we take over for a short period as a backup system."

Mel Trask held up his hand. "Hold it, hold it, Dave. You heard Lori today, that system is so backed up all over the globe that it's all but invulnerable. Not only that, *it doesn't stumble, it doesn't miss a beat. Come on now.*"

David shook his head as if dealing with a dull child.

"Mel, Mel, sometimes your naiveté amazes me. Global's people may have given our wide-eyed Lori a grease job about how invulnerable that operation is. But there isn't a computer in the world that can't be tampered with one way or another.

"You remember Colonel Burns, the Army's electronic

spook genius?"

Mel Trask nodded.

"He tells me that they have a top secret piece of electromagnetic equipment that can block out any kind of an electronic transmission in the world.

"They can garble phone transmissions, radio and TV transmissions and even microwave line-of-sight transmissions. They can effectively block out a whole city or even a whole region like they did in Desert Storm. Now tell me we can't make that system skip a beat."

Mel Trask shook his head slowly, partly in disbelief and partly in awe of his friend's deadly drive to stop John Garland and Global Computer Trading. "But how do you know where all the systems are in order to block them out?"

David said "We know for a fact that one of them is in Toiyabe, Nevada. Lori saw that one and worked on it herself. We will know in a few hours where the one in Virginia is that we've been invited to check out. Colonel Burns should also know by then through his telephone line tracking equipment where all the other ones are located. It's just a matter of hours."

Mel shook his head again at the amazing pit bull-like tenacity of Malcolm. "Does this colonel have enough equipment to cover all of these areas?"

David smiled as he leaned back and looked at Mel through lidded eyes. "If he wants to retire in six months to that lifetime of luxury he aspires to, he damn well better have."

Dick Simon, who had been quietly watching and listening to the exchange thought to himself how David Malcolm's attitudes and mannerisms looked snake-like, and shuddered.

CHAPTER TWENTY-FOUR
THE SET UP

Georgetown Health Club
Georgetown, Maryland
March 5, 11:30 a.m.

Lori had often used the club's private secretarial service offices for her business when she worked out before going home from the office. Not many people were aware of the offices and phone lines maintained for the health club's better customers, and Lori was sure that the phone lines were safe.

She tucked a stray wisp of her blond hair under her sweat band as she dialed the private number for John Garland's office. She felt a twinge of excitement as she heard John's warm, vibrant voice answering. "This is John, can I help you?"

"John? Lori."

She could almost see his smile as he said "Yes, I know, I'd know your voice anywhere, beautiful lady."

She couldn't explain the funny thrill she felt and it took her a moment to compose herself. "John, I left the meeting with the President a short time ago. I'm calling you from my health club in a private office where I am confident that the phone line is safe."

"Good thinking. How did it go?" he asked.

"Well, I could tell the President was impressed and he had already been contacted by Senator Mitchell and others. He also saw a tape of the hearing, so I know he was intrigued with the whole thing.

"Naturally, he has to take every precaution and he asked if he could have some experts check out the system."

John interrupted. "Yes, I know. Buck Raymond called me about thirty minutes ago to make arrangements for a team of computer people from four agencies and some people from Malcolm's bank to drive down to Alexandria, Virginia, and check it out."

Page 153

"I'm worried about Malcolm's people. He virtually *told* the President that his bank people had to be involved and he lit up like a Christmas tree when he got his way. I have a bad feeling about this man."

"Don't worry, Lori. I am fully aware of the things he is capable of and what his personal attitude is. We have taken every precaution and later, when we have more time, I'll tell you why no matter what he does or tries to do, it will not make one bit of difference.

Our team has spent years thinking about all the possible scenarios and what we have to do to protect the operation from all negative possibilities. What are you going to do now?"

Lori leaned back and closed her eyes as she talked.

"Well, first, I'm supposed to call Malcolm this afternoon and give him more information on my trip and findings."

John interrupted her. "I'm sure that one of his questions will be to ask you where the computer center is located. I would be pleased if you would tell him anything he wants to know except the precise location of our computer center.

If you just told him that the computer center was located in a section of the mine administration operation, that isn't untruthful and suggests that you mean the mining company administration building."

"What if he tries to do something to that building and the people in it thinking he is putting the computer out of business?"

"Provisions for that possibility have already been made. No one will be injured and nothing important can be damaged unless you think a sort of movie set is important."

Lori laughed. "You didn't!"

"Oh, but I did," John answered.

Lori shook her head as she smiled. "You're unbelievable, Mr. John, but I love it. What's next? When am I going to see you again?"

"Well, first of all, we want to accommodate the President and his experts at the backup computer center in Virginia.

I want him to be satisfied that this system will work as a monetary system and gain his support as quickly as possible because we don't have much time left."

"I know, John. I did my best to convince him today."

"I'm sure you did. Did you read the papers or watch the news on television today? There are serious problems developing all around the world. There was a riot in the loop in Chicago when banks couldn't accommodate the withdrawal demand requirements the President announced two days ago. In London, a large part of the financial district was trashed for similar reasons.

"The state police in Toledo, Ohio, had to rescue a bank president and his staff when some unruly mill workers threatened to take them out and hang them. The situation is getting dangerous and the fuse is growing shorter. I'm sure the President and the Congress are aware of all this and know they must act within the next couple of days."

Lori sat on the edge of the desk. "I know, John. I have been following the news, too. Our office received word from London that the Prime Minister has advised our President that they are willing to tie into the system completely if the U.S. comes in."

John broke in excitedly. "Yes, and the Scandinavian countries announced today that they are tying Global into their monetary system as of tomorrow, and I've been told by Charlie Ross that we received a message from Saudi Arabia that an emissary from that country will contact us sometime this afternoon to learn how they can sign up."

Lori sighed. "Oh, I wish there was more I could do. I feel so helpless."

"Beautiful lady, you're doing just great. But there is more you can do. I want you to call some of the senators and congressmen and give them your views. I will fax a list of their names to your office. Also contact Senator Ketchall and ask him who you might help convince before the open floor votes. That will help immensely in swaying enough votes to ensure the bill's passage."

Lori shook her head. "Can't they see they'll lose if it doesn't get implemented right away?"

"Apparently not, at least, not yet. I've dealt with people like that from time to time. Their preoccupation with self is so great, they cannot see the forest for the trees. Like the man said, 'Vanity, vanity, all is vanity.'"

Lori slumped down on the desk before her and wistfully said, "Oh John, I wish you were here."

There was a long silence on the other end of the line and finally, in a very quiet voice, John said, "Lori, I wish I were, too, and I may be there before you know it. Whatever happens . . ." he paused, "whatever happens, I . . . please have faith. Everything is going to work out. I'll call you when I get in."

Lori brightened. "When will you get here?"

"I don't know yet, but soon. When I call, if you're at the office, the call will be from Uncle John in case anyone is listening. I have to go now, beautiful lady. Take care."

There were tears slowly rolling down Lori's cheeks as she whispered, "I will, John. Please be careful." She slowly lowered the phone to its cradle when she heard the line click. She felt drained and then, with a new resolve, she straightened her back and dabbed the tears from her cheeks with the towel over her shoulder. She got up from the chair with a renewed determination and said to herself, *we're going to win because we're right.* And with that, she walked out of the room.

CHAPTER TWENTY-FIVE
NOW YOU SEE IT, NOW YOU DON'T

Potomac River
Alexandria, Virginia
March 5, 1:30 p.m.

Charlie Ross was standing on the bridge of the small modern freighter that was tied to the last wharf downstream from Alexandria, Virginia. He had flown in with his crew from Reno in a chartered jet to meet the freighter as it came up river from Chesapeake Bay.

The freighter was unloading the last of twenty-five large cargo containers that had been specially built by Global some two years earlier. The containers were designed so that one side could swing up to become a roof while the other swung down to become a floor, all interlocking with each other to become a series of offices or one large office. Trailer trucks were hauling them to an isolated warehouse and office building in a commercial district three blocks from the river.

In one section of the warehouse there was a complete computer layout put together to look like a Global system but composed completely of old surplus computer equipment the government had sold at auction several months earlier. The equipment nameplates had been removed and replaced with nameplates that duplicated the type of equipment that Global's systems used.

As the trucks arrived, a part of Charlie's crew positioned the containers on the floor of the building. As soon as the containers were all inside the building, the crew went to work and quickly unlocked the swing-out sides and hooked them together until they formed a large office similar to the one that Lori had seen in Nevada but sitting within the warehouse with the reception office and door area abutted to the building's main door entrance.

Inside the crates were all the computer and electronic

equipment of a typical Global Trading Company operating system bolted to the carpeted container floors. Two containers were loaded with office furniture that was quickly positioned throughout the newly erected offices.

Part of the crew plugged telephone lines into prearranged phone outlets located at intervals on the floor of the building. Others were stringing electrical cables outside the container walls and hooking them up to outlets built into the walls of these special containers.

Precisely one hour and fifteen minutes after they had begun unloading the ship, Charlie Ross walked in the front door of what was, for all intents and purposes, a typical Global Computer operations office.

There was a fully furnished reception room complete with receptionist, ringing phones, a company logo on the wall spelling out 'GLOBAL COMPUTER TRADING COMPANY' and a very impressive, fully operational computer operations office beyond.

Charlie walked through the reception office, into an office corridor that minutes before had been the sides of a shipping container and then to a door marked 'Computer Operations Center.' Sticking his card in the door and announcing his name, the door swung open to reveal the busy activity of a Global trade settlement and credit accounting operation, all authentic and looking as if it had been there for years.

Charlie winked at Bob Trainer, his assistant, and said, "How's business?"

Bob winked back and said, "Busy as usual and getting busier all the time."

"Any glitches?"

Bob shook his head. "None that I can see. The equipment and lines have all been checked and tested and are working perfectly. The lines are all hot and operating and the trade volume is up 120 percent over yesterday."

"Well, try to look pretty. We have video cameras rigged all over the place and we're broadcasting what they pick up back to the ship where it's all being videotaped for posterity."

"You think anybody will try anything dumb?" Bob asked as Charlie sat down at a terminal.

"Not while the government's experts are in here checking out the system, and probably not until well after they're all gone. By that time we should be packed up and back on the ship sailing down Chesapeake Bay.

"Of course the cameras, which the boss figures are expendable, will still be here taking neat pictures of any activity that might take place. Should be interesting.

"I've got a list here of all the names, addresses, social security numbers and stuff like that on all the people the President is sending down. Let's get busy and check 'em out. See if we have any strange people in this bunch."

Charlie keyed in a code and a modem number. The screen flickered for a few seconds and then began scrolling requests for access codes. Charlie keyed in a code and the screen then invited the user to list names for requested background checks. Charlie dutifully listed all the names before him beginning with the two men from Case City Bank.

One by one, screens came up with information on each name that was printed out on a nearby printer. All the names checked out except one man from the Case City Bank.

The message kept flashing, 'still checking.' Finally, it repeated the known information, street address, phone number, zip code, vital statistics until it got to 'profession or skills.' There the screen showed a flashing 'unknown or unlisted' message.

Charlie printed out the information and then turned to Bob. "Looks like we hit a ringer. The date the information was entered into the FBI computer on this Ben Sessions from Case City Bank is today." Charlie began massaging the keyboard as he spoke.

"Let's sign in with TRW Credit Reports. Those guys will track a pole cat if he owes money."

When the information screen came up, Charlie keyed in the data on Ben Sessions. In ten seconds, the screen began filling up with data. Charlie began reading off the screen out loud.

"Unmarried, moved five times in two years. Owes money but has a six figure bank account as of day before yesterday. He has worked at various branches of the Case City Bank in three countries as a special assistant to the chairman. No known relatives."

Charlie looked at Bob. "Sounds like a company security agent, wouldn't you say?"

Bob nodded his head. "And a guy we better keep our eyes on."

The phone beside Charlie buzzed and he picked it up. "This is Charlie. Yeah. Okay, thanks."

Bob looked at Charlie. "The troops comin'?" he asked.

Charlie nodded as he looked at his watch. "Yep, they'll start arriving about 4:30. We've got an hour to check out the place and see if everything's ready. Didn't someone bring all this morning's printouts?"

Bob nodded. "They're still in the box, Charlie. But we'll get it all unpacked and put away like it would normally be in case they ask to see records for the last ten days. It's all on file and of course, on the backup tapes."

"Well, let's get some office paraphernalia and personal junk scattered around. We brought boxes of stuff like coffee cups with names on 'em and pencils half used up. Get everybody to help unpack and carry the stuff back to their desks so it will look like what one would normally find laying around on top of desks and in desk drawers. Anybody check the toilets?"

Bob grabbed a phone and started dialing an extension. "I'll get Darrell to go through that stuff and make it look lived in. We also put some doodle pads full of messages and junk in the boxes along with a few personal photos, a pinup calendar and even an old Penthouse magazine and a couple of those grocery store check-out stand whiz-bangs. Hello Darrell, here's what I want you to do . . . "

Washington, D.C.
March 5, 2:30 p.m.

Lori was shuffling through some papers on her desk with one hand while holding the phone with the other, waiting for an answer to the ring. Finally she heard Dave Malcolm's voice come on the line. "This is David Malcolm."

"David, this is Lori Young."

"Oh, Lori, I tried calling you earlier but you weren't in your office."

"David, after a trip like the last two days, I had to unwind a little to get my head clear. I went to my health club and took a swim and had a massage."

"Feel better now?"

Lori looked at a news clipping of John and said, "Yes, thanks, lots better David. What else do you want to know about that computer system?"

"I would like to sit down with you for a few minutes if you don't mind. I hate to discuss something like this on the phone."

Lori thought for a moment and then a small smile crossed her face as she said, "David, why not come here to my office. I have a very descriptive log I finished on the plane ride back last night and this morning. I also have a map of the Toiyabe Canyon area and a lot of other documentary information I picked up while there."

She could almost see David smiling and rubbing his hands in anticipation. "Splendid idea, Lori. I'll be there in fifteen minutes. See you then," and he hung up without waiting for an answer.

Lori reread the information John had prepared for her which he had titled, "Good honest answers and directions are often the best misdirection someone can use when dealing with a Machiavellian mind."

She smiled and shook her head in admiration as she put the document away. *Mr. John Garland sure knows the kind of people he's dealing with,* she mused. *He would have made a great CIA operative.*

The buzzer on her intercom was a signal that someone had just arrived. She absent-mindedly straightened up her desk and got up as her secretary came in to announce the arrival of David Malcolm and a Colonel Burns.

Lori motioned her to show them in. Her secretary opened the door and held it for them as she asked them to enter. David came in with his usual unctuous smile in place.

"Beautiful Lori, it's such a wonderful reprieve to be in your presence."

'Horse puckey,' she thought to herself as she smiled at Malcolm.

"Lori dear, this is Colonel Burns. I took the liberty of bringing him along. He is an old friend and the Army's top electronics man. You two have a lot in common."

'Fat chance,' Lori mused but then smiled and extended her hand to the colonel as she nodded toward a chair. "Please sit down, Colonel." Turning to Malcolm, she said, "I have no problem with Colonel Burns' presence if you don't, David."

"Thank you, Lori. I just wanted to go over some things before our computer expert goes down to Alexandria to examine that system of Global's."

Lori pulled over a stack of files and a map and said, "Fine David, fire away."

"First of all, the system you evaluated, was that actually located at Garland's mining company?"

"Yes, it was located at the mine although separated from the mining company's administrative operations."

"Did they hesitate showing you any part of it?"

"No, David, as a matter of fact they wanted to show me more than I had time to see."

David's face showed surprise before he answered. "How do they send and receive their data for the computer center from such a remote area?"

Lori spread the map of northwestern Nevada on the desk and said, "Well of course they had a huge bank of phone lines, some of them fiber optic, but apparently most were conventional.

"Then they had radio communications, the likes of which I've only seen at military bases. There was also a large communications antenna and two communications dishes on the peak above the mine."

She stood up to look at the map better and both the colonel and David stood up to see what she was describing. She pointed to Dome Peak above Toiyabe Canyon with a heavy heart but did not let her feelings show in her face or voice.

"There," she pointed, "is Toiyabe Canyon. If you look closely at this topographic map you can see that the canyon is shaped like an hour glass. The lower portion is the community of Toiyabe Canyon, a company town where all the workers live. Then the canyon walls rise and pinch together to form the funnel part of the hour glass. After you pass through that narrow part of the canyon it widens out again into sort of a bowl with the shaft leading to the underground mining operation at the upper end of the bowl. On the left and going down the slope from there is the ore treatment mill and smelter.

"From the uppermost part of the bowl going down the right side is the mine equipment maintenance building. Then the parts and tool room department building. Then the power generators and underground fuel storage and finally the mining company offices and administration building.

"At the very head of the canyon and above it is Dome Peak. It is one of the highest points in the area and on it are various radio and television repeater stations, the FAA flight control repeater, the Fallon Naval Air Station flight control repeater station and, finally, the antenna and dishes for the mine and Global's computer operation."

Malcolm looked surprised. "You mean all of these operations are bunched up on one tiny peak and share less than what appears to be about ten or twelve acres of ground?"

Lori nodded her head. "I believe Mr. Garland said something to the effect that if some foolish person wanted to take out Global's communication system for some misguided reason, they would have to be prepared to take on the U.S. Navy, the FAA, four major networks and some secret government communications operation as well."

Malcolm and Colonel Burns exchanged glances and then looked back at the map. "Lori, you sure did your homework. I admire your thoroughness. How in the world did you find out all about this in less than two days?"

Lori thought back to her trip to Perspective Peak with John the day before. "Mr. Garland was proud of what his team had accomplished and he personally drove me up there to show me."

Malcolm shook his head in disbelief. "The man is incredible."

Lori said very softly, "Yes, David, he is."

David turned and looked at her for a moment before continuing. "Well, let's talk about the system's operation for a moment. You told the President earlier today that the system was foolproof. That's hard to believe. It would seem that all electronic systems are vulnerable to some degree. I mean, suppose that power station had an accident?"

"According to Charlie Ross, manager of the computer operation, they have a massive, advanced, battery-backup system that would provide operating power for up to two weeks if necessary. Incidentally, the mining company has a contract to provide power to the various government agencies who maintain communications systems on that peak and they have required the company to set up an elaborate security system for both the power station and the closely guarded, underground, backup system."

David and Colonel Burns again quickly exchanged glances, none of which was lost on Lori as she smiled to herself at their discomfort.

"I presume that they broadcast communications to the

satellites from that location?"

"Yes, apparently they do. Sometimes, during the time I was observing the system's operation, the whole operation would become idle and act purely as a backup system while one of the other operations somewhere else in the world became the central processing unit for the entire network."

The colonel shook his head in amazement. "Incredible, it's an incredible system."

Lori looked at the colonel and nodded. "You're right, Colonel. And while I was there, I watched the last stages of a test being conducted on a sort of system clone of their big mainframe. The clone system was constructed solely from a series of microcomputer CPU's based on powerful new processing chips.

"A Japanese company had already built several hundred of these super microcomputer-based systems to Global's specifications and was delivering them to locations around the world to await a full network test."

Lori could see Malcolm's face drop as he fought to control a tic in his eye. She had purposely dropped this bomb on him in hopes of discouraging him from attempting any violent action against John or Global.

Finally, David Malcolm rose and motioned to the Colonel to follow suit. "Well Lori, you have done the usual exceptional job you are so well known for. I shall certainly tell the President and the Secretary of your work 'above and beyond the call.'"

David proffered his hand to Lori as he said, "Thank you so much for this enlightening information and for allowing the colonel to be present. I'll be in touch with you later."

Lori led the way to the door of her office and smiling, opened it for them. "Thank you, David. It was a pleasure to be of service and I hope it provides what you need for your decision making. And it was a pleasure meeting you, Colonel."

As she closed the door behind them, she leaned against the door and thought, *Oh God I hope I poured a ton of ice water on his devious plans. Dear, dear John, be careful.* Finally, shaking her head, she pushed herself off the door and headed for her phone.

CHAPTER TWENTY-SEVEN
EVEN GOOD GUYS CAN LOBBY

Capitol Hill, Washington, D.C.
March 5, 4:00 p.m.

Senator Ketchall and Tom Ballard were sitting in the senator's office with their eyes glued on the television in the corner. The picture on the screen showed riot police on horseback swinging clubs at crowds of screaming, rock-throwing people as the announcer described the scene.

"And in the Trafalgar section of London, mounted police have been trying to control mobs of screaming people that are attacking one of Britain's largest financial institutions, who are hysterically demanding to withdraw all of their savings."

The announcer continued, "Meanwhile, in New York City in front of banks like the one shown here, people are quietly waiting their turn in teller lines in order to draw out the government-decreed allowable amounts from their bank accounts.

"There has been some violence, some work stoppages and civil unrest reported in parts of Los Angeles, San Francisco, New Orleans, Miami, Pittsburgh and St. Louis. However, in most parts of the country it appears that citizens are taking a 'wait-and-see' attitude—waiting to see what Congress and the President offer as a solution.

"The New York Times today reported that its consultants' analysis has shown the computerized monetary system of dollar-based electronic credits now under consideration by Congress could easily save the nation's assets from any serious losses.

"At this point, the proposed system is not yet well understood. Cokie Roberts is standing by at the Treasury Department in Washington to tell us what she has learned about the system."

The TV screen's scene shifted to the well-known political analyst. "Mike, the Secretary of the Treasury has announced

Page 167

today that analysis by the National Science Foundation and the department's own computer people suggests that switching from a paper-based currency to an electronic credits based currency would not be all that difficult.

"He pointed out that businesses everywhere already utilize electronic cash transfers by using customers' ATM or credit cards in computerized cash registers. So it isn't altogether new to anyone. However, the Secretary pointed out that a decision must be made quickly before the situation gets more serious."

Senator Ketchall aimed his remote control and turned off the TV. "Things are disintegrating by the minute, Tom. Congress has got to act right away. What is the latest count after that big lobbying effort by the PAC boys today?"

"Well, before those guys began intimating big losses in campaign funds, we almost had it locked up. Right now, I don't know. At last count we were about neck and neck and that's not enough."

Senator Ketchall shook his head. "First of all, I am convinced the President is with us on this thing. What bothers me though is that the whole world is about to blow up around us and here we sit watching ostensibly grown, responsible men waffling between the survival of an orderly society or pleasing their major source of campaign funds. I wonder if they realize that if they don't get this thing on line immediately, all their campaign funds put together won't buy them a dog catcher's position.

"We need John Garland here in person. No one can sell this thing better than he can. Not only that, we need to get him and his story on every media vehicle possible. Did you get a hold of him as I asked?"

"Yes, Senator, and he said he would get on his way immediately. That was about 12 o'clock our time and he said he'd be here in about three and a half hours, give or take a few minutes. Seems he has a jet at his disposal."

The senator looked at Tom. "Private jets don't usually fly that fast, do they?"

"If I'm not mistaken, this is a jet out of Fallon Naval Air Station. Seems they have some kind of quid pro quo working."

"That must be a hell of a quid pro quo. But, if it'll get him here in a hurry, I'm not going to ask the Navy to explain. Now Tom, it's time for us to do a little lobbying of our own."

"Yes sir. What do you suggest?"

"Let's start with a list of every congressional powerhouse that thinks like we do. Call all your counterparts in their offices, tell them Garland is on his way here for a personal appearance. Then ask them to help us line up newspaper, TV and radio for a full scale media 'dog and pony' show tonight at around 6:30. That will be right after the major local and national news shows and should give this thing some immediate coverage as a news special. It will also hit all the early morning editions of every newspaper."

Tom interrupted. "But, Senator, you don't even know if Garland is prepared to present anything at a big media event like this."

The senator smiled. "I've known John Garland for a long time. I've heard him speak extemporaneously on this subject a dozen times and every time, he had everyone in his audience hanging on every word. Better still, they understood every word he said and even better yet, they *believed* every word he uttered. The man is so sincere, real and articulate, that he could have run for any public office he wanted and won hands down."

"Why didn't he?"

"Why didn't he what, Tom?"

"Why didn't he ever run for public office?"

"I asked him that a few years ago and he said that he could better serve the nation and his fellow man doing what he was doing. That being a politician was too restrictive and did not permit a man like him to be effective.

"I didn't really believe that statement at the time. I was still a federal judge then and thought how I might help change things if I were a politician. Since becoming a senator however, I've often thought about what he said."

"Okay, Senator, let me get started and it might help if you talk to some of the big guns yourself. How about calling your friend at ABC and maybe the editor you know at the Wall Street Journal."

"Don't worry, I will. Meantime, those computer experts the President wanted to send over to one of Global's centers to analyze the effectiveness of the operation should be on their way. See if we can tie their findings into the media event."

"I'll work on it and now I better get started."

With that Tom Ballard left the room and Senator Ketchall turned to his phone to get the ball rolling.

CHAPTER TWENTY-EIGHT
THE STING WORKS

Alexandria, Virginia
Global's temporary office
March 5, 5:30 p.m.

The phone at Charlie Ross's elbow rang. Without turning from the computer screen in front of him he punched the speaker button on the phone. "Yeah, Charlie here."

"Charlie, the troops are beginning to arrive. Sherrill is taking them into the conference room and giving each of them the handouts we prepared."

Charlie looked at the clock on the wall. "How many still to come Andy?"

"Two. The guy from the Treasury and somebody from the IRS."

"I'll be over in a minute."

Charlie got up and went over to a seemingly blank wall with only a clock and calendar on it. Touching an unseen button, he swung the clock out from its back to reveal a small computer panel. He punched a red button that said 'start recording,' and pushed it back against the wall until it clicked and walked out of the room.

As he walked into the lobby he saw a man and a woman sign in at the visitor and security register, show their I.D. and receive visitor badges.

He walked over to them putting his hand out. "Hi, I'm Charlie Ross, operations manager here."

The first man shook his hand and said, "Jack Taggart, data processing manager IRS, and this is Carol Belkert, same GS and job at Treasury."

They shook hands and Charlie motioned them to the conference room. "Follow me please, the rest are already here." He opened the door for them and as they passed through there were greetings and acknowledgments from those who knew each other in the close community of the world of computers.

One of them waved at Charlie. "Hi, Charlie, remember me? Del Adams, we used to work together over at Mines."

"Sure, Del, how could I forget, you're the one who told me I wouldn't last six months at my new job right?"

Del smiled sheepishly. "Obviously, I was wrong."

"Ladies and gentlemen, for those of you who don't know me, let me introduce myself. My name is Charlie Ross and I'm the operations manager for Global Trading Company. Since time is of the essence, I will be brief as possible in outlining the basics of the system to you. Much of what you want to know, both the technical specs and the software operations, are outlined in the material you've been given.

"The system you are about to see and test has been six years in the building. The concept actually took a lot longer than that. Right now, it's been operating as a full-blown network system for a little over two years.

"There were a few minor glitches in the beginning that did not, however, affect the overall system. What we have developed here is a system combining all the essentials in both hardware and software so as to provide unlimited access to a very complex database and as accurately as possible, to mimic the human mind's operation in several basic areas. Among other things, the system has been designed to employ so-called 'fuzzy logic' when it has to deal with input that might employ more than one action or answer.

"The first area is the ability to accurately determine where, in a vast memory complex, the system should store information for later retrieval. The second area is how to quickly locate a specific memory area in order to retrieve information for appropriate action relating to that specific transaction.

"The third area is the ability to make numerous complex mathematical conclusions essential to a specific transaction and then properly apportion each segment of that transaction to the appropriate accounts.

"A fourth area is the system's ability to create a vast, non-duplicating code for each business, government taxing agency, data outlet and, finally, each individual who may use this system. This non-duplicating archiving code is capable of having a quadrillion individual accounts at present and can be increased by the square if necessary.

"That capability suggests that the system could accurately handle accounts for every individual, every known government agency and every business entity on earth. Furthermore, it can accurately keep an error-free track of all these accounts at the present rate of over six billion transactions per hour.

"We are presently completing benchmark tests on a new system we have developed composed entirely of microcomputer CPU boards based on powerful new chips operating at extremely high megahertz.

"The benchmark tests are almost unbelievable for their speed and artificial intelligence ability. Networking together several hundred of these much less expensive central processing units in massive parallel systems should increase the system's ability a hundred fold."

The persons assembled in that room were all the most knowledgeable computer systems people in government and they sat dumbfounded at what they had just been made privy to. Finally, one of them raised his pencil to gain Charlie Ross's attention.

"Mr. Ross, what you have just told us is almost Buck Rogers or Star Trek stuff. I mean, we have been doing research in various areas of this, but not in our wildest dreams did we think we would get to this point for at least another ten years."

Charlie nodded his head and smiled. "Quite true and six years ago I would have said you're right. But right now, I'm going to take you next door and show you a system capable of doing all these things now. Shall we go folks?"

Charlie led the way to the air conditioned main computer rooms where he first conducted a tour of the computer hardware for them, explaining the system as they went.

"What we have here are multiple paralleled mainframes in

tandem operating under an artificial intelligence software I described to you earlier.

"They are all hooked up via a complex communication network that is duplicating all signals on several different modes of communications to avoid any possible interruption.

"We have several of these systems scattered around the globe, each duplicating the other to ensure backup and uninterrupted operation as well as to guard against any loss of information. I might further point out that we have the most advanced anti-virus safeguard built into this, which employs a cryptography system that changes almost daily.

"The granddaddy system incorporating the Cray 1000 mainframe is located in an isolated area of Northern Nevada. However, these subsystems can almost duplicate what the Cray can do."

Charlie studiously avoided looking at the Case City Bank representative, knowing that the video cameras would be tracking him.

When the group had finished asking questions concerning the computer hardware, Charlie led them into the busy and fully staffed data center where men and women were sitting at screens and keyboards monitoring the activity flowing into the system and answering phone call inquiries from around the globe.

"This is the operations center. Mainly, we randomly monitor transactions with a special checking software to make sure that all transactions are accurate, properly completed and archived.

"Also we answer inquiries concerning how one signs up for Global's services and assign business, government or personal code numbers and access codes to those who do sign up.

"Most of that is actually handled by sales offices in New York, Los Angeles, Toronto, London, Paris, Brussels, Zurich, Istanbul, Rome, Melbourne, Hong Kong, Tokyo and several others.

"Incidentally, in just the last five days, inquiries have

jumped from 50,000 per day to over a half a million a day. And that comes from every country on the planet."

The group was impressed with the description of the operation to the point of being speechless. Charlie gestured toward ten empty seats in front of ten terminals.

"If you will each take a seat at a terminal, I will explain how you can access the system and monitor its activity. I believe that each of you was advised to have someone from your offices standing by to call in on a special number and access code in about five minutes. They can enter any transaction you wish, regardless of how complex, so that you could follow the handling of it here."

The assembled group all nodded and began to seat themselves in front of screens.

"Also, when you have completed that, I will give you a temporary access code that will permit you to pull up any data from the archives you might wish. The access will be by agency or industry and not give specific names but codes known only to Global's code group. This is being done to maintain customer confidentiality.

"Should the government sign on as a full-scale user, then specific information will be available to each agency relative to its legitimate right to know as dictated by the present laws. Access codes will then be replaced by names of the data sources.

"You may use plain English for any inquiries or use any computer language you feel comfortable with. The computer understands all languages and is able to interpret. The front slash key brings up the main menu and then pull-down sub menus are available on any of the main menu subjects. You simply state your requests in English at the appropriate menu screen.

"Finally, I will ask each of you to develop a personal message or code that will be transmitted with date and time and this system's personal 'fingerprint' to your agencies every fifteen minutes to prove that it can operate reliably without loss or interruption.

"Now it's about time for your associates to call in transactions. Please key in the code you gave your office and key in a request for the computer to monitor all transactions displaying those codes."

With that the group began its observation and testing. The blinding speed with which transactions were entered, calculated, completed and archived was awesome. Carol Delbert from the Treasury department asked, "How do you slow this thing down Mr. Ross? I can't even follow what it's doing?"

Charlie smiled. "Just key in the request to 'print to screen' and hit the 'enter' key. That will cause the transactions to be printed out screen by screen and after you have read each screen just hit any key for the next screen until the statement 'End of transaction' comes up."

She nodded and turned her attention back to the screen.

Forty-five minutes later, after the experts had observed, tested and thrown everything at the system they could think of, the representative from the Federal Reserve stood up and said, "Mr. Ross, I've never seen anything like it, we could put our government's entire operation on this one computer system and save a ton of money." He shook his head again. "Man, I've never seen anything like this, I've never even dreamed anything like this would be available in this century."

Charlie laughed. "Glad you like it. We're pretty proud of it ourselves."

One by one the visitors rose, making last-minute notes for their reports, and shaking their heads in disbelief at what they had witnessed.

Del Adams, the man Charlie had worked with in Washington years before, came over to shake Charlie's hand.

"Charlie, this outfit sure gets my approval and then some. There is no question in my mind that it can accurately and efficiently handle anything you can throw at it, much less act as a monetary and trade system. Boy, would I love to work for an outfit like this."

He shook Del's hand and said, "I'll keep that in mind."

Charlie shepherded the group into the lobby and out the front door where they got into their government vehicles or chauffeured cars and began heading back to Washington to make their reports.

When the last car had pulled away, Charlie went back inside where the receptionist gave him the message that the last car had passed a specific check point and no untoward activity had been noted by the TV cameras thus far. Charlie thanked her and reached over the counter to a microphone sitting on her desk.

"Folks, this is Charlie Ross. I'd like to compliment you on a magnificent performance. And now, like they say in the movies, 'strike the set,' pack up and let's get out of here and get back to our regular location. On the double folks."

The reverse procedure of activity took place in an obviously well-organized and rehearsed operation. The furniture was all moved back into the two empty containers that had temporarily been the reception lobby and the conference room.

The walls of the other areas folded up and locked in place to become shipping containers. Cables and phone lines were unhooked and rolled up and trucks began hauling Global Computer Trading Company operations office number two back to the ship from whence it had come.

CHAPTER TWENTY-NINE
THE SIMPLEST EXPLANATION IS THE BEST

Washington, D.C.
A phone booth on Capitol Hill
March 5, 6:15 p.m.

The phone in her apartment was ringing for the sixth time when Lori breathlessly answered, "Hello?"

"Lori, this is John."

Lori felt her heart jump. "John, where are you?"

"I'm in Washington. I flew in at Senator Ketchall's request."

"Yes," she responded, "but what are you doing here?"

"Watch your TV set about twenty minutes from now. Any major network will do."

"John, what are you going to do?" she yelled.

"Calm down, Lori. I'm just doing what is required of me. It shouldn't take more than an hour. When that's over, I want to see you."

Lori caught her breath. "Oh yes, yes, where? When?"

"I'll call you, beautiful lady. Just be ready to leave your place when I call."

"I will, I'll get ready now. Please be careful John."

"Believe me when I say I am. Do you have a VCR that can tape the special broadcast?"

Lori looked at her television set absently. "Yes, yes I have one."

"Good, do me a favor and tape whatever comes on."

"I will."

John hesitated for a moment and said, "I've got to go now, beautiful lady, see you in a little while."

Lori hung up thoughtfully and stood there for a moment. Then she rushed over to the television set, dug out a tape from a cabinet below, and put it in the VCR. Turning on the set to the local ABC affiliate, she set it to begin taping in ten minutes, then turned to the bedroom to get dressed.

John walked out of the phone booth and down the corridor to the waiting Tom Ballard who was anxiously pacing the floor. He looked up when he heard John's footsteps.

"Oh good, we've still got about ten minutes. You sure you don't want makeup Mr. Garland?"

John shook his head and smiled. "No thanks, Tom, I don't need it. I don't sweat."

Tom looked at John as they walked quickly toward the chamber where the assembled House and Senate were gathering and shook his head.

"Boy, I'd be sweating like a stuck hog if I were getting ready to address the House and Senate, the President and probably 25 million people. Man, I don't know how you do it."

They stopped before a small door leading to an anteroom behind the chamber in which John was about to face the assemblage Tom had described.

John turned to the Senator's aide. "Tom, talking to thousands of people is no different than talking to one person when you have something important to say about which you feel strongly." Then with a wry smile, he added, "The only difference is you may have to talk a little louder if there are no microphones."

Tom took a deep breath, opened the door and they walked into the anteroom. Senator Ketchall was there with his counterpart, Speaker of the House Boyd. They shook hands and Congressman Boyd asked John if he was prepared for his talk.

John smiled at him in his relaxed manner. "Ready as I'll ever be."

The congressman had little beads of sweat off his forehead as he said, "Boy, I hope it's good because our you-know-what is on the line tonight."

John shook his head in acknowledgment and said, "In more ways than one, I'm sure."

Just then the door opened behind the dais and a page whispered to Senator Ketchall, "Sir, they're ready out here."

Ketchall nodded and the two congressmen squared their shoulders and put on their best faces and headed out the door.

Tom Ballard said, "The senator will press a button that lights that red light up there over the door when they're ready for you." John nodded.

* * *

As she dressed, Lori kept running in from the bedroom to the living room to see what was happening on the TV set. She finally settled herself down on the couch and put her long legs up on the coffee table as she watched the end of the second edition of the local news.

She knew a situation comedy was scheduled to come on after the commercial break and that it would have to be something of major importance to preempt that commercial money-maker.

Right on the half hour, the announcer broke in to say that the usual programming would not be seen in order to broadcast a special address to the nation by the leaders of both the House and Senate.

The announcer was saying, "This is a most unusual address in that the President and all the Cabinet members will be present at the request of the House and Senate leaders. There is no advance information of what the emergency meeting is about except that it has a bearing on the monetary emergency and the upcoming vote in both houses Monday on whether or not to support and utilize a computerized monetary system.

"We take you now to Washington, where correspondent Brit Hume is standing by in the Capitol."

The picture switched to a long shot of the chamber filled to overflowing with the heads of the nation's government. The correspondent's voice could be heard though he could not be seen.

"We are in the Capitol Building waiting for Senator Ketchall and Congressman Boyd to bring the session to order. They are just coming up on the dais to take their positions."

The Vice President gaveled the session to order and nodded to the Senator. Ketchall and Boyd stood and thanked the gathered assembly for their attendance. Senator Ketchall then continued. "Mr. President, members of Congress, ladies and gentlemen, we have asked you, the leaders of our nation, the media and the people of the United States to join us tonight to hear and consider some words that could make the difference between the survival and growth of an orderly society and the possible disintegration of all this country stands for.

"Unfortunately, the present monetary situation has come upon us without much warning and that has left little time for dissemination of intelligent information or discussion of various possible solutions.

"All of us present here tonight, the heads of our nation's governmental departments and the heads of state of most countries, agree that something must be done immediately.

"Many suggestions for a solution have been presented to the President and the Congress and all have been evaluated to the degree possible within this short span of time.

"Congressman Boyd and I, as well as a substantial number of our fellow legislators, feel that there is a possible solution available that has a proven track record. And from what our investigators tell us, it has an extraordinary capability to quickly switch over to a full-scale monetary system without incurring a loss to anyone.

"The system presently operates as an international computerized trading and transaction settlement system. The problem is that there is little time to provide everyone with a simple explanation of its operation and why it will work.

"In order to circumvent that we have asked the gentleman who conceived this system and directed its development to come before us in this chamber tonight and give us all a better understanding of his unique system and why it represents a viable solution.

"Mr. President, members of the Congress and ladies and gentlemen, I introduce John Garland, chairman of the board of trustees of the Global Computer Systems Trust."

John walked up to the dais, nodded to both Ketchall and Boyd and turned to the camera and microphones.

"Thank you, Senator Ketchall, Congressman Boyd, Mr. President, members of Congress and ladies and gentlemen.

"Unless someone among you has been living in a cave this week, you are no doubt aware of the serious monetary problems created by the Latin American default on foreign debt.

"I am here tonight at the request of the House and Senate leaders to describe what I feel is a viable system capable of quickly assimilating all the data necessary to become operational within days without incurring loss to any bank depositor or currency and coin holder anywhere. I further feel that it would help restore confidence and order to our monetary system immediately.

"In order to explain why I feel that way, it is important to have a clear understanding of certain basic facts and conditions.

"Let me begin with my perception of what a monetary system is."

Lori leaned forward, intently focused on the TV screen and John's words as he continued.

"The monetary system of this or any country provides an orderly method for the creation and circulation of a medium of exchange. The conventional meaning of a 'medium of exchange' is what we call 'money' of varying denominations representing a certain basic underlying 'face value.'

"Forgive me for reducing this to its simplest terms, but I feel that it is important that everyone can clearly comprehend the facts that outline our present situation.

"Each of us, individually and collectively, must be able to survive. That is to say, to the extent possible, we must have basic food, clothing and shelter. The more advanced the society, the more is required for basic survival such as, for instance, transportation, communication and energy.

"Collectively, these things represent survival for modern human kind.

"The largest majority of us must work to produce some goods or service with which to earn 'money' which we use to buy those things we consider essential to our survival as well as those that bring us comfort and pleasure.

"Obviously, trading our physical labor or mental abilities directly for a basic need such as a pair of shoes or a shirt could be done occasionally on a very small scale. But it would be impractical to try to trade that output or asset value for say, rent, electricity or gasoline on a large scale.

"That means that we must be able to trade our individual output and assets for some sort of universally recognized and accepted medium of exchange whose unit value is accepted by all who utilize it.

"We call such a universally acceptable medium of exchange 'money' and use that medium of exchange to purchase or pay for those things we either need or want.

"In the United States that medium of exchange has, to now, been our currency and minted coins and all those instruments that represent such coin or currency. If I have deposited an amount and currency in a bank account, then my check to a merchant represents my currency and is the medium with which I exchange my productive output or assets for those things I need for my survival and comfort. In other words, it is a part of, or represents, the medium of exchange.

"The international acceptance of this medium of exchange and its orderly transfer and flow throughout society is handled by the monetary system we use. In order for the people of an entire nation to accept that medium of exchange or money at so-called face value, they must feel confident that they will be able to purchase something of equal value to the labor or output expended by them in acquiring the coin or piece of paper currency.

"In other words, for the medium of exchange, and the monetary system which controls its orderly flow, to have meaning and acceptance by everyone, everywhere, all people must be able to have total confidence in its value."

Miles away, David Malcolm and his guests were glued to the TV set as they, too, hung on every word that John spoke.

"In countries, many of them Latin American countries suffering from runaway inflation, almost no one has confidence in their country's paper money anymore because it no longer has a stable face value.

"Their paper currency may have been able to purchase one pound of sugar today, but tomorrow, inflation may have so eroded that currency's buying power that it is then only able to buy one half an pound of sugar.

"Therefore, everyone quickly spends every cent they are paid in currency to buy something that has a basic value that could then be used for barter or exchange for something of equal value the following day. Saving cruzeiros or pesos or other forms of paper money is out of the question because tomorrow will have less purchasing power than did yesterday.

"One of the major reasons for such a loss of confidence is that a government that administers the monetary system for its country keeps printing more paper money than should be in circulation. It does this in order to pay its mounting day-to-day operating costs and thus, reduces the total value of all paper money in circulation throughout that country by the amount that is printed.

"Paper money acting as a medium of exchange must represent things of real or intrinsic value in order to have a stable face value.

"Once a government chooses to ignore that principle, or external forces override that principle, the paper money it prints loses its value at an ever spiraling rate until it is worth little more than the printed scrap of paper it really is."

At a bar in New York, Dick Simon and Mel Trask were observing the reaction of the bar's patrons as they sat spellbound following every word of John Garland's dissertation on the TV set behind the bar. Mel turned to Dick Simon and said, "I must hand it to the guy, he really knows how to present his subject matter." They turned back to the broadcast as John continued his presentation.

"Now let us examine our present crisis. For years, our banks and banks in other developed countries, have been lending substantial sums of money to under developed or Third World countries to be used by them for the development of low cost energy, good roads, improved methods of agriculture, modern transportation and communications systems and new industry.

"The theory was that once those loans were invested in such projects, the countries receiving such loans would be able to develop new industries that would hire more people in better jobs. They would be able to sell and export more of their output, would be able to feed, cloth and house more of their people, and would then be able to generate the taxes with which to pay off those loans.

"Unfortunately, for one reason or another, theory and reality often did not match in final results. The money loaned often did not get spent for the projects planned and therefore did not generate the prosperity envisioned.

"A large number of the borrowing countries, many in Latin America, fell far behind in their debt repayments and even in their ability to just pay the interest on their debts. Inevitably, there came a day when a number of them got together and decided that the only way out was to declare a moratorium on their debt.

"Federally imposed banking rules throughout most of the free world require that a bank that has a bad or uncollectible loan must write off that loan as a loss, even though such a bank may, in fact, later recover such a loan.

"In the case before our nation today, the amount of those loans was so massive that writing them off and lost income from yearly interest payments has caused a great number of banks to lose all their working capital, at least on paper. Thus they were technically considered insolvent.

"News of this technical insolvency throughout the nation and the world caused many depositors to lose confidence in their banks, even if their banks were not affected.

"The first reaction by too many depositors was, 'Let's get our money out of the bank before it shuts down or goes out of business.'

"Soon that generated other losses of confidence until it turned into a massive chain reaction causing a run on the banks' deposits not unlike the bank panic of the '30s.

"When that happens, banks soon run out of paper money to pass out to the demand depositors because at no time is there ever enough paper money in circulation to let every depositor draw out every cent he has on deposit.

"Unfortunately such bank runs are not based on fact but are the result of irrational hysteria. Those banks are usually not truly insolvent or out of assets in the form of deposits and loans. They simply didn't have enough paper currency in circulation to cover an irrational, hysterical withdrawal demand. And if the Treasury Department, the only agency permitted to print paper money, were to run its printing presses day and night for a year, they still could not print and get into circulation, enough paper currency and coins to meet such a massive hysterical demand for withdrawals.

"The result? People everywhere begin to lose confidence in paper money. Not because a small amount of inflation has caused more paper money to be printed and not even because of runaway inflation, but because their isn't enough paper currency and coins in circulation to satisfy their immediate demands.

"Which brings me to a basic point to help you understand why the Global system is an answer to this crisis.

"That point is simply this: Money, paper currency, coins and the monetary system that administers their flow, are only as good or as valuable as the users are willing to believe they are.

"That means that the monetary system and its medium of exchange must be beyond manipulation or control by any one person, group of people, political power or government. Moreover, it must also not be affected by any set of circumstances such as those that confront us today.

"It means that such a monetary system must be honest in developing value for its medium of exchange and must be based solely on the underlying basic or intrinsic value of the goods or services it represents, whether the medium of exchange be a paper currency, coin or electronic credits.

"Finally, the medium of exchange and the monetary system which governs its flow and face value must be completely reliable. One must be able to count on it not to lose its value nor can the system that governs its flow ever break down, or make a mistake in accounting or forget one single transaction. Finally, it must be totally accessible to anyone, anywhere, anytime."

Jack Brockman, sitting in the gallery of the Capitol building with several members of his staff, turned to his administrative assistant and whispered, "I hate to admit it, but I am getting a whole new insight into the monetary system I've been administering all these years."

His aide nodded and they turned their attention back to John's explanation.

"That brings me to Global's system. It has presently been an operating international trade settlement and barter system for over two years.

"It is composed of a network of computers that span the globe throughout 135 countries with seven central computers spread out around the world, each of which contains a duplicate of every transaction of each of the other six computers in its memory.

"The operating system was developed so that it cannot be tampered with and that every transaction must be honest and straightforward in order for it to be processed.

"This system is presently the fastest and most reliable computer system in the world, capable of handling hundreds of millions of transactions every minute of the day, accurately and reliably. And it is able to credit every account without mistake or loss.

"More important, it is solely owned, operated and administered by its users and depositors. When it was set up, it was organized as a trust, registered in every country where such a trust can operate. Its ownership is held in trust for all the people who use it and is administered by trustees elected by the users of the system in each country in which it operates.

"The trustees are chosen for their intelligence, honesty, wisdom and unimpeachable integrity. When such persons agree to act as trustees, they are generously compensated by the trust to insure that they will not be tempted by financial pressures.

"Any profits the trust generates over and above its modest operating costs, are redistributed to each account holder pro rata to the size of their account and amount of usage they paid for. In other words, all those who use it, own it much like a federal credit union.

"Because it operates in an honest, straightforward manner and cannot be manipulated, it cannot be subjected to government-induced inflation, deflation or to illegitimate monetary transactions.

"Paper currency, coins, precious metals, rare objects of art that can be purchased with paper currency without leaving a trail to the purchaser lend themselves to criminal activities for profit ranging from bribery and fraud to illicit drug traffic, hot checks, stolen credit cards, fencing of other stolen property and every other kind of illicit activity.

"This is possible because the current medium of exchange can be secretly accumulated, secretly transferred from one to another, hidden, transported, laundered and ultimately used to acquire power, wealth and even respectability.

"But a computer system that deals only in electronic credits, where each transaction is verified and indelibly recorded in an electronic memory, does not lend itself to secret accumulation of wealth, secret transportation or secret payments for illicit purposes as do paper currency and things of value purchased with paper currency.

"If you think about this for a moment, you will recognize that not only would that save society hundreds of billions of dollars in misdirected, misused or hidden funds, but it actually encourages a discipline of honesty and integrity for all of society. Moreover, its use would cut the cost of government operations drastically.

"Such a system can be the basis for restoring respect and confidence in government, our medium of exchange and monetary system, our banking system and our whole society.

"If such a system is adopted internationally, it will open lines of communications between peoples of the world as never before. Cooperation on major issues confronting the planet would suddenly become solutions on a worldwide basis. World cooperation, prosperity and peace would finally and inevitably become a reality.

"I believe, with all my heart, that this proposed monetary system and medium of exchange is a viable answer to our present crisis and that it can be put in operation within seventy-two hours of the time the decision to use it has been made.

"I have no doubt in my mind, that men of good conscience will have no qualms in voting to adopt such a system. I must also assume that anyone hesitating to vote in favor of its adoption may well have personal questionable motives in mind.

"Finally, I would like to point out that whenever a radical idea, concept is presented that is expected to be beneficial to the greatest majority of a people, there will also always be those who violently oppose such a plan for the perceived danger it presents to their vested interests, political and financial powers.

"You can expect such people to use everything at their disposal to remove, control or destroy such a threat to their interests. Fortunately, there is one earthly power that no amount of money, political power or violence can overcome and that is the power of the people.

"It is my sincerest hope that I have presented the facts to you in an understandable manner. If that has been so and you believe as I do, then I hope you will let your representatives in government know your feelings on this issue. You are the power that can make it happen. The final decision . . . is yours.

"Thank you, and I sincerely wish for all of you the best outcome possible."

With that John bowed his head to the audience, turned and bowed to the men behind him and quietly walked off the podium out of camera range.

Lori sat spellbound as she watched what was probably the longest moment of silence in television history. No announcer broke in, no commentator spoke, the audience sat stunned and then, slowly, waves of hand clapping swelled as people began to stand up. The sound continued to rise until it was a deafening roar.

Finally the voice of the Washington correspondent broke in. "Ladies and gentlemen, you have just heard John Garland addressing an emergency joint session of Congress at one of the most dramatic moments in our history.

"After hearing Mr. Garland's presentation tonight, it is doubtful that any congressman would dare go on record with a 'no' vote on the computerized monetary system bill scheduled for a full Senate and House vote Monday."

Lori's shoulders slumped and she closed her eyes and shook her head as she turned off the TV and rewound the VCR. Her head was reeling from the kaleidoscope of thoughts that flooded her mind. The bill would surely pass now. But the frustration and growing hatred of desperate men like David Malcolm would also now be totally focused on John Garland and his system.

She stood up and walked to the window trying to clear her mind. Looking out into the night at the twinkling lights moving along Potomac River Drive, she wondered what sensible thing she could do.

How could they protect the system? What could be done to protect John Garland? *Damn,* she thought, *I finally meet the man I want more than anything in the world and he stands up and makes himself the target of every evil group in the country.*

The phone rang and Lori jumped. It would be too soon for John's call. She ran over to the phone and picked it up, her heart beating wildly. "Hello?"

"Miss Young?"

"Who is this?" Lori asked.

"Charlie, Charlie Ross."

Lori looked confused. "Charlie? Where are you calling from? How did you get my number?"

"A mutual friend gave it to me in case I had to get hold of him this evening."

"Oh! Where are you? What's wrong?"

"Nothing is wrong, Miss Young. Everything turned out just like we figured. Someone blew up the building in Alexandria and burned it to the ground."

"My God, Charlie, what are you saying? Was anyone hurt?

"Oh no, the building was empty, we had cleared out the whole system and all the people a couple of hours before it happened and we got the whole thing on film. Just tell our mutual friend I'm on the short wave frequency and to give me a call when he gets there."

"Charlie, wait, don't hang up..." But it was too late, Charlie was observing his own phone time limit to avoid traces and had hung up.

Lori sat down on the couch and put her head in her hands feeling woefully inadequate and thoroughly confused. The phone rang again and as she picked it up she knew it would be John.

"Lori, can you pack a few things to cover a weekend and meet me at the place you called me from earlier?"

At first Lori was confused at what place he meant and then she remembered her call to him from the health club. "Oh! Oh! Yes, I can do that. Charlie called and needs to talk to you. He said that . . . "

John interrupted her. "I already know what he wants to tell me and where to reach him. Just get over to that place as soon as possible and I will explain everything then. Bye," and he hung up.

Lori ran into the bedroom and picked up what she called her 'war bag' which she always kept packed with some leisure clothes and toiletries ready for the occasional emergency trips her position called for. She zipped open the top of her bag and stuffed in the video tape, grabbed her keys off the dresser and headed out the door.

On her way down the elevator she decided against taking her own car in case she might be followed.

CHAPTER THIRTY
THE COLDEST NIGHTS OFTEN BRING ABOUT THE WARMEST MOMENTS

Washington, D.C.
Lori's Apartment Lobby
March 5, 7:30 p.m.

When Lori's elevator reached the lobby she ran to the doorman. He hailed a cab and Lori got in and told the driver to take her to the Willard Hotel downtown. She told the cab driver she was in a hurry as she handed him twice the normal fare.

The driver pulled up in front of the hotel and she dashed out with her 'war bag' hanging from her shoulder, ran through the lobby and out the other entrance. She jumped in another cab waiting at the cab stand.

Pressing a twenty in the cabby's hand, she directed him to her health club in Georgetown some ten minutes from there.

As the cab pulled up to the entrance of the health club, she jumped out and started for the entrance. She heard John's voice behind her.

"Over here, Lori." Turning she saw him sitting behind the wheel of an older model car. He opened the door and got out to greet her as she frantically looked around.

"Don't worry Lori, no one followed you. I was watching."

She ran over to him, dropped her bag on the sidewalk, buried her head in his chest and put her arms around him.

"Oh John, John, what is going on? Where are we going?"

John put his hand under her chin and gently pulled her head up and kissed her. "Beautiful lady, nothing is going on that we can't handle." He picked up her bag and put it in the back seat and opened the door for her.

John tooled the car through the narrow streets of Georgetown until they were on a parkway heading out of the Washington area toward the Maryland countryside.

"Where are we going?" Lori asked again.

"A friend of mine has a beautiful summer home on Chesapeake Bay. Normally it's closed for the winter. He thought it would be a safe place for a well-earned restful weekend. How does it sound so far?"

Lori leaned over and put her head on John's shoulder.

"This is all so crazy. I don't know what to say. I don't know what to think. I don't understand what is happening to me. I don't even know what I'm doing here. For the first time in my adult life, I'm completely confused."

John looked down at her head on his shoulder and said, "I'm suffering from a touch of that myself. The way I feel right now, I don't care if the monetary system comes apart at the seams or human kind is about to slide into anarchy. There are certain things I need to find out, things both of us need to find out about each other that only have to do with you and me. By God, we need some uninterrupted time alone for that."

The intensity in his voice and the emotion with which John said it brought Lori's head up to look at him. This was not the calm, composed collected man she was used to seeing. And for some reason she couldn't identify just then, that pleased her.

Lori began to feel more relaxed as they drove. Somehow, John's presence made her feel that all would turn out well. She looked at him and asked, "What was Charlie talking about when he called me?"

"Something we had anticipated. It all began when it became obvious that Global's system was seriously being considered by congressional leaders and the President. It was obvious that eventually we would have to make one of the operating computer centers available for observation and testing.

"Charlie and his team had long ago been thinking out various scenarios for protecting the system and its hardware. One of those was to construct a fully operational, portable operations center.

"We felt that there might be violent resistance from those

the system threatened and that, when all else failed, we would be vulnerable to the possibility of physical damage.

"So Charlie designed this portable Global Computer System Office with all the essential hardware and furniture contained in a series of specially designed shipping containers that could be opened up and hooked together to form a complete office just like the one you saw in Nevada.

In fact, all the offices have been standardized so that they all look and operate the same. Any one of Global's operating teams can walk into any of the other offices and feel right at home. Nothing new to get used to.

Lori looked at John staring intently at the road. "You mean you anticipated the possibility that you might need a portable office?"

John glanced quickly at Lori before answering. "What we anticipated was the possibility that we would have to demonstrate the system's capability somewhere in the vicinity of D.C.

"We searched for, and located, a relatively isolated warehouse which, in this case, happened to be in Alexandria, Virginia, three blocks from a dock on the Potomac River. Global bought the building and fitted it out to accommodate Charlie's portable unit about two months ago.

"Later, after we met you, all of us were positive that your report would result in someone wanting a first-hand look. So the containers were shipped to Norfolk, Virginia, Wednesday just after you left Reno.

"There the containers were loaded on a small ship Global owns and early this morning it sailed up the Potomac, docking at Alexandria early this afternoon.

"By 4:30, the containers had been off-loaded and trucked to the warehouse, set up, hooked up and operating with a full crew, ready to receive visitors, looking for all the world like they had been there for years."

Lori shook her head in amazement. "That's incredible. But what was that business about the warehouse being blown up and burned to the ground?"

"Naturally, Charlie checked out the backgrounds of people who would be attending the 'show and tell.' One of them had a manufactured background. He was one of the men sent by Malcolm's bank to observe the system. Anticipating the possibility of problems, we installed video cameras throughout the Alexandria building. They were hooked to a video broadcasting unit that beamed the output to the ship and a recording system.

"As a result, we were able to monitor both the approaches to the building and the interior. We had also purchased a lot of government surplus computer equipment as junk and set it up to look like the operating system that had been brought there in containers except that it was slightly offset from the space where the containers had been set up.

"Charlie told me that forty minutes after they had vacated the building, the man representing Case City Bank at the 'show and tell' showed up in a van. The cameras had clearly captured his face when he was in the Global office earlier and got two good shots of him when he came back in the van. Not knowing that the building was now empty, he placed a suitcase behind the warehouse where a gas line entered the building and then went up a fire escape and placed a second suitcase on the roof directly over where the Global computer system had been and then left.

"Twenty minutes later, the explosives in the suitcases went off, the building was demolished and the burning gas line caused a fire that was so hot that it probably destroyed all evidence of what happened. Except, of course, the video we have."

Lori looked shocked. "My God . . . David didn't care who might have been in that building. That's conspiracy to commit murder, John."

"Yes, I know. It's also conspiracy to destroy a whole society because of a perceived threat to his personal gain."

John turned the car off of the two-lane blacktop they had been following onto a dirt road bordered by winter-dormant trees. The fields were cold and covered with frost. As they drove over a slight rise, they came upon a lovely country home with bay windows and a barn in back. Evergreens grew all around the place and there was a light on in what appeared to be the living-room window. John pulled the car around the back and pulled under a canopy.

They got out and John opened the trunk to get out his bag. Lori looked around. "Where are we? Whose place is this?"

John picked up his bag, closed the trunk and walked around the car to get Lori's bag out of the back seat. He began to explain as they walked to the back door of the house.

"We're at the summer home of a very old friend of mine. A man I went to school with. We joined the Navy together at the beginning of World War II and served on the same ship when we got out of boot camp. He saved my life on one occasion and I got him off a burning, sinking ship on another. You might say we owe each other our lives. I guess we've been almost like brothers over the years."

John put down the bags and leaning down, fished out a key from behind an old-fashioned milk delivery box and opened the door. Standing aside he held the door for Lori, grabbed the bags and followed her in.

John saw that his favorite brand of coffee was on the counter beside the coffee maker. He put down the bags and went to the counter to make a pot. Lori went to the cupboard to find cups and silverware.

As the coffee began to perk, John continued.

"I called him before I left Nevada this morning and told him what I was going to do. He felt there would be a lot of heat on me and on Global's operation and suggested I come up here for at least the weekend and stay out of sight. He knew this would be the last place Malcolm or any of his associates would look."

Lori brought cream from the refrigerator and a bowl of sugar from the cupboard and sat down at the kitchen table to await the coffee.

"Who is this friend of yours, John?"

John looked at her for a moment before he answered. "His name is George Talbott. He is the operations vice president for the Case City Bank."

Lori looked up from her cup in amazement. Then shook her head in disbelief. "No wonder you always knew what was going on at Dave Malcolm's office. John, I don't mind telling you I'm a little confused and more than a bit frightened.

"I've always prided myself on self discipline, on the ability to submerge all personal feelings and drive myself to learn, to understand, to develop goals for my life."

Lori's voice grew quieter as she continued. "When my father and mother were killed in an accident many years ago, to keep from falling apart, I forced myself to go on working toward the things my parents and I had decided were meaningful.

"I loved them deeply and missed them in a way that was beyond description. But over the years, I got over the grief and did my best to become a whole, adult human being again.

"I love being a woman and being treated like a woman just as I want to be respected as a human being and as a capable person. For some reason however, I only received that recognition from older, self-confident men. Otherwise, I always felt I was being seen as some kind of obscene caricature. Because of that, I had almost no social life other than government and embassy functions and a few 'real people' friends I enjoyed being around."

John poured coffee for both of them and sat down at the kitchen table with her.

"It's funny," he mused, "but when I first met you I sensed that. Please go on."

"Well, then I met you. You kept pushing into my thoughts much as you say I did in yours. For the first time, I felt totally confused about everything . . . about my career . . . about my associates in and out of government . . . and most of all . . . about my personal feelings."

Lori dropped her head and a tear slowly rolled down her

cheek and dropped onto the kitchen table. John picked up her hand in his two hands and said, "Look at me, Lori."

Lori lifted her head to look at John with tears brimming in her eyes.

"Lori," John continued in a quiet voice, "I'm confused too, and disturbed. Meeting you has awakened feelings in me I had forgotten I had. Thoughts of you keep intruding in what had been a very, very directed, goal-oriented mind.

"For years I have been a disquieted observer of the slow disintegration of all the decent elements of our society. It pained me to watch the 'now' generation followed by the 'me' generation. To see selfishness replace consideration, and greed slowly supplant charity and be held up as a character trait to strive for."

John rose from his chair and held out his hand to Lori and said, "Come, let's go into the living room. I think I hear a fire crackling in the fireplace. George must have had his caretaker come over and do all these thoughtful, little things."

Lori picked up her cup and they walked into the comfortable living room where the warm glow of a log fire beckoned them. John put his cup on the mantel and leaned his shoulder against it as he continued his unburdening.

"For some reason, I guess it was about fifteen years ago, I envisioned many of the things that are coming to pass today. My wife was gone, my children grown and living their own lives and I had a business that kept me physically busy while allowing me the financial freedom to pursue my goals.

"What I saw and experienced gave me a gnawing feeling that something had to be done to re-instill values and beliefs that were slowly dying all over the world.

"The loss of confidence in elected officials and governmental systems. The loss of belief in things that were part of our spiritual being. The loss of belief in ourselves. The turn by so many, to chemical escape from reality.

"It all ate away at me until one day, while sitting on Perspective Peak pondering these things, I began to envision the system that we now call the Global Computer Trading system.

"It was not the nuts and bolts that intrigued me but the ultimate effect it might have on the peoples of the world as a pivot around which to re-establish faith . . . confidence . . . honesty, self-respect, concern for others. All those elements that go to make up a healthy global society. A society that one enjoys and is proud to be a part of.

"After that day, I concentrated all my efforts on developing the Global computer system. It became sort of a 'Holy Grail.' My mind was dominated by developing it, making it efficient and selling it to others. I permitted nothing extraneous to intrude."

Lori had seated herself on the bench-like base of the elevated fireplace and was looking up at John, engrossed in his story.

"And then one day, you walked into my life. A bright, beautiful, intelligent, sexy woman with extraordinary insight and awareness. You were sensitive, understanding and had a great sense of humor. Your intellectual depth is awesome.

"In one, short, twenty-four hour period, you so captivated me that you overshadowed almost every other thought in my mind. I found it difficult to concentrate on the situation at hand. It was as if I had been waiting for you all my life and when you showed up, I didn't know what to do about it.

"So you see Lori, I, too, feel confused, disturbed, unsettled and at the same time I feel a joy and a passion for you I have never experienced before in my life.

"At odd moments throughout the last two days I felt like abandoning all this work and effort and just grabbing you up in my arms and . . . and . . . God knows what."

Lori slowly got up from the ledge carefully putting her cup down and turned to fix her gaze on John, her eyes filled with a warm love for this man.

She put her arms around his neck and pressed her body against his shamelessly. He slipped his hands around her back and their lips met in a moment of overwhelming intensity.

It was as if all the world had slowly melted away and only the two of them were left standing in some formless void, clinging to each other with all their strength, feeling the fires of their passion and the emotions of their growing love for each other.

John picked her up in his arms as if she were a child and carried her wordlessly into the bedroom. It seemed to them as if they were dream walking, oblivious to anything but each other. They shed their clothes automatically as if hypnotized, and made passionate, uninhibited love.

Each moment seemed to lift their spirits, emotions and passions to new heights until, at last, they lay exhausted in each other's arms, murmuring words and sounds of love until they both fell into a deep, untroubled sleep, still in each others arms as if molded together.

CHAPTER THIRTY-ONE
WHAT A DIFFERENCE A DAY MAKES
INSIDE AND OUT

Somewhere on the Maryland shore
March 6, 8:00 a.m.

The sounds of smooth Dixieland music floated into the bedroom causing Lori to roll over and open one eye to the ceiling. It took her mind a moment to become fully awake as she started into a sitting position. And then, memories of the night before flooded her consciousness and she relaxed and laid back down, stretching luxuriously and smiling a small satisfied smile of remembrance.

She yelled out, "John, is that smell coming from the kitchen that evil-tasting coffee you make?"

She could hear cups rattling and then John stuck his head around the corner of the door frame and said: "Evil-smelling? Lady that is the second-best smell in the whole world."

She looked at him coyly and said, "What is the first, Mr. John?"

He looked at her with a lascivious grin on his face and said, "You are, my love," and ducked back out of sight.

She raised her arms above the covers and stretched again, marveling at how wonderful she felt. At that moment John came in wearing a too-small and too-short robe belonging to their host and carrying two cups of coffee.

She laughed at him and said, "Are you starting a new style or did you just find that one in a rummage sale?"

They both laughed as he handed her the saucer and cup and sat down beside her. For a long moment they just looked into each others eyes as they sipped their coffee.

Finally John said, "My God, you're beautiful, Lori. I love you so much it hurts."

She put her cup down on the bedside stand and seductively said, "If it hurts that bad, can I kiss it and make it better?"

He slid his cup beside hers, shrugged out of his robe and slid into bed beside her saying with mock gravity, "You will be gentle won't you?"

Lori laughed until tears came to her eyes and then they held each other fiercely like two teenagers on an exciting journey of exploration and discovery.

The phone rang seven or eight times before either of them stirred. Lori murmured, "Let it ring, don't answer it."

It stopped ringing and then started again. John said, "Hold my place, I'll be right back." He jumped out of bed, pulled on the robe and ran for the phone.

Lori could hear John talking but couldn't discern the words. Since she knew that probably only two people knew where he was, she assumed the call spelled trouble. Lori slipped out of bed and went into the bathroom with her robe and cosmetics case.

When John got off of the phone, he came back to the bedroom, saw the empty bed and heard the shower running.

Walking into the bathroom he said, "Pardon me lady but there is a water shortage and everyone is required to shower with a friend."

He heard Lori giggle. Dropping his robe on the floor, he pulled back the shower curtain and stepped in with her. They embraced and kissed, oblivious to the spray of the shower splashing over them. She looked at him coyly and said, "Pardon me, sir, but do you know if this sort of thing is allowed in here?"

"Only between consenting adults."

They laughed joyously, feeling as if they were both twenty years younger.

Lori wriggled happily against John's wet body. In a few moments she said, "Are you sure you're over sixty?"

John smiled at her and said, "Sixty-four to be exact."

Lori looked at him. "You don't look sixty-four and you certainly don't act like you're sixty-four. You sure you're not 'joshing' me?"

"Depends on what you mean by 'joshing,' but if we keep this pace up, I'll probably look and act like I'm ninety by the end of the week."

Finally, John heaved a big sigh and said, "Unfortunately, I have to interrupt this program for a commercial." He turned off the shower and handed her a towel and grabbed one himself.

Lori looked at him alarmed. "What is it, John? What's happened?"

"That was Charlie on the phone. Apparently someone with extremely advanced electronics has pinpointed four of our operating systems and several of our COMSAT dishes, our phone lines and antennas and has blacked out all communications to and from them along with a substantial part of the communities where they are located."

Lori groaned, "Oh no, I thought we could have this weekend to ourselves. What are you going to do?"

"For now, our equipment has automatically switched all communications to our units in Switzerland and Sweden where this electronic blackout equipment cannot cross the borders in order to get close enough to be effective—at least for the time being.

The problem is that we haven't had an opportunity to upgrade the communications capability of those remaining operations. When the business day begins on Monday, they may not be able to carry the increasing traffic load by themselves, and trades and settlements could be backed up for hours."

Lori grimaced as she watched John's face in the mirror as he shaved. Though her mind was on the problem just described, she was idly looking at John's strong youthful-looking body and thinking, *He's damn sexy for sixty four.* Forcing her mind back to the problem at hand she said, "It appears that someone, read that David Malcolm, is trying to discredit the system's reliability before the vote on Monday."

John stopped his shaving and looked at her in the mirror. "No doubt, but what bugs me is that whoever is doing this has blocked all communications on Toiyabe Peak and the Navy is going crazy trying to figure out where it's coming from. I can't figure anyone, even Malcolm, having the technical capability and equipment to do this."

Lori had pulled on a Levi jump suit and turned the sink over to John's shaving. She started out of the bathroom and suddenly turned back to John whom, she noted, was watching her in the mirror, and said, "Colonel Burns!"

John looked back at her in the mirror and said, "Who?"

"Colonel Burns. I just remembered. Right after he and David left my office I had my assistant get me a background on him. He is in charge of the Army's electronic snooping division. It's part of Army intelligence, and I remember reading in the file that some of their duties are to electronically black out enemy communications."

John shook his head. "David must be crazy, completely crazy. Subverting the Army to do his dirty work. He can't win in the long run. In the meantime, we've got to do something to shut off that electronic blackout before Monday."

Lori felt a little thrill as she heard John say 'we.' She pulled on her sweater and called back to John in the bathroom, "I'll get my assistant on the phone. Our agency has quite a lot of pull and we can take the Secretary's name in vain without his approval. I'll find out what unit Colonel Burns is attached to, who his commanding officer is and who, in turn, is that man's commanding officer. I also know the Secretary of Defense and his wife on a social basis. I can call him as well as the chairman of the Joint Chiefs of Staff. By the way, how many phone lines does this place have?"

John walked to the door of the bathroom, now dressed in a pair of Levi's and a pullover sweater. "One, I believe. You pick up the phone in the living room and I'll pick up the hall phone and see if they're on the same line."

She walked into the living room and John went to the phone in the hall. She could hear the click as he picked up the phone in the hall and said, "Guess what?"

"What?" Lori asked, feeling a small flutter of alarm.

John smiled and said very softly, "I love you. That's what," and hung up.

Lori closed her eyes and for a moment, feeling relief and then whispered to herself, "Thank you, Mr. John." Then she called out loud to him, "I'll make my calls first."

"Go ahead," he answered from the kitchen as he thumbed through his address book looking for Senator Ketchall's weekend numbers.

Lori and John spent all morning alternating on the phone, calling people in and out of government who could help.

Senator Ketchall wanted to call in the FBI but John convinced him that because of procedures that governed the FBI's operation, it would not accomplish what they needed soon enough. Senator Ketchall agreed and said he would concentrate on the Secretary of Defense and the Joint Chiefs of Staff.

Lori spoke to the brigadier general who headed Army Intelligence and told him she had already revealed the same information to the Army Chief of Staff, just in case this general was on Malcolm's payroll. He would now be concerned about covering his ass. The general assured her that he had given no authority to Colonel Burns to use any government property for this sort of activity. He sounded genuinely shocked and disturbed. He assured Lori that he'd look into the situation immediately.

John talked with the commander of the Fallon Naval Air Station in Nevada to reveal the reasons for their communications blackout and urged him to alert his superior in Washington to raise hell with the Army. The captain at Fallon thanked him and assured him they would tear someone a new asshole.

Then John called the Swede to alert him to the situation and have him organize their neighboring rancher and mining friends to help locate the equipment being used. He also suggested the security system around the perimeter of the canyon be armed and all the area residents be alerted to the situation and the possibility of trouble.

Finally, John called George Talbot in whose home they were staying. He quickly sketched out what was going on and what had happened to the warehouse in Alexandria. Talbot immediately recognized the name of Malcolm's private strong man and assured John he would search out the records on Colonel Burns and see if he could pinpoint a payoff of some kind.

It was almost noon by the time Lori and John had finished their telephone counterattack. They were both exhausted from hours on the phone and were sitting on the couch in the living room. John finished recounting his results and Lori was reading off her list of results and reactions to John. As she closed her notebook she said, "You think we should drive back to the city?"

"No, not today anyway. I don't care if school keeps or not, today is our day. We can tilt at windmills tomorrow. But today, beautiful lady, I just need to be with you.

"Today we need to share our innermost thoughts. We need to share our fears and joys, hearts and bodies. I want to spend this first day of the rest of our lives loving you and making love to you and I want to experience your love for me and your making love to me. On this day, nothing on God's Green Earth can be more important."

Lori couldn't speak for a moment. His words had filled her with an emotion so powerful she couldn't organized her thoughts enough to say anything. She had not experienced emotions this powerful since her mother and father had died. Sensing this, John put his arm around her and just held her. They sat that way for a long time. Finally, Lori spoke in a quiet voice.

"I don't think I need to find out any more than I know right now. I need you and want to be with you the rest of my life."

John's face had a soft, gentle look as he said, "Thank you."

Lori thought for a moment and said, "You know, I just thought of something. If any one of these people I talked to on the phone today is in David's back pocket, I am, as a former

President once said, 'in deep Doo Doo.' "

John frowned. "That's the last thing I wanted to have happen, Lori."

She smiled archly at John and said, "Oh, I don't know. It's not all that bad. As I see it, that makes you responsible for me now and if I were you, I wouldn't leave me out of your sight for one minute."

John looked at her, leaned over and pulled her over toward him until her back was laying in his lap and she was looking up at his mock grimace.

"Is that so?" He leaned over and kissed her gently. "Well, in that case let's fool around a little bit." He leaned down and kissed her again.

She put her arms around his neck and pulled him back to her fiercely and said, "Little bit, hell, let's fool around a whole bunch." She kissed him passionately. When they came up for air, she murmured, "Don't you think we ought to build up our energy with a little lunch?"

They both laughed and Lori got up to go to the kitchen, dragging John along by his hand. Looking over her shoulder she said, "You know what I don't understand?"

"What?"

"Why the heck I'm so happy when we are in so much trouble?"

"Beats me."

They both laughed and went into the kitchen to build up their energy.

John and Lori spent the rest of the day talking, sharing things that each thought the other should know and experiencing the elation they felt for having found each other. They were delighted to find how many things they had in common, the kinds of music, the books, the food, the ocean, the outdoors, nature and simplicity.

The love they felt for each other was almost overwhelming and seemed to grow with the shadows of the waning day. Their unspoken, growing commitment to each other was so obviously total that it filled them with a feeling of comfort and a joyful happiness people their age seldom experience.

They were sitting on the couch together with Lori snuggled up to John, her head on his shoulder, his arms around her, gently stroking her hair as she listened to his voice.

He was telling her of his life and experiences when the shrill ring of the phone interrupted their intimacy. It brought them harshly back to the reality of the moment.

John reluctantly sat her up and got up from the couch to answer the phone in the hall. He picked up the phone apprehensively, not wanting this day to end. "Hello?"

"John? This is George Talbot."

"What's up, George?"

"Trouble. Shortly after I talked to you this morning, I began to worry about my phone line, so I called in a guy on my personal payroll who checks for bugs on my communications systems. He found a live bug on my home phone transmitting every conversation. It was the same type I have found on the bank's phone systems from time to time, installed there by one of Malcolm's people."

John clenched his fist. "Damn, damn, damn. So he obviously knows what we talked about and where I am, right?"

"Right, but he doesn't know that *we* know yet. That's the only thing in our favor at the moment. And that's not all, John Boy. I just heard on the news on the car radio that the Army has uncovered a plot by a Colonel Burns to use the Army's top secret electronic equipment to black out all communications on the Global Trading system. The colonel was arrested and is being questioned by Army Intelligence."

John nodded his head. "That was probably the result of a call I made to the Army Chief of Staff."

Talbot continued, "I don't know, but shortly after that, one of my trusted people called to let me know that Malcolm's gone bonkers. He's been on the phone calling key people on the bank's payroll to galvanize some sort of a telephone, telegram and fax assault on Congress, the President and God knows who else.

He's openly threatening them with blackmail about under-the-table political campaign funds and quid pro quo favors in return if they don't act to turn down Global's system. Now that's irrational as hell and an irrational man is a dangerous man."

"Where are you calling from?" John asked.

"Right now I'm calling from a phone about a mile and a half from the house. My wife I was going to the convenience store for something."

John thought for a moment. "What do you figure our head start is from the closest place he might have someone?" John was calculating the driving time from Washington the night before.

George looked at his watch and said, "Near as I can figure it, five hours at the outside."

John looked at his watch and said, "What time was it when I called you?"

"My best recollection is that it was about 12:45. It's 4:20 right now so that was about three hours and thirty-five minutes ago. Figure it would take the tapper time to make a trace on your number, then a little while to get hold of Dave. Then maybe forty-five minutes for Dave to figure out what he's gonna do. And then another thirty minutes to lay it out for whoever he got hold of to do it. Let's say an hour and a half to institute any kind of plan.

"Assuming that Washington is the starting point for whoever has been assigned to do whatever, we're talking about three hours from the starting gate to you."

John looked at his watch again. "I've got maybe an hour then."

George answered him, "Right. Now the road you came in on from Georgetown would be the same road anyone else would be coming in on. If you were to turn right coming out of my driveway instead of going back the way you came, you would wind around bearing northwest at each cross road you come to until eventually you'd wind up on the outskirts of Baltimore. Take you about an hour and a half."

"I don't have a map in front of me George, but what are my options from there."

"Unlimited old buddy, unlimited. That area is a rabbit warren of roads and highways. You could be back in Washington in forty minutes from there."

"Thanks, George, I'll be in touch the minute I light. By the way, do you know Lorelei Young?"

"You mean the under secretary of Commerce?"

"Yes. If anything happens that I can't handle, look out for her. She's accidentally in over her head in this situation."

"Will do. Where should I look for her besides her office?"

"I don't know yet, but she will call you using our old code."

"Gotcha. Take care, I don't want to be gone too long."

"Wait, George." John yelled, "What about your own ass?"

George laughed. "I've covered this old ass years ago. That slimy bastard knows if he ever tries anything with me and mine, enough garbage will show up at different newspapers and federal prosecutor's offices to put him away for a hundred years. I would have already used it to help you out except that he has too many of his associates in on this that could carry on without him to do you any good."

Lori's body was rigid with fear and apprehension as she heard John hang up the phone with a bang, muttering to himself. John walked into the room with a dark look on his face. It was the first time Lori had ever seen anger in his face.

"That son of a bitch has ruined the most beautiful day I've ever had. Lori, we've got to pack and head back to Washington by way of Baltimore. That was George Talbot. He found a tap on his phone, the kind Malcolm uses on his employees at the bank, and he's sure that by now some kind of trouble is on the way out here."

Lori jumped up from the couch and threw her arms around John's neck, clinging to him fiercely. "I'm going everywhere you go. It's not fair, we just found each other. It's not fair." She started to cry, tears streaming down her cheeks.

The tension went out of John's body and he held Lori to him stroking the back of her head and murmuring, "Don't cry, my wonderful lady. I won't let anything happen to us. It just means it's time to start thinking about how to bring this whole thing to a conclusion so you and I can ride off into the sunset without worrying about the likes of David Malcolm. Let's get our things together and get going. We'll think out a plan of action on the way."

He tilted her head up and kissed her with a love and passion that made her forget about everything but the two of them.

CHAPTER THIRTY-TWO
HALF TIME AND THE SCORE IS TIED

To Washington via Baltimore
March 6, 5:15 p.m.

As they drove through the countryside approaching Baltimore from the east, indications of confusion were everywhere. There were signs on many store windows reading, 'closed until further notice.' Many gas stations were closed or had signs in their windows, "cash only." Those that remained open had lines of cars.

John had just finished telling Lori how to contact George and what code to use in the event there was a need to get some trustworthy assistance in the east. He explained that George knew his private network of friends and how to contact them.

Lori shook her head. "I told you, Mr. John, I am not leaving your side."

"Lori, you're still the under secretary of Commerce and I'm still the chairman of the board of trustees of Global Computer Trading. Neither of us could ever live down not responsibly taking care of our obligations before we disengage ourselves in an honorable manner.

"Furthermore, it may become necessary for us to separate for a short time in order to do our jobs and help bring this thing to a conclusion."

She looked at him and in a tiny voice said, "Just for a little while maybe?"

He looked at her for a moment and smiled, shaking his head as he said, "Oh Lord, Lori, I love you so much."

She looked at him and smiled. "Don't worry, I'll be a good girl. I'll discharge my obligations and do whatever you want or need me to do."

John reached over, pushed the center armrest back up out of the way and pulled her over toward him until their bodies touched.

They drove on in silence as he began thinking through a plan of action. She sensed his need for quiet and just sat pressed against him, taking comfort from the touch of their bodies and the sense of his presence.

As they drove into the outskirts of Washington, John began unfolding the kernel of a plan to Lori who eagerly joined into the planning with parts that she could handle and help with.

"Where does Malcolm stay when he's in Washington?" he asked her.

"I understand he keeps a permanent suite at the Mayflower Hotel."

"We need a safe place to operate from. Some place that has phones, a fax maybe, a place to cook and sleep and a place that is not easily entered by uninvited guests. Got any ideas?"

Lori thought for a moment. "What about an embassy? They're about as invulnerable as a vault if they're on your side."

"Hmmm, that's a hell of an idea. Their phone lines are usually pretty tap-free too. Especially if they're not considered a political threat."

Lori thought for a moment. "Which country is your strongest booster, I mean for Global's system as an international monetary system?"

John screwed up his face in thought. "Let's see, Switzerland? No, too obvious, Malcolm knows we have an operations office there."

Lori said, "What about France? Didn't you say Courdelet was a good friend of yours?"

"That's it!" John smiled as his mind raced ahead.

Lori looked at him. "The French Embassy?"

"No dear heart. Courdelet's office or his house. His old comrades in arms, the Legionnaires from his Algiers days are all a part of his staff at the International Monetary Fund offices in Washington.

"They love intrigue and they're not afraid of a fight. Those ex-Foreign Legionnaires are worse than the Turks when it comes to spoiling for a fight."

He wheeled the big car around in a U-turn and headed for 14th and J streets. He pulled up at a drugstore that had a phone booth inside and jumped out of the car to make the call.

On the third quarter, he finally located Courdelet and told him the circumstances as briefly as possible and what he needed.

Alphonse Courdelet responded with the enthusiasm of a long-frustrated Legionnaire itching for some action. His mind worked like a well-oiled machine as he detailed a plan.

He told John that Martine, his old aide, would pick them up at the Lincoln Center parking lot where John would leave his car. They would be driven into the IMF building basement garage and be taken up to one of the four apartments the IMF maintained in the building for visiting members who wished to remain incognito while in the U.S.

Each apartment was equipped with several tap-free lines and fax machines. Downstairs, there was a worldwide radio communications center and computers available for their use. Security would be doubled and they would help *'La Cause'* in every way.

John smiled at the old soldier's enthusiasm and his expert planning and said, *"Vivre la Cause."*

Lori could see the smile on his face and knew *the plan was coming together.*

They reached the IMF basement without incident even with Colonel Martine driving the IMF staff car as if he were negotiating a mine field in a jeep.

Alphonse Courdelet greeted his old friend with an enthusiastic embrace saying, "You have saved an old soldier from death by boredom, *mon ami.*"

John introduced Lori to Alphonse who graciously bowed and kissed her hand and then led them to the elevator that took them to the floor where the apartments were located.

He unlocked one of four doors leading off the corridor and ushered them into a sumptuously decorated suite complete with a study that had phones, typewriter, an old teletype and a fax machine.

Courdelet led the way to a comfortable furniture grouping and beckoned them to sit down. Martine efficiently took a yellow pad and pen from the desk to make notes. Courdelet said, "Let us begin with an update of what has taken place to this moment."

John nodded and began his account of what had happened since the first of the week. He also related what some of the likely actions might be in light of the bombing of Global's shell building in Alexandria.

When John had finished his precise account, Courdelet leaned back in thought. "It would seem that there are a number of things that need to be done. The first is to diffuse Mr. Malcolm's plan to discredit Global's system.

"From the afternoon news, it appears that the Army's electronic blackout operation of the system has already been lifted. Now we must make sure that there are no further interruptions to the communications between Global and its customers.

"Next priority is to make an international show of force by bringing together every organization and country willing to adopt Global's approach to a computerized monetary system, *n'est pas?*"

John and Lori looked at each other with smiles. The old soldier's enthusiasm had driven out all negative thoughts and they were now cooking on all burners.

John said, "Let's add to that all the senators and representatives ready to vote in favor of the bill before the House and Senate Monday."

Lori chimed in, "And then advise all the wire services, every television network news show producer and anchor with a joint news release that will clue in every newspaper and TV news show Sunday night, Monday morning and Monday night."

Martine was dutifully making notes of everything said and then looked up to add, "And what about this crazy man who blows up buildings without regard to human life? Surely he will not be sitting on his hands?"

Courdelet nodded. "Truly a dangerous man from what you have described my friend. People used to the immense power that man wields, do not give up such power easily. Once it becomes clear they cannot win, they throw every asset into seeking revenge. Martine and I have experienced such insanity several times."

They all nodded in agreement and Martine elaborated on an incident he and the general had experienced in Algeria that caused Lori to turn her head away in disgust. The general stood and said, "We must plan a way to protect not only Global's operations, *mon ami,* but we must also plan to protect both you and the lovely *mademoiselle* from this man until he and his organization are put to rest."

John stood up and walked to the window, looking out at the cold night. Finally, he turned and said, "Sometimes there are more ways to skin a pig besides feed it butter."

General Courdelet laughed. "That is a quaint saying my friend, surely it does not come from France?"

John smiled. "No General, it comes from the deep south where people speak in quaint sayings but its meaning is clear. Instead of focusing on protection, although that is certainly called for in this instance, I believe that there might be other ways to change this situation from its present status to one more favorable."

Martine smiled and said, "I do remember that we did convince an irrational Arab one time, but unfortunately he died shortly after we were able to change his mind."

Courdelet shot a warning look at Martine and turned to Lori, asking her to forgive the colonel for his indelicate remark.

John looked at the group and said, "David Malcolm needs to be reached, to be confronted with the facts and made to see reason. What he obviously fails to recognize is that his own bank and companies he controls can only survive if the computerized monetary system is accepted by everyone and immediately put into operation."

Lori added, "And at this point, Global's system is the only

system acceptable to the majority. I think that is what bugs David. He has never been denied his way before. He has never lost control before."

John looked at Martine. "I believe, Jacques, that sometimes it is even possible to bring someone to accept reason without being so near to death."

Martine shrugged his shoulders and smiled.

Courdelet said, "First things first. I will have a dinner prepared for us by the staff. Then we shall organize our plan for immediate action. Jacques and I have already alerted all the members of the IMF that we are publicly declaring our total support for the Global system.

"Jacques, you will please look to the safety of our friends and arrange to provide an unobtrusive security for them when they must leave these confines."

Everyone nodded in agreement whereupon Alphonse and Jacques bowed and left the apartment with shoulders squared, anxiously looking forward to organizing and carrying out the first part of the campaign. Finally, they were once again able to engage in a meaningful fight of which they could be proud.

After the old general and his aide left, John called Senator Ketchall and asked him for the number of a phone line he knew to be 'clean' where he could call him in a few minutes. The senator gave him a number. When John reached him there, he brought him up to date and outlined the plan to the present.

Lori contacted her assistant and said she was spending the weekend with friends and might be in late Monday.

John had found a radio station that was playing light classical music and had carried their bags into the bedroom of the apartment.

When he returned to the library, Lori was just hanging up the phone. He could see that she was her old self again and the fear and apprehension had been replaced by resolve. It showed in the way she talked and held herself.

In that moment his heart filled with his love for her and he walked up behind her, lifted up her hair and kissed her on the nape of her neck. He could feel her shiver. She turned around and put her arms around him and buried her head in his shoulder.

They stood, holding each other like that for a long time, communicating only through their feelings.

Finally, Lori said, "John, we are going to win. *We are going to win.*"

John tilted her head up and smiled gently. "Yes, my love, we are going to win. And after that, we are going to disengage ourselves from anything we don't feel like doing anymore, and then, you and I are going to live happily after."

Lori took a deep breath. "Oh John, that sounds so wonderful. Everything's changed so drastically in the last five days it's hard to believe. It all seems to center around our being together. I love you so, Mr. John."

The music on the radio had changed to a Strauss waltz and John slowly began to dance Lori around the room with mock ceremony. She laughed gaily as they circled lightly about the room and when the music ended John bowed, she curtsied, he kissed her hand and when he stood up he pulled her to him and they embraced more passionately and kissed each other almost with a quiet desperation.

The telephone again interrupted their moment. It was Courdelet announcing that dinner would be served downstairs in the first-floor dining room in precisely twenty-three minutes. John muttered to himself, "He could have added 'which should be enough time to finish anything you might be doing.'"

Dinner was a potpourri of planning, discussion and reminiscing between old friends. Except for the planning part, Lori spent most the time listening with fascination.

Typical of the French Èlan, there was never any suggestion on the part of Courdelet or Martine that they were at all aware of anything unusual in John and Lori's being together. It was accepted as if it had always been so and was the most natural thing in the world. It made both John and Lori feel at ease, and they appreciated these two courtly, dignified gentlemen even more.

Over coffee and liqueur, they planned their schedules for the next day and how they would mesh and interact for maximum effect.

When all was settled, the two Old World gentlemen escorted Lori and John to the elevator as if they were visiting dignitaries and with equal courtliness, bid them both good night.

As the elevator door closed on them Lori sighed with appreciation. John looked surreptitiously at the ceiling and pinched Lori on the butt.

Lori, shocked at first, looked up at his mischievous smile and said, "How dare you. I'll give you thirty minutes to stop that."

"Only thirty minutes?" he said in mock disbelief.

She shrugged her shoulders and leaned against him saying, "How about all night?"

They both laughed, recapturing the carefree feelings of the night before and earlier that day.

The elevator door slid open and they walked to their apartment door and as John fished for the key he said "You know, I've been wanting to do that since the first night I saw you."

"Do what?" Lori asked.

"Pinch that beautiful, sexy butt of yours." He laughed as she hit his shoulder saying in a mocking voice, "Oh you . . ."

CHAPTER THIRTY-THREE
THE GROUND SWELL GROWS

Washington, D.C.
Sunday morning March 7, 9:15 a.m.

Sunday morning was a flurry of activity for Lori and John. Between telephone calls to gather support for the Congress and the President in their decision-making vote on Monday, they alternately read a dozen Sunday editions, from the New York Times to the Washington Post and watched special newscasts describing the flow of events since yesterday.

Jacques Martine had thoughtfully brought them a breakfast cart loaded with enough delectable food to feed an army and all the newspapers. Judging from their appetites, Lori and John had worked up quite a hunger since dinner the night before.

A newscaster on a local station was describing a scene at the entrance to the White House service gate where a line of delivery vehicles were waiting to deliver a flood of messages from all over the world.

"Word from inside the White House," he said, "is that over 90 percent is in response to John Garland's appearance before Congress Friday night, urging the President to accept the proposal for the changeover to a computerized, electronic monetary system.

"We are told that the Western Union computer outlets in the White House are backed up several hours, printing out messages of a similar nature from all over the world.

"Meanwhile, on Capitol Hill . . . "

John switched the set to another channel where similar news was being disseminated. He switched again to the Public Broadcasting channel where two congressmen and two of the computer experts who had tested the Global system Friday, were being interviewed by a senior news anchor on their views of the Global Computer system.

The two experts were ecstatic about the system's capability. One of the congressmen was in full agreement while Senator Tim Fourchette was saying that he felt a study of the system's reliability was needed before he could, in good conscience, embrace the system.

Lori looked at John and said, "Tim Fourchette is Malcolm's man in the Senate and what one might call a 'yellow-dog conservative' instead of a 'yellow-dog democrat.'"

John smiled at her and squeezed her hand. "Think his views have a chance?"

Lori smiled back and said, "You've heard about the snowball in hell?"

They both laughed and turned their attention back to the papers.

The editorial section of the Post had a banner headline proclaiming 'Time To Act, No Time To Wait.' Lori showed it to John who quickly read it, nodding his head. "Strong support. I haven't run across one paper yet with an opposing view."

Lori looked at him matter-of-factly, shrugged her shoulders and shook her head. "How can there possibly be an opposing view when the facts are so clear, so simple and so undeniable? John, it's a landslide in favor of a straightforward idea. There can be no other outcome."

Lori leaned over and switched to another channel just as the newscaster began reading a statement handed him.

"This just into our newsroom. The International Monetary Fund just released a statement that the moment the United States signs the bill accepting the new monetary system, the countries represented by the IMF will sign up to become a part of this new international monetary system. The countries include France, Great Britain, Germany, Japan . . ."

Lori squeezed John's arm in excitement as she bounced up and down on the hassock she had pulled up to the television set.

The phone rang and John jumped up to answer it. It was Martine, who told him that Senator Ketchall was returning his earlier call. "Put him through please, Jacques."

The Senator's normally quiet voice came on the line with a shout. "John, that you?"

"Yes, Senator, I'm here."

"John, listen to me, it's a stampede. We've got tons of mail, telegrams, faxes, phone calls. Every phone line is jammed. There are only sixteen hold-outs on the bill and two of those are out sick."

John quickly motioned to Lori to come over and listen to the phone with him as he continued.

"I hear you, Senator, and that is fantastic news. That obviously means that there can be no question of the bill not passing both houses."

"It will pass, in fact, a 'no pass' is out of the question now. The President just called me a few minutes ago to tell me he fully supports the bill and he'll sign it the minute it hits his desk."

Lori hugged John and he held her hand tightly, laughing.

"That's fantastic Senator, it renews one's faith in the system. It looks like it's time for me to head back to Nevada and start organizing the transition from our end. There's a big job ahead of us to make a fast, smooth changeover."

Senator Ketchall laughed joyously. "Boy, I feel like we've really accomplished something worthwhile for a change. You just tell me what you need and I'll get Congress to authorize the funds for it."

"All I need is the best computer brains in government and the financial industry in an organized and directed effort toward this common goal. We already have a transition plan on paper that we will immediately start distributing to the key people in government and private industry."

"What about Lorelei Young?" the Senator said. "She impressed me as the one who ought to head up government's transition team."

Lori and John exchanged looks. "You're right, Senator. She's already impressed me more than you'll ever know. Yes, she is definitely the perfect one for the job ahead."

"Good, I'll get hold of her and tell her to get started."

"I've already taken the liberty of doing that Senator. I think I may have gotten her motor running."

Lori pinched John on the butt and whispered in his ear, "You wonderfully dirty old man."

"Good, call me when you get to your office in Nevada and let me know if there is anything I can do."

"Right, Senator, I'm on my way, and I'll call you some time tomorrow."

"And John, take every precaution for your safety. You have become the focus of all those who stand to lose as a result of this bill's passage. They're all going to focus on you as the man who is the cause of putting them out of business."

"I know that, Senator. I'll be careful."

John hung up the phone slowly, got up, took Lori's hand and pulled her up to him. Tilting her chin, he looked into her eyes for a long moment. And then quietly said, "Beautiful lady of my life, as much as I hate the thought, this is one of those times we're going to have to be apart."

Her eyes were moist, but she held her composure. "Yes, I know. But the quicker we get started, the quicker we can get on with our lives."

John smiled at her, leaned down and kissed her gently on the forehead and said, "Spoken like the trooper I know you are."

He paused for a moment as he looked at her intelligent face and the warmth and love that seemed to emanate from her eyes.

"Since we met, it seems I'm always rushing to pour out my thoughts to you. I'm really not always this wordy, but it's important to me that you know how I feel about some things before we leave here."

Lori smiled coyly as she said, "You mean there's more?"

John smiled and shook his head. "I'm serious, Lori. It's just that I want you to know that I not only love you emotionally and physically, but I love you in a spiritual sense as well. I respect you for what and who you are, just the way you are and I want you to be the best that you can be.

"I want to be able to share your joys, successes, pains and sorrows, and I want you to know that I will always be there for you under any circumstances."

Lori took John's hand into her own and looked at it as she carefully chose her words. Finally she looked up at him.

"It seems like I've always been waiting for you to come into my life. We've only known each other a few short days, but it seems like I have known you forever.

"I have never felt more comfortable or happier with any other human being. In this short span of time, you've awakened feelings and emotions in me I didn't even know I had. You've given me joy . . . and pleasure . . . and peace I've never experienced before and you've instilled thoughts and ideas that move me in ways I can't even begin to describe.

"This morning I am looking ahead to a life with a man I not only love more than anything in the world but I respect more than anyone I have ever known. I want desperately to share everything with you and yet, I love you so much that I would never want you to be anything but what you are, nor do I ever expect your constant attention. I know that we both need our own moments and that others have the right to make demands on our time for the things we do best.

"Even though the last thing I feel like doing right now is seeing you leave this town without me, I know neither of us has a choice. So, as they say in the movies, 'let's get a move on, soldier.'"

They quickly packed. Then John called Martine and Courdelet telling them what had occurred and that he and Lori would be leaving in a few minutes.

They made arrangements that Martine would drive them both to the Washington airport and, after John departed, Martine would take Lori to her apartment.

Martine assured John that he would arrange for a surreptitious security watch at both her apartment and her office and he, Martine, would personally take charge of this assignment.

John thanked his old friends and then asked Martine to dial George Talbot's home and ask him to call the Currency Trade Communications Office in ten minutes for some important financial information.

That was a prearranged code telling his friend Talbot to get to an untapped phone and call John's beeper and leave the number.

John was just zipping up the last of their bags when the beeper went off. John quickly punched up the number on a cellular phone and waited for the ring. George answered it on the first ring.

John quickly outlined the circumstances and what had taken place. He asked George if he had been able to keep track of Malcolm since their last communication.

Talbot told him that the last information he had was that Malcolm was heading for New York for a meeting with some business associates.

"And about the man who bombed the shell building in Alexandria, he's dropped out of sight. Everyone from the FBI down is looking for him. No trace. But I've been monitoring some special coded accounts Malcolm uses to fund questionable operations."

John said impatiently, "And?"

"And there is one in particular that had been used to fund our bomber friend. I noticed that this morning, a very large sum was transferred from that account to a hotel-casino in Reno. Indications are that the funds have already been picked up."

"Doesn't sound too good, does it George?"

"No, it sounds like he might be there working on something very unpleasant."

"Just track Dave for me the best you can and let me know where he lands. As for that bomber guy, Charlie has already sent videotape of him to the FBI as well as all our people around the country. I'll take care of my end, you make sure you take care of yourself. Like the man says, it ain't over 'til it's over."

"Right. I'll talk to you over our private wire when I get back to Toiyabe Canyon."

John hung up the phone, picked up his and Lori's bag, then stopped, put the bags down, put his arms around Lori and held her tightly. He kissed her with all the love in his heart and then quietly said, "I love you more than anything, Lori. Always know that."

Reluctantly letting go of her, John bent down, picked up their bags and they went to meet Martine.

CHAPTER THIRTY-FOUR
DISSENT IN THE RANKS

New York City
March 6, 3:00 p.m.

Mel Trask was walking up and down the expanse of his spacious office, carrying his phone back and forth as he talked.

"I don't care about my board seat. I don't care about the loan call. I don't give a damn about our joint ventures, Dave. I am backing off. You have gone completely off your rocker, old friend. The stuff you've pulled is way outside of the courts I play on."

On the other end of the line, David Malcolm was stuttering he was so mad.

"Listen to me, *listen to me, Mel.* You're in this up to your ass with me. You and Garvin and Murdoch and Esterbrook, you're all in this up to your neck, my friend. I have tapes of everything we've discussed. If I go down, we all go down."

Mel Trask flopped down in his chair and put his feet up on the desk.

"Not me Dave, you don't have me agreeing to use the U.S. Army to black out anybody's communication. You don't have me agreeing to some ridiculous idea like bombing a Global office. If I can't buy the business I want, I don't need it bad enough to try any other way. This is your play. I'm bugging out. From here on in you're on your own."

With that Mel Trask swung his feet off his desk and emphatically hung up. Punching a button on a flat console he said, "You in your office, Dick?"

The voice of Mel's ever-present vice president came over the intercom. "I'm here, Mel."

"Good, make a note to get in touch with that federal prosecutor tomorrow morning, what's his name? You know, the guy we offered to back for a try at the governor's job?"

"Bob Calliani."

"That's the one. Tell him I want an appointment to talk to him about something I found out on that Alexandria, Virginia, bombing and that communications blackout. Tell him I want to give this information to him as a friend, anonymously."

Dick Simon smiled to himself as he scratched out 'we' on the pad in front of him and said, "Right, Mel."

CHAPTER THIRTY-FIVE
THE DOMINO EFFECT

Westchester, NY.
March 6, 4:00 p.m.

Corbin Esterbrook was adjusting his tie in a mirror, getting ready for an early cocktail party he and his wife planned to attend at the Westchester Country Club when the phone rang.

Corbin went over to the bedside table and picked it up.

"Hello, this is Corbin. Oh yes, put him on please." The still-irate voice of David Malcolm came on the line.

"Corbin, I need your help here in the city right away. I have to discuss a plan with you. When can you get here?"

Corbin looked at his wife and smiled as he answered.

"I'm sorry, David, but my wife and I are just leaving for a very important function we've planned on for weeks. I just can't get away."

"Corbin, you better come if you know what's good for you."

"David, are you threatening me?"

"Look, Corbin, we have to act now to protect our businesses or we may very well lose everything."

Corbin looked at the ceiling for a moment before answering.

"David, I'm afraid that, come what may, I want no part of what's going on right now. I am prepared to make the best of the situation and accept the Global operation as the best thing for all of us. In fact, I had the company's vice president for public relations issue a statement to that effect just a few hours ago."

"YOU WHAT? ARE YOU MAD, CORBIN?"

"Perhaps it is you who are mad. It seems you've forgotten the art of doing business with both sides."

With that, Corbin depressed the phone cradle and then flashed it. His butler came on the line at the switchboard downstairs and Corbin said, "If Mr. Malcolm, or anyone, calls back right now, tell them we've just left. And, Willis, have the car brought around. Thank you."

Corbin and his wife looked at each other meaningfully and walked out together.

David Malcolm was all but frothing at the mouth as he paced in his office. His mouth and eye were twitching and his hands were clenching and unclenching violently.

"That sonofabitch, that sonofabitch," he kept muttering over and over again.

CHAPTER THIRTY-SIX
BROTHERS UNDER THE SKIN
OFTEN SUFFER FROM THE SAME RASH

New York City
March 7, 6:15 p.m.

The voice on the intercom on David Malcolm's desk sounded disconcerted. "Mr. Malcolm, this is Don Frazer, chief of building security, and I'm calling from the main lobby entrance security station."

The chief of the bank's building security had been called to intercept the latest visitors and personally OK their being permitted to enter the building lobby.

"Yes, yes Frazer, what is it?"

"Sir, there are three men out there who just arrived in a limo. I beg your pardon, sir, but they don't look like the type of people you let into a bank building at night. I can see that at least two of them are armed. Shoulder holsters I'd say. They insist that you asked them here for a meeting."

"Well, what are their names Frazer?"

"Names, sir?"

"Yes, yes, what are their names?"

"Uh, the only one that gave his name is Mr. George Castellani. The other two, he says, are with him."

Malcolm sighed. "Send them up on my private elevator please."

"Yes sir."

"And Frazer, there will be two more gentlemen arriving whom you may think are odd looking—Mr. Gacho and Mr. Rivera. They also may have some bodyguards with them. Please send them up when they come."

Frazer shook his head in disbelief. "Yes sir, if you say so, sir. I'll be right here with some extra men if you need me."

"Fine, fine, Frazer. Thank you," and Malcolm impatiently switched off the intercom and went to the private elevator entrance in a small hall off his office.

He cursed himself for not having had a special sealed-off entrance built in the garage to his elevator that anyone could drive up to without getting security clearance.

The doors opened and George Castellani stepped off followed by his two ever-present bodyguards.

Malcolm put on his best banker face, stuck out his hand to a limp, disinterested handshake and heartily welcomed Castellani.

"Long time, no see, George. How've you been? You look like you put on a little weight."

Castellani looked at Malcolm. "Cut out the crap, Dave. You got me called out of a show my wife and I been waitin' two months to see so this better be good."

"Listen George, I'm really sorry about that. I'll have two more tickets sent around any time you want to go back and see it. Please come into the office."

They all walked into the sitting room area of the office and sat on the couch and chairs while Malcolm went over to a sideboard liquor cabinet and asked if anyone wanted a drink

They all shook their heads negatively. The scene from Malcolm's office at night was impressive—even for Castellani. The whole city of New York spread out before them with the Hudson and East rivers framing the city lights. It almost appeared unreal.

David walked back into the sitting area and sat across from Castellani, his long legs stretched out before him and a drink in his hand.

"Let me get right to the point, George. A great number of ventures such as yours stand to be put out of business if this new electronic monetary system is put in place."

"My people been in business for over a hunnert years all the way back to the old country, Dave. What do you mean we stand to be shut down?"

"Well, George, most of your dealings are in cash. Very large amounts of cash. As I recall, last year, through the business networks and accounts I helped you set up, your were able to bank and reinvest over $3.2 billion just in Manhattan alone."

George Castellani's eyes became lidded. "Yeah, so?"

"So, George, under the computerized monetary system there would be no way such business fronts could be set up that easily, that much cash pumped into the banking system and, shall we say, 'legitimized,' without being picked up the very first day.

"If the Global Computer operation becomes our next monetary system, there won't even be any cash on the streets to buy the kinds of goods and services you sell."

The intercom buzzer interrupted David's discourse on street-money economics and Frazer's voice could be heard saying. "Mr. Gacho and Mr. Rivera are on their way Mr. Malcolm."

Castellani let out a sigh. "You bringing them two snakes into this, Dave?"

David smiled. "George, how you talk. The stuff they sold you last year accounted for at least a billion and a half of your income."

George Castellani looked at David sourly. "I don't recall asking you to keep books for me, Dave."

David got up and said, "Excuse me." He went to the elevator lobby to greet his new guests, returning in a few minutes with Gacho and Rivera in tow followed by five Latin, strong-arm types, all obviously armed.

David waved them to the remaining chairs and stools by the sideboard.

"Gentlemen, I believe you all already know each other?"

Castellani nodded to the two men and Gacho raised his hand in recognition while Rivera offered no recognition.

David continued, "Raoul and Pepe, I was just explaining to Mr. Castellani that if this new Global Trading network is installed as a monetary system, it will replace all currency now in circulation and there will only be numbered accounts for every business and individual in the country.

"There will no longer be any street money or cash in circulation anywhere. Currency will be worthless. The customers you usually sell your imported goods to will no longer have anything to pay you with.

"You, I, all of us will be out of business overnight. Do you understand that?"

Raoul Gacho pulled a slender cigar out of a case and said, "David, both Mr. Rivera and I are university educated and we can both read English very well. We have been following this situation since long before anyone in this country was even aware of it. I am sure that Mr. Castellani has also had no trouble being informed of it as it appeared here."

Malcolm visibly colored as Raoul Gacho continued.

"Now, I am sure that your bank would come under the umbrella the President and the Congress have proposed in the new bill, which means that every depositor you have would receive an amount of credits equal to the amount of cash he now has on deposit with you, is that correct?"

"Yes, essentially that is correct."

Raoul Gacho smiled as he continued.

"Correct me if I am wrong, David, but I believe that means that all the assets Mr. Castellani, Mr. Rivera and I have placed in your bank and its various branches through your costly, but very efficient, laundry service, will also therefore show up as credits in the same accounts, of equal value to the present dollar value. The computer system will simply become the central accounting operation for your bank from now on."

David looked pained. "Yeees, that is a simplified way of putting it."

Raoul continued, "Essentially then, none of our present cash assets are in danger of being lost. It is only any future business that will temporarily be interrupted."

David showed some irritation. "You say temporarily, Raoul, are you aware of how difficult it will become to sell your product to those who have no visible means of support, or if they do, how hard it would be to explain the payments of say, a hundred dollars a day, while on welfare?"

"Perhaps, but we have had experts working on some alternatives. We may have to reduce our business volume somewhat at first, but we are exploring some interesting possibilities."

David shook his head. "I really don't believe you gentlemen understand the full complexity of this situation and its total effect.

"For instance, every individual and every business will have a federal number for their accounts. The government will have a specified limited access to the entire database of these numbers.

"They can, on a daily basis, have the computer search that data base and pull up reports on every number and cross check its transactions to and from each source and recipient, and prepare a report on that activity.

"They can then program the computer to flag all unreasonably large amounts of money flowing to a single account or group of accounts and track it backward to find out what the business is based on that can generate such a huge cash flow.

"If your business had been subject to this computer system before, they would have flagged your accounts within the first five weeks of business and probably had you before a grand jury within ten days."

The men sat quietly looking at each other with poker faces while digesting Malcolm's information. Finally, Pepe Rivera nodded his head in Malcolm's direction.

"He has a point, *amigo*. These kinds of transactions will be very difficult to hide or disguise."

Castellani looked at Rivera and then Gacho. "Yeah, he has got a point. It might take some time to figure a way around this. I mean, even if we start investing in a slug of businesses that we can use as fronts, it's still gonna cost a lot of time, a lot business and money."

Gacho looked at David thoughtfully. "In other words, you are suggesting that the only way to protect our interests is to stop this man and his system from operating. Am I correct?"

"You are correct, Mr. Gacho. You are quite correct. If for some reason, that system is proven vulnerable or unreliable within the next four days, Congress and the President could not permit that new system to be put into operation."

Gacho looked at Malcolm quizzically. "Then what do you suggest, David?"

"First, let me point out some facts. We now know that Congress and the President have agreed to put the Global system into full scale operation starting sometime next week based on the knowledge that the system is 'fail safe.' I also know from personal experience that nothing, so far, has been able to immobilize that system or interfere with its operation.

"That means someone on the inside, who can, in effect, pull the switch and turn off the system on purpose, has to be reached.

"If that switch can be turned off within the next four days, Congress and the President cannot permit that system to operate for fear of paralyzing the country."

David got up from his chair and slowly began to walk back and forth as he outlined a daring and dangerous plan.

CHAPTER THIRTY-SEVEN
NOW IS THE TIME FOR ALL GOOD MEN

Toiyabe Canyon Nevada
March 7, 7:30 p.m.

The flight from Washington to Reno was a flurry of planning and discussions. John had contacted Charlie Ross and Bob Trainer on the sea-going Global operation and had them meet him at the airport for the flight to Reno on a chartered jet. It was a well-equipped plane with communications systems including cellular phones that allowed them to make arrangements ahead.

After their arrival, each went their separate way to start setting up for the transition operation ahead.

John arranged for Mrs. Hanson to bring in some kitchen help to prepare dinner for a meeting of all of the key Global operations people whom they had alerted for this final planning session. Included at this meeting were all of the Delta mining people and neighboring ranchers, Indian tribes and prospector friends.

The dining room at the lodge seated 125 people. All but two seats were filled with the men and women who had worked so hard to make Global Computer Trading Company an operational success.

As the last dish was cleared from the tables, John stood up and his friends and co-workers.

"Folks, if you will please give me your attention, we are on a short fuse and have an awful lot to do in the next few days.

"As you know, this is the moment we've all been working toward. Congress and the President have agreed to sign a bill embracing the Global system as the new monetary system and protecting it against interference.

"The United Sates was the 'linchpin' that brought together over 120 countries throughout the world to adopt the Global system as an international monetary system.

"Obviously there are appropriate adjustments for each country's currency value in relationship to all other values in accepting Global's non-political method of adjustment to our electronic credits.

"The congressional bill calls for the transfer of all paper currency, bank accounts and other types of accounts, to electronic credits. There are, of course, some caveats dealing with questionably large amounts of cash that might represent illicit drug money or cash hoards from other illegal activities. These will be handled on a case by case basis.

"All of you have been fully indoctrinated in the method worked out by Charlie Ross for a relatively smooth transition from our present electronic marketplace and barter system to, what will now become, the international monetary system.

"There are a number of aspects I want to make you fully aware of. First, of course, are the methods we will be using and how we are going to interact with the various governments to bring about the appropriate transfer of credits from paper currency and checking accounts.

"In the United States, our direct liaison will be the under secretary of commerce, Lorelei Young, whom many of you met several days ago when she visited our Global operations center here. She is already busy setting up for the first agency tie-ins and will be in her office all night tonight. Her number is in your material.

"She will be working closely with Charlie Ross and Bob Trainer. In the beginning, we will give her passwords and access codes, which she will then assign to the various government agencies, banking institutions and private banks.

"Each of them will be permitted to access specifically assigned data bank sectors within Global's main data bank for the purpose of keying in or dumping data into our data files for compilation and cross referencing."

One of the operation's managers from Global's Zurich office raised his hand to interrupt. "What about checking the validity of the data we receive?"

John nodded approvingly at the awareness of the man as he continued. "At the outset, all data will be accepted at face value until auditing and cross referencing can be completed.

"Through the use of direct computer memory bank download transfers and optical character reader transfers, we should have a sufficient data base loaded within seventy-two hours to begin actual operations.

"The IMF office in Washington will act as liaison for all member governments and handle any problems or questions that arise. They will be assigning the same type of access codes and passwords for their members.

"There have been key banks in various countries designated as direct contacts for ironing out any problems or difficulties we may run across. Lists of their names, locations and phone numbers will be found in the material you have in front of you.

"Time is of the essence. People throughout the world don't understand what's going on beyond the fact that their assets and savings are in jeopardy. Many of them are already reacting in a hysterical manner.

"Worldwide hysteria of that sort builds on itself until it becomes a feeding frenzy. The hysterical mass begins destroying everything and itself without realizing it. By our best estimate we have about four days in which to head off that sort of a reaction.

"When we leave this room, the foreign operations will begin, starting with the most sophisticated, computer-oriented countries, where we can accomplish the data base transfers the quickest, and show the citizens of those countries that they have lost nothing.

"That will have a calming effect on some of the smaller, less-organized countries and buy some time for the more troublesome transfers."

An attractive woman representing the Toronto office stood up and asked John, "When does all this start, Mr. Garland?"

John turned toward her to answer her question. "The congressional bill in this country is expected to hit the President's desk by 10 a.m. Eastern time tomorrow.

"By mutual consent with several agencies such as the Federal Reserve, we are going to begin transferring data at 12:01. Eastern Standard Time tonight, giving us a head start on this country and having the data transfer legally take place on the day the bill becomes law.

"Each of you will be heading up a different transition team, which is detailed in the material in front of you.

"Now for the bad part. We have all been aware that Global's system represents a danger to certain segments of society—drug dealers, the Mafia, multinational profiteers who can only operate through the bribing of government officials, terrorists who must have access to under-the-table cash, just to mention a few.

"Many of you found this out when Global experienced a communications blackout on five of our operations centers over the weekend and Charlie told you about the mock operation being blown up Friday night.

"I have reason to believe that there will be some kind of concerted, last-minute attempt to shut down Global's operations in an effort to convince the federal government not to allow Global to become this country's monetary system.

"We need every one of our operations centers up and running to accomplish the data transfer essential to monetary operations before mass hysteria can take hold.

"We have taken every precaution conceivable to avoid any interference with the operations of our system and our government will be ordering every federal police agency and military service into a full security alert status as of tomorrow at 10:30 a.m., right after the bill becomes law.

"It will probably take twenty-four hours from that time for these forces to be totally and effectively deployed. That means Global's operations centers will be vulnerable during that time period except for our own security methods.

"We will have taken every possible precaution, many of which you are already familiar with. I believe these precautions and capabilities will be adequate.

"There is, however, one thing I wish to make clear. Whatever we do to protect Global and its people and operations, it must not include overt aggressive action on our part. We will defend ourselves in whatever way is necessary at the time. We may employ violent actions to defend ourselves. If that becomes necessary it is my hope that those of us who will be concerned with our security can and will use methods that can contain any attempted violence against Global's operations and its people until such time as the government forces take over.

"Be aware, be calm and follow all the protective procedures you have so diligently been practicing. And now, we are about to engage in an activity that may well be one of the most important and meaningful ever undertaken on a worldwide basis. I know every one of us expects it to be successfully deployed.

"I want you to know how much I care for and respect each of you for your dedication and your unstinting efforts in the development of this plan.

"In time, the whole world will come to honor you all and pay tribute to that dedication and courage."

The room exploded in an enthusiastic response and John held up his hands for quiet.

"I would like the security people and mining employees to stay on for a little security planning session after the computer operations people leave.

"Those of you who were flown in from other cities will be ferried back to Reno where you are either ticketed on domestic flights or will have charter flights return you to your operations centers.

"And now it's time to stop blowing smoke about what we're going to do *and do it!*" He smiled at them as the computer team got up with their instruction packets and headed for their various places of assignment.

Mrs. Hanson and her team of cooks and waiters swooped into the dining room, cleaning the tables for the security meeting and setting out cups and coffee pots.

Swede Hanson; Johnny Honey Umptewa, son of the chief of the nearby Paiute tribe and a lifetime friend, Bill Carder, Mine supervisor; Harry Hutch, the head of mine security; and Dan Burke, chief of the Reno airport security, all sat at the head table with John.

"Ladies and gentlemen, Swede has already clued you all in on what we may be facing. At this point, the only official assistance we can look to is the Fallon Naval Air Station, because of its air traffic control and radio communications repeater towers behind us on Dome Peak, and Dan Burke, whose airport police at Reno will be watching for the arrival of people that look suspicious.

The Navy will monitor all air traffic between Salt Lake City, Elko, Tonopah, Reno and Winnemucca. Their radar system can track even a hedge-hopping helicopter. They will give us a warning about any aircraft they pick up straying beyond normal air corridors in this direction. They will also scramble Navy aircraft to intercept any aircraft that appears to be placing their communications equipment in jeopardy."

Harry Hutch raised his hand for attention and John nodded to him to speak. "How do you want us to set up security here, boss?"

John looked at the ceiling for a moment before speaking.

"Let's start with surface access. There are only two roads in and out of Toiyabe Canyon. The one out of Austin to the north and out of Gabbs and Ione to the west. All other approaches are across a lot of bad desert and a mountain range or two.

"The road out of Gabbs and Ione is just a dirt road and has to pass a lot of ranches and tribal range land. You've all been given reliable, portable, two-way radio communications equipment so we will be able to track anyone coming through Gabbs many hours before they even got close.

"If someone tried to come across country out of Tonopah, it would take them at least a full day if they knew what they were doing and chances are they won't."

Bill Carder interjected, "What do you think these folks might try to do?"

"I have no idea what some of these people might do, Bill. But I do feel certain they will try to do something to disrupt Global's operation.

"I want you all to be fully aware of several things. First of all, these people controlled enough wealth and power to field a well-equipped air and land force of terrorists with all the latest and deadliest weapons. Second, they have none of the conscience or compunctions of normal members of society. They are capable of doing anything to anyone without regard to conventions or concern.

"Therefore, we have no idea what to expect. I only know that people like that will fight tooth and nail to protect their power and income base and use any weapons they think will help.

"Officially, our government cannot and will not be able to provide us any security or protection until the congressional bill becomes law or until violent force has been used against us. Until then, and probably for the next day or two, we will be on our own and very vulnerable.

"Since this is our key computer center, I have reason to believe that this will be a primary target. We all agreed earlier that we have a reasonable chance to defend ourselves on the ground since we have only one road into the canyon from the end of the blacktop south of Austin and northeast from Ione.

"Since we anticipated problems when we built this place, we have designed our underground operations center to be sealed off from the surface on this side of the mountain range.

"We have underground living quarters stocked with three months of food and water supplies. We have an underground water source that supplies us with underground power and water. There are seven hidden, filtered air shafts to the surface on both sides of the range and one escape tunnel to the east side of the range. All of these are well hidden and unknown to anyone but us.

"If there is an air attack, it would be on the mining operations area, the administration building and the power plant and, of course, our TELSAT and COMSAT dishes, our microwave dishes, our antennas on the peak above us and our conventional phone lines."

Sam Boyd, Global's international coordinator, said, "What happens if someone knocks out these communications?"

"Well, Sam, very few people were aware of the fact that long ago we started to lay down buried fiber-optic lines that run underground along the railroad right-of-way, by special arrangement with the railroad. These lines run into Reno and Salt Lake. Every time the railroad dug up and repaired the road bed, we'd be out there laying our fiber optics. It took us six years, but I think we have an invulnerable link to the outside world as a result.

"Our automatic switching terminals in Salt Lake and Reno can tie us into different phone networks every five minutes on a constant basis so that a phone tap to trace our source is impossible. We have not utilized that system of communications in order to keep it secret in case of an emergency. We may face such an emergency soon.

"I wanted you to know about the backup system so that you wouldn't try anything foolish that might risk your lives in order to protect our regular phone lines or our antennas and communications dishes. Now let's talk about the road access to the canyon.

"As you know, the road into Toiyabe Canyon is a mining company road that was built with BLM permission beginning at the edge of Belle Caster's ranch.

"Swede, Randy, our head powder man, and I, have worked out a little trick that should sidetrack anyone coming in on that road long before they reach Toiyabe Canyon.

"Right after this meeting, two of our graders, a couple of D-8's and a front-end loader are going to re-route the mine road at the Box Canyon draw and doze it right into the Box Canyon. Anyone who's never been up here before wouldn't know the difference between the two canyon entrances or the road.

"Our regular road is going to be dozed out of existence temporarily and we'll push some boulders over it and dump a bunch of tumbleweed around. The berm cut will just make a smooth curve into and up the draw right into the mouth of Box Canyon, and we'll doze the road right up to the end of that canyon.

"It'll take a vehicle fifteen minutes or so to get to the end of that canyon before they realize they're in a box.

"Swede and Billy will set some charges under that big sheet of volcanic flow hanging over the top of the entrance and after the strangers are about at the end of the canyon, they'll blow the overhang and block the canyon entrance.

"We'll have some of you stationed up around the perimeter of the canyon to make sure no one climbs out till the Congressional bill becomes law and government security arrives.

"If they have radio communications with them, they'll have trouble getting a signal out of that deep canyon. We can intercept the communications and determine who they're trying to contact and intercept any strange communications from outside the canyon to try and track who's transmitting and where they're located."

A weather-beaten sheepherder stood up and said, "What d'ya want us to do Big John?"

"I figure all you ranchers and sheep herders will be able to spot anyone trying a cross country approach and warn us on your radios.

"The cities in which our communications routing offices are located will all be well guarded by local law enforcement while all of our overseas operations are already under twenty-four hour guard by the military in those countries.

"I don't feel those operations are in any jeopardy. Because this is the main operating base where our top people and the main computers are located, I believe this is where they will try to hit first.

"The minute the military shows up here to take charge of security, I will be leaving for Washington to help the national and international transition operation. In my absence, Charlie Ross will be in charge of the Global operations. Bill Carder will be in charge of the mine operations, as usual, and Harry Hutch will handle all security for the area."

Harry raised his hand again and said, "What if worse comes to worst, Boss?"

"Well, Harry, everyone is already familiar with how we seal off the fifth level where we have our operations center in case of any serious problems. We must protect the operation against shutdown at all cost.

"Folks, we need your eyes, ears and courage as well as restraint. I want no violence unless there is a clear and present danger of violence against us, and we need to defend ourselves.

"There isn't a man or a woman here that can't outsmart some city slicker—no matter what kind of arms or equipment they have. I'm relying on that ability to avoid bloodshed whenever possible. Meantime, the success of this whole thing is as dependent upon you for the next twenty-four hours as it is on anyone working on the computers.

"I appreciate all of you and what you're willing to do and I can only say that some day, the whole world will thank you for what you're doing here now. Go get 'em folks."

CHAPTER THIRTY-EIGHT
THE BEST LAID PLANS OF MICE AND MEN
ARE NO BETTER THAN THE PLANNING RAT

Reno, Nevada
March 7, 9:30 p.m.

Ben Sessions did not look like the Ben Sessions last seen in Alexandria, Virginia. He had on jeans, khaki shirt, a sudden sun tan and looked for all the world like an exploration geologist.

The sign on the outside of the meeting room at the Airport Plaza Hotel read, 'Geologic Exploration Conference—by invitation only.'

There were some thirty men assembled in the room, looking ill at ease in work clothes and boots. Many were obviously Latin, some were rough-looking Anglos and some looked like they hadn't seen sunshine in years. The walls were covered with maps and aerial photographs of Nevada.

Ben Sessions was sitting at a conference table across the front of the room. One of the men in the front row looked balefully at Sessions and said, "What the hell you got us in a place like this for? We can't even get a drink sent in here, man."

"The reason we are meeting in this conference room is that there are at least ten of these a week in this place and we don't look suspicious pinning maps on the walls and getting together in a large group like this."

One of the other men, obviously of Latin origin, sat shaking his head with distaste.

"I don' like this *pinche* set up meng, de FBI office is in de buildin' nex door. For what you do this?"

Ben looked at the group with disdain before he answered.

"Because it's the safest damn place to meet. Just listen and learn. You gentlemen are here to take part in a ground assault on a place called Delta Mining Company located in Toiyabe Canyon about 150 miles east of here. Since there are no airfields near Toiyabe Canyon on which to land an assault force, three different teams will be coming in from three different directions.

"We've purchased four used four-wheel-drive Suburban wagons, two four-wheel-drive Jeep station wagons and two four-wheel drive pickup trucks. They're all in top condition and all have been fitted out with extra fuel tanks and five-gallon water cans.

"About two hours ago, a container was off-loaded from a private cargo plane and is now on the other side of the airfield in a mini-storage place. It should have all the hardware and ammunition in it we need. We're going to split up into three groups."

Sessions walked over to a colored BLM map of northern Nevada. Pointing to Tonopah, he said, "One group is leaving tonight for Tonopah, located right here. It will take about five hours driving time. Get a motel and catch a few hours sleep and then head out at dawn on this road here."

He pointed to an old mining road just north of Tonopah and traced it until it met a BLM trail heading northwest into Big Smokey Valley just to the east of the range.

"The roads are all marked with a highlighter pen and, as you can see, they come in about two miles south of Toiyabe Canyon. There's no road connecting the canyon and that last few miles, but there is an old sheepherder trail from there to the canyon around Shoshone Peak. Sheepherders drive pickup trucks into that canyon over that trail all the time.

"The second group will take Highway 50 into Austin, here. From there you follow this road south past Bunker Hill Peak, past the edge of the Yomba Indian Reservation, through some ranches and then connect to the private Delta Mine road here."

He pointed to connecting roads on the map. "It winds up some draws and then into Toiyabe Canyon.

"Just before you get there, pull off into this area here and make radio contact with us. We're sending some choppers and other aircraft in and they will direct you from there.

"We've got two targets. First, the communications antennas and dishes on the peak up here. Next, the mine administration building and all the buildings east of it.

"We've managed to get our hands on some of the Army's latest and best mortar hardware, guaranteed to take out both of those targets with no more than a couple of well-placed rounds. You'll also have the latest Stinger ground-to-air missiles."

One of the Latinos interrupted Ben Sessions asking, "Who's gonna teach us how to use them things?"

Sessions pointed to two of the men in the front row and said, "Ron Daigle and Sam Del Veccio here are both ex-Army ordinance people who know how to handle this stuff. They'll check out each team on how to use 'em.

"Randy will go with the Tonopah team and Sam with the group out of Austin. They'll handle the mortars. After the hit, a chopper will pick up the crew out of Tonopah first and get them over to the little airfield at Austin. One of two twin-engine planes will be waiting to fly each crew out to Salt Lake and from there you'll catch commercial flights out.

"The second crew will head back out to the blacktop, dump the Jeeps and get in the Suburban parked there and head for the same airport where the second plane will repeat the process.

"OK, roll up the maps you're each gonna be using and meet out in the back parking lot where I've got the vehicles waiting. Then follow us over to the mini storage and pick up your hardware and get going."

With that the men all got up and started their assigned tasks.

CHAPTER THIRTY-NINE
NEVER SEND A BOY TO DO A MAN'S JOB

Mt. Dome, Toiyabe Range
March 7, 7:01 a.m. Dawn.

"Delta Mines, this is Billy John Eagle, come in Delta Mines." Billy John was sitting on a flat-top boulder looking south across the barren desert sink between him and Tonopah.

"This is Harry at Delta Mines Billy, go ahead."

"I'm up at the old sheepherder camp on the southeast side of Dome Peak. There's a bunch of guys in a couple of Jeeps, sunk up to their axles in soft sand, sprayin' sand all over tryin' to get out. Over."

"Billy John, do they look like prospectors or ranchers? Over."

"Naw, they look like they just walked out of a casino on South Virginia Street. Over."

"Okay, Billy, keep an eye on them and let us know if they get unstuck. Over."

"Harry, from the looks of it, they'll be stuck there forever unless they walk out. Over."

"Okay, Billy, keep us posted. This is Delta Mines out."

Harry put down his radio mike and picked up the phone to report to John Garland.

John answered on the second ring. "Garland here."

"This is Harry, John. Billy John Eagle just called in from the southeast side of Dome Peak. He spotted a bunch of city slickers stuck in the sand out on the big sink north of Tonopah. From his description, these Jeeps will be there awhile unless somebody gets 'em out."

"Thanks, Harry. Looks like our suspicions were correct. Keep me posted."

"Will do."

John toggled the phone while checking his watch. It would be 10:10 a.m. in Washington he thought, as he dialed Lori's private office line. After an interminable wait, she finally came on the line.

"Hello, this is Lorelei Young."

"Lori, it's John. Are you all right? You sound very tired."

"Oh John, thank you for calling, and yes, I am tired. I had a cot set up in my office for cat naps, but so far, the cat's been too busy."

"I know, the crew here is working at a feverish pitch to keep up with all the data downloads, but it looks like it's working without a hitch so far."

"Good. I've staggered each agency so that as soon as one gets organized with the proper memory segment and starts the download, I get the next one on line. We've had to get some of the agencies to get newer phone modems to accommodate high-speed data transfers."

"Lori, has there been any sign of possible external problems or attempts to interfere with this operation?"

"None yet. How about you?"

"One of our lookouts just spotted a couple of Jeeps full of obvious tenderfeet stuck in a sand desert trying to get to the backside of Toiyabe on an old BLM trail. Don't know who they are yet, but they're out of commission for now anyway. The airport police reported the arrival of some known Mafia types and a couple of suspicious-looking Latino's who fitted a drug profile last night, but that's it."

"John, I'm worried. It's not like Malcolm and his friends just to give in. I have bad feelings about this."

"Do you have security in your building Lori?" John asked.

"We have the usual government security guards at all building entrances and an extra patrol on this floor. Besides, I got Martine a special security pass and he is all over the building like a ghost. He gave me a powerful little FM walkie talkie that matches the wavelength of one he carries on him and he checks with me every hour. So far he has called to check on me from the roof, from the basement, from the air conditioning system and every place but the ladies room. The man is incredible."

John laughed. "Yes, I know. That's what the Algerians thought, too. I feel better knowing he's there watching over you. Please try to get some rest, my beautiful lady, and be on your guard every minute. I have no idea what someone may try to do, I only know in my bones that someone will try something to stop us."

"Don't worry John, I am staying in the office until this transfer is well on its way. I expect to hear from the White House any minute that the bill has been signed into law. After that, it should be too late to do anything. You be careful too my darling. I can't wait 'til this is all over."

John sighed as he said, "Like the man says, 'it's not over 'til the fat lady sings.' Stay alert even after the bill is signed."

Lori leaned back in her chair and closed her eyes. "Promise me something darling?"

"Anything," John answered gently.

"Promise me you'll take me back to that house in Maryland and do it all over again but this time with the phone unplugged."

John laughed. "I promise."

They both hung up with the same emotional feelings.

The phone on John's desk rang again. Harry's voice brought him abruptly back to reality.

"Big John, Swede just called in from the Box Canyon. They got four car loads of hot shots boxed up there. Swede says that when the blast went off, they jumped out of their vehicles and unloaded some heavy duty mortars, a couple of bazookas, what looks like Stinger missiles. And they're all armed with automatic rifles or machine pistols."

John sighed. "Looks like the party's beginning. Do they know how to get out?"

"Not yet, but they been shootin' up at the rim not knowin' where the targets are."

John carried the phone with him to a map wall where a topography sheet of the Box Canyon was pinned.

"Tell Swede to keep 'em pinned down 'til the cavalry

arrives if he can."

"Will do. Swede says Johnny Honey Umptewa has a plan to disarm their heavy artillery. I wouldn't worry about our guys boss, if Johnny says he has a plan, it's got to be a doozy."

"I believe you, Harry, stay in touch with them and let me know what is going on."

"Right."

Immediately after John hung up, the phone rang again. He picked it up and barked, "Garland here."

"This is Commander McVey at Fallon Naval Air Station Mr. Garland; Our radar has been tracking three large choppers that left Reno a short while ago on a flight plan to Battle Mountain. They've just changed course and are heading directly for the repeater on Toiyabe Peak about twenty minutes from you. Hold on a second . . . be right back to you!"

There was a pause while the talk button went off and then clicked on again.

"The radar just picked up what appears to be two F-15s from the general direction of Stead Air Force Base. We can't get any confirmation from the Air Force or the Air National Guard and they're hedge hopping three or four hundred feet off the ground. Do you know anything about the Air Force or Air National Guard jumping in with some help?"

"No, but I sure hope they are. What protective action is the Navy planning on Commander?"

"We're scrambling two fighters and two chopper gun ships to try and intercept them before they get to the peak. Our radio communications are trying to raise them now."

"Good, I'll watch for you and them. I don't know what we can do since we don't do ground-to-air-missile warfare. But we'll take whatever precautions we can. Keep us posted Commander."

"Yes sir."

John toggled the phone again and raised Harry Hutch. He explained what had been reported and asked if the community and the mine buildings had all been evacuated.

"Yes sir, we got everybody out before dawn on company busses except for the security people and those folks down on level five. We've sealed off level five, started up the air filter systems and have the standby power system up and idling in case the surface power goes down."

"Good man, Harry. Tell everyone to keep their heads down and pray a lot. Talk to you later."

He hung up and shook his head. He felt leaden from lack of sleep but knew he had to be wide awake right now. He headed out of the door of his study down to the lodge kitchen where he found a pot of his favorite coffee on tap. He poured and swallowed a couple of mouthfuls and headed out the door.

Looking up toward the low peak on the north side of the hour glass pinch to Toiyabe Canyon he saw a flurry of activity just below the peak and then, looking beyond the peak, he saw two civilian choppers approaching Toiyabe Canyon just above the desert floor.

* * *

At that moment, on the canyon rim high above the trapped vehicles below, Johnny Honey Umptewa was tying a half stick of dynamite to an arrow. He pushed a cap with a very short fuse Swede handed to him into the dynamite stick and laid it beside four others like it.

"Okay, Swede, you have Billy lay those other four arrows down that way along the rim but out of sight of the canyon floor, about sixty feet apart."

Swede nodded and motioned to Billy Carder, the mine's powder man, to carry out Johnny's orders.

Johnny picked up a large bow leaning against a pinion pine and strung the arrow.

"Swede, you sure this cap'll go off in ten seconds?"

"Johnny, I been shootin' rock for forty years, I can tell you to within a gnat's ass when that thing will go off."

Page 261

Johnny smiled. "OK, Kimo Sabe, here's the plan. You light the fuse and start counting. I creep up to the edge of the rim, on the count of eight, I aim and let go. Then we run like hell to the next one and start all over again."

Swede got out his ancient Zippo lighter, almost lost in his huge hand, and said, "Say when, great warrior."

Johnny held out the bow with the notched arrow in it to Swede and said, "When."

As soon as the fuse sputtered to life Swede started a measured count.

Johnny bent down and crept up to the edge of the canyon rim until he was looking down into the barrel of the mortar cannon on the canyon floor. He carefully aimed and on hearing the count of seven, drew back the bow, aimed and fired. He then ducked and ran over to the next fused arrow.

Halfway there, they heard the explosion followed immediately by a second explosion.

"Bingo," Johnny said smiling at the Swede. The Swede held up his thumb in salute, and lit his Zippo. The sound of machine gun fire from below was followed by splattering rock and shreds of pinion pine branches in the area they had just vacated.

As soon as the firing stopped, Johnny motioned for the Swede to light the next missile fuse. The Swede obliged and began his quiet, measured count. Johnny crept up to the canyon rim peering through the shrub at the edge.

He could see that the other mortar and one bazooka had now been moved behind a truck whose bed was loaded with what appeared to be ammo boxes. He aimed at the ground just below the truck's gas tank and at the count of seven, let fly and jumped back to join the running Swede to the next arrow.

Again, the first explosion was followed by a second almost immediately and then several other earth shaking blasts, this time accompanied by screaming and yelling.

The sound of a jet thundering over them caused them to look at each other and then follow the path of the jet. They thought it was probably one of the Navy jets from Fallon heading down Toiyabe range towards the mine.

Swede shrugged his big shoulders and said, "Looks like the cavalry got here a little late, Tonto."

Johnny shrugged his shoulders and said, "We ain't finished yet Kimo. Let's get the next round ready while I skinny up to the edge and spot the next target."

Johnny crawled up very carefully to a low greasewood bush and, taking care not to move the bush, slowly raised his head far enough to see over the edge. What he saw caused him to throw caution to the wind and signal Swede and Billy to come look.

They ran over to the canyon edge and looked down. There, all the remaining guns and ammunition had been thrown in a pile, four men lay on the ground dead or wounded from the ammo and gas tank explosion and the rest were all leaning against the remaining vehicle with their hands spread out on the vehicle top and standing spread eagle.

One of them was yelling, over and over again, "WE GIVE UP, D'YA HEAR ME, WE GIVE UP. DON'T BOMB US, WE GIVE UP."

Swede checked out the canyon cautiously for hidden marksmen. He looked at Johnny Honey Umptewa and Billy and said, "It must'a been them jets. They think we called in the Air Force to bomb 'em."

Johnny and Billy smiled and Johnny said, "No use to tell 'em different, huh?"

Swede shook his head and then yelled down to them, "Take off all yer clothes except yer shorts and throw 'em in the back of the truck where we can see 'em all."

The men below quickly complied even though the temperature was just at 40 degrees. When they had completely undressed, Swede said, "OK, the guy standing nearest to the tailgate, turn around real slow, then take your shirt out of the truck bed, shake it out real good and put it back on."

The man did as he was directed. Then Swede continued,

"Now take out yer pants and do the same thing."

Little by little, one by one, Swede checked out all their clothes for hidden weapons, then had them dress and move on toward the canyon mouth. Billy and the two men on the other side of the canyon stood guard on those who were dressed and waiting.

Suddenly the sound of three enormous blasts in rapid succession shook the ground.

Johnny looked at Swede and Billy. "What the hell was that?"

* * *

Back at the mine, John was standing outside the lodge following the flight path of the jets overhead trying to establish their markings when he saw them drop a bracket of bombs aimed dead at the communications dishes and antennas on the peak.

He watched in consternation as the whole peak blew up after the jets were out of sight.

"What the hell?" he yelled and pulled his walkie talkie out of his belt holster and yelled for Harry Hutch. "Harry, can you see what's going on from up there at the draw?"

"Yeah boss, them F-15s obviously ain't on our side and the Navy boys are comin' in from Fallon right behind 'em."

Just then two Navy jets thundered overhead apparently chasing the F-15s.

After the noise subsided, Harry's voice came on again.

"Better find some cover boss, them two choppers comin' out of Reno are comin' up the road, strafin' as they go and they look like they're carryin' some racks of rockets . . . "

Harry's voice was drowned out by the choppers overhead and then the firing of their rockets was followed by earth shaking blasts.

John stood transfixed as he watched the mine administration building, the power house, the fuel dump and the mine elevator building all disintegrate into balls of flame and smoke.

The two Navy gunships had arrived and were firing air-to-air missiles at the unknown choppers. One of the two choppers erupted into a ball of flame just over the communications peak and the other one dropped down over the ridge of the range and disappeared.

"Harry, can you hear me. This is John."

"Yes sir, I can hear you."

"Are our guys OK?"

"All but the two I stationed just below the communications peak. Looks like they went out with the blast up there."

"Damn, you see any ground activity?"

"No sir, Swede just reported in that he's got a bunch of guys that were all set to come up here bottled up in Box Canyon. He says for us to come and get 'em."

"Can you see where those two F-15s are?"

"They're long gone and the Navy jets are right behind 'em, but they're out of sight. Want us to get the fire fighting crew up there?"

"Just the elevator building and shaft. We need to get that fire out and salvage what we can. I think they only got the top of it and they don't think it's too important anyway. They believe they hit the operations center when they hit the admin building. They don't know it's underground."

"OK, boss, the boys are already heading down to the fire equipment, and they should have enough water up in the upper reservoir to handle that. Harry over and out."

John headed back to the lodge to get on the phone. Fortunately the lodge, situated below the hour glass canyon from the mining area in the town area of the canyon, was not on their target list, at least not yet.

When he got to his study and toggled the phone it came up dead. He quickly unplugged the phone from the conventional phone plug outlet and rolled back a small cabinet to reveal a second phone plug that tied into the secret fiber optics lines.

Dialing quickly, he heard the line connect and Lori's voice come on.

"This is John again. Lori, the war has started. Get your transfer operation people and equipment moved to a secure place immediately. I have reason to believe you may be in serious danger."

Lori's voice was frightened and strained when she answered.

"What . . . what happened?"

"Someone in Air Force F-15s just blew up the communications peak, then two chopper gun ships followed in and destroyed the mining complex.

"Two of my security people are dead and we're trying to put out the fire on the shaft elevator building."

"Oh my God, what happened to Charlie and his operations crew?"

"We already had that sealed off before all this happened, they're OK, and, as you probably know, they're still in operation. Right now, we're the only ones that know that.

"I want you to put out the word that there was a slight interruption while some switch-over took place. If there are any informers on your end, I want them to think that Toiyabe Canyon is out of business."

"I will. I will. But are you all right?"

"I'm fine, Lori. Don't worry about this old man. I was born a survivalist. It's you I'm worried about."

"Ever since we first discussed this, I've been looking around for a safe operating place. This is a terrible thing to say, but I don't trust anyone in our government anymore. Ever since the colonel, two generals and I don't know how many others showed up on Malcolm's payroll, I've been paranoid about everyone. To tell you the truth, the only place I feel safe is the IMF building as long as Alphonse and Jacques are in charge."

There was a pause as John thought and then said, "Bingo, that's the place. Get on the phone and call Alphonse. Tell him what we've discussed and ask his help. Call Martine on your walkie talkie and get him organized. How many people and how much equipment do you have to move?"

Page 266

"About eight people and ten terminals that we can tie into our computer here in the building by phone lines. No one needs to know where we are and I'll leave a dummy operation running here so no one will be aware of what we're doing."

"Perfect. Get rolling and tell Martine what happened so that he's on guard for anything no matter who they appear to be. If they can get someone to fly two F-15s against us, there's no telling what they can subvert. And, Lori . . ."

"Yes, John."

"I love you . . . gotta go now," and he hung up.

A moment later, Harry called him on the walkie talkie to tell him about the men Swede and his crew had trapped and captured in Box Canyon. John called the Naval Base to report the trapped men and the damage suffered as well as get a report on what happened in the air fight.

The base commander told him that one of his choppers had been hit without casualties and had to land in the desert beyond the Toiyabe range. They had shot down one of the F-15s and two choppers with air-to-air missiles and the other F-15 had disappeared, flying low beyond their radar net.

They now knew that the two F-15s had been stolen from McClellan Air Force Base in California that morning by two Air Force captains showing authentic-looking special orders signed by an Air Force general, which had been verified by phone with a now missing general.

There was an inter-service air search underway at that moment to locate the missing F-15 and other teams were examining the wreckage of the other F-15 and the two choppers to see if anything could be found to give them a lead.

"Your security chief, Mr. Hutch, told us about the men over in the Toiyabe sink south of here and we have some choppers over them now. We'll take them over to the base brig and hold them for investigation."

John smiled and said, "If you wait just a minute, the Swede will bring you about eight more of 'em together with some traceable, stolen, Army weapons."

Page 267

"I better have another chopper come over to help carry the prisoners."

John shook his head and smiled. "Boy, I sure hope the fat lady sings pretty soon."

Puzzled, the base commander said, "I beg pardon, sir?"

"Nothing, Captain. By the way, I wonder if you could justify flying a couple of men and I back to Washington on one of your hot jets, one more time?"

"Mr. Garland, in view of the situation and the Presidential order that just arrived here, I'm sure we can justify just about anything you want."

"Thank you, sir. I'll have my chopper fly us over to your base as soon as I can get my men and some things together for the trip. Call me if there's a hangup."

CHAPTER FORTY
THE WORST IS ALWAYS YET TO COME

Andrews Air Force Base
Monday, March 7th, 3:45 p.m.

John marveled at how light the landing was in this incredibly fast machine. They had flown the 3,000 miles from Fallon Naval Air Station to Washington in just over three hours. He gave a thumbs up sign to the lieutenant as he, the Swede and Johnny unbuckled and climbed out of the cockpits.

A jeep picked them up from the plane and took them to the operations building down the field where they were met by the watch commander.

He had a message for John from George Talbot in New York asking that John call him ASAP. The commander directed John to an office where he would have privacy and John dialed George's private line.

George answered the phone on the first ring. "George, I just got in. I'm at Andrews Air Force Base just outside D.C. What's up?"

"John, Malcolm shot out of his office about two hours ago on his way to Washington. The building's chief of security showed me last night's visitor list for Malcolm's private elevator—five Mafia guys, two of the biggest known dope dealers from Columbia and their assorted bodyguards. I don't know what's going on, but it's got to be trouble."

John rubbed his brow. "I know part of what's going on and I'll explain that later. Right now I need to know where Malcolm was going."

"His chauffeur said he heard him on the car phone telling his Washington lobbyist to have a car pick him up at the airport and take him to his private suite at the Mayflower. It's the one on the top floor I told you about."

"Thanks, George. I'll call you later when I get time." As John hung up the phone the watch commander stuck his head in the door and said, "There is a call waiting for you from your Nevada office. It's a Mr. Ross."

John nodded and picked up the phone. "This is John, Charlie. What's up?"

"David Malcolm is on the line calling for you. Harry put it through to me like you told him to do with all calls. I told him you were around here assessing the damage and I would have to locate you if he would hold. He's holding."

John nodded to himself. "Good, patch him through but stay on the line and record the call."

There was a momentary switching sound and then John said, "Garland here."

"Ahh, Mr. Garland, this is David Malcolm calling. I understand you had a bit of a problem there."

John closed his eyes for a moment before answering. "Nothing we can't handle, Mr. Malcolm."

Malcolm answered sarcastically, "Oh really, I understand it was quite devastating."

"Yeah! Obviously I'm pretty busy now. Give me your number and I'll call you back."

"I don't think this can wait, Mr. Garland."

The tone of Malcolm's voice gave John a leaden feeling in the pit of his stomach.

"All right then, go ahead."

Malcolm's unctuous tone suggested a cat who had just swallowed a canary. "As you well know, Mr. Garland, I don't want your system operating unless we, that is, I, am in charge of its operation. Since you've so cleverly arranged to put that possibility out of my reach, I'm afraid you've left me only one option."

John hesitated to ask the question he knew he must. "What option is that Mr. Malcolm?"

"Since you, Mr. Garland, are the only one with the authority to shut down Global's operations, you must exercise that authority as soon as possible and keep it shut down for the rest of this week."

"I'm afraid I can't do that, Mr. Malcolm."

Malcolm's voice was hard and sharp as a razor's edge when he answered. "I'm afraid you must, Mr. Garland, or you will never see Lorelei Young alive again."

It took all the strength John could muster to regain his composure before answering. "What do you mean?"

"I mean that one of the most sophisticated, well-trained terrorists on four continents has Miss Young in his custody right now, waiting to hear from me as to *what* to do with her . . . and *how to do it*. Do you understand Mr. Garland?"

John had a sinking sensation in his gut and his brain was reeling. If the phone had not been made of strong plastic it would now have been crushed in his grip. Finally, he regained control and answered.

"How do I know this is true?"

"Oh, I'll give you time to check it out, say forty-five minutes to place a call to her office. I think you'll find that they will tell you that the President sent a special car for her with a security contingent to escort her to an emergency meeting. They were, of course, my people in disguise."

John stalled for time to think.

"If it is true, it's still going to take a couple of hours for me to reach every operating system around the world and for them to verify my orders."

"I'll call you back in exactly forty-five minutes from now, Mr. Garland. We can discuss the rest then. Oh, and Mr. Garland, don't even think of doing something foolish like calling the FBI. I am the only link you have to Lorelei Young!"

John dropped his head to his chest until he heard Charlie's voice on the line. "I got it on tape boss. Want me to call the FBI or something?"

"No, Charlie, there isn't time for that. I know where Malcolm is. I'm less than twenty minutes from there now. He doesn't know I'm in Washington. You get hold of DEP-COMM's security and check out Malcolm's story. Then call Alphonse Courdelet and tell him what happened. Have him contact Martine, who's supposed to be guarding Lori. Tell him I'll call him back in the next thirty minutes. I'll call you as soon as I can."

He hung up the phone and whirled to talk to the waiting watch commander.

"Do you have a car with a siren and red light available?"

"Yessir."

"I need it with a driver who knows the city backwards. It's not only a national emergency, it's a matter of life and death."

The officer jumped into action. "Yessir, follow me."

Swede and Johnny, carrying all their baggage, ran to keep up with John as they asked him, "What's up Big John?"

"I'll tell you on the way," and they all piled into the car. The car was weaving its way through the Washington traffic at breakneck speed, lights flashing and siren wailing. The young driver did indeed know the short cut to the Mayflower Hotel. John turned to him and said, "Turn off the siren when we're a couple of blocks away."

"Yes sir, we're about two minutes from there now."

John looked at his watch. 4:20 p.m. It was exactly fifteen minutes since Malcolm had given him his deadline. He dug into his flight bag until he felt the holster containing his automatic pistol.

He pulled it out, jacked a shell into the chamber, pushed the safety on and clipped it to his belt under his wind breaker. The Swede looked at him sideways in a quizzical manner and shrugged his shoulders. John told him Malcolm had kidnapped Lori and was holding her as a hostage to get him to shut down the Global operation for a week.

"You want me and Johnny to go up with you boss? We've both got guns with us."

"No, stay with the car. I'll need your help when I get back down here."

"Yes, sir, we'll be here and we'll be ready."

The car turned into the hotel's basement garage and stopped at a barrier. An attendant looked out of his kiosk win-

Page 272

dow. John affected his best "general" look and said, "General Daniels, I'm expected and I wish to remain incognito."

The attendant nodded politely, used to the clandestine visits of admirals and generals in the venerable old hotel's garage. The opened the barrier for the Air Force VIP car.

John directed the sergeant to the private elevator area and jumped out to punch the button. The door slid open immediately as if waiting for him.

Twelve floors later the door slid open silently at its destination and John looked toward the door he had been told was Malcolm's special suite. Then he walked to the apartment next door, pulled out his pocket knife and quietly forced the lock on the door.

Inside, he quietly checked out the apartment. It was unoccupied. Taking a glass from the butler's pantry, he went over to the wall between the two apartments and placed the glass against the wall and his ear to the glass bottom, quietly listening for a moment. Aside from footsteps pacing back and forth, he heard no sound.

Going to a bedroom window that faced the street behind the hotel at the wall between the suites, John opened it and looked out. The old hotel had built the suites after the initial construction so the suites sat on the original roof, inside of a low parapet.

He climbed out onto the roof in the cold air, walked quietly to the bedroom of the adjoining suite. Carefully looking in, he saw it was empty. He checked his watch. He had fourteen minutes of Malcolm's deadline left.

Using his pocket knife again, John inserted it between the upper and lower window and worked the blade back and forth until he had pushed open the window latch. Raising the window quietly, he climbed inside. Once inside, he paused again to listen for sounds of voices. There were none. John said a silent prayer that Malcolm would be alone and then slowly inched the door open so he could see the small entryway and the room beyond. Malcolm was standing at a window, drink in hand looking down on the darkening city below.

John took the automatic from its holster and silently walked into the room toward Malcolm. Malcolm must have sensed his presence because he started to turn just as John reached him. John's left fist shot out with a 195 pounds of mad mining engineer behind it and connected with the point of Malcolm's chin. Malcolm fell like a sack of potatoes. John rubbed his fist and then picked up the phone and dialed the number of the International Monetary Fund.

The IMF operator answered and John identified himself and asked to speak to Alphonse Courdelet. The general came on the line immediately.

"Where are you, *mon ami?*"

"I'm at Malcolm's hotel, what did you find out?"

"They are both missing. Miss Young left her office over an hour ago, supposedly for a meeting with the President. Martine cannot be found, and he does not answer his walkie talkie. I did not alert anyone until I talked with you."

John nodded his head. "Good. Did Charlie tell you what Malcolm said?"

"Yes, that is why I am very concerned. I checked with the Commerce building security saying that I was trying to locate our man, Colonel Martine. He said he had not left the building and I suggested that he may have left with Miss Young.

"The security man said that two secret service men had picked up Miss Young in a White House limousine to take her to the meeting with the President. Jacques Martine was not with them."

John took a deep breath before answering. "That means Malcolm's man got Lori and Jacques is probably still in the building somewhere, tied up or dead. You better call DEPCOMM security back and tell them to start looking for Martine. I'll know where Lori is in a few minutes. Call you back when I can."

As he hung up the phone, John felt Malcolm stirring at his feet and leaned over and searched him for weapons. He removed a small automatic from Malcolm's side pocket and dropped it into his own jacket pocket. Then he pulled Malcolm up and sat him on the couch.

Malcolm slowly returned to consciousness and groaned as he sat up on the couch. His eyes widened when he recognized John standing over him with a gun.

"How did you get here? I just talked to you in Nevada!" He looked at his watch to verify the time and then slowly focused his eyes on John.

"Where is Lorelei Young being held Malcolm?" Malcolm shook his head and said, "I don't know. The men holding her will allow you to talk to her to verify her condition."

John's face became rock hard as he looked at Malcolm.

"Mister, you subverted the army, stole military planes and destroyed my mining complex worth several million dollars. You caused at least two of my people to be killed and several to be injured to say nothing of the Navy's losses. Why did you do all of this and then kidnap Lori?"

"Because we knew that all that would not shut down your system. We needed a diversionary tactic."

"You son of a bitch, you did all that just for a diversionary tactic? Normally, I don't believe in violence, but once in a while I run into someone so arrogant and so psychopathic that violence is the only thing they understand and respect.

"I'm holding a gun on you that can splatter your brains all over that couch and you're giving me this bull shit?"

He reached down and grabbed Malcolm's nose between his thumb and forefinger, squeezing and twisting it until Malcolm had tears streaming down his face and was screaming in pain.

John then grabbed Malcolm by his shirt front and picked him up to his feet as if he only weighed a few pounds. He drove his fist into Malcolm's midsection so hard that it disappeared, doubling him up in excruciating pain.

John continued talking in a deadly, cold, quiet voice.

"Arrogant assholes like you have no compunction about killing as many innocent people as necessary to get your way.

You think nothing about trying to destroy a system that can save the world from financial chaos just to satisfy your greed and lust for power."

Malcolm was rubbing his nose and mumbling, "I'll make you pay for this. I'll make you pay."

John grabbed Malcolm's ear and twisted it until it felt to Malcolm that he would pull it off his head. He screamed again and fell to the floor crying. John grabbed him by the collar and pulled him to his feet again.

"You're going to tell me where you're holding Lorelei Young or I'm going to pull your nose off your face and your ears off your head. I'm going to make you feel so much pain you'll wish you were dead. *Do you understand me, asshole?"*

To give emphasis to his words he twisted Malcolm's other ear until he fell to the ground screaming. He reached for Malcolm's throbbing nose and lifted him back to his feet by it. The pain was excruciating and Malcolm screamed for John to stop.

"Stop, stop . . . I'll tell you!"

"Start talking."

Malcolm told him that a man known only as 'Colonel K' had his men pick Lori up at her office, posing as secret service men. She went willingly because she thought it was legitimate.

"I have no idea where they went or where they are. I only have the number of a cellular phone . . . that's how I reach them to let them know if you're going to go along with the plan."

"And if you don't call within that time?"

"They'll kill her, dump her body and get out of town."

When Malcolm stopped, John grabbed his ear again and twisted. "And if you call on time what happens?"

Malcolm said, "They will set up a method for you to verify Miss Young is alive."

John's mind was reeling at the audacity. "Let me have that phone number."

When Malcolm hesitated, John reached for his nose again

and Malcolm quickly gave him the number.

John picked up the phone with his left hand and dialed Alphonse's number. The operator quickly put him through. John told Alphonse what had happened to Lori but that he still didn't know what had happened to Jacques.

He told Alphonse, "I'm going to set up a meeting with them on the premise that I won't send out the orders to shut down Global's operating system until I can personally verify that Lori is OK."

Alphonse thought about that for a moment. "That could be very dangerous, *mon ami*. Surely there is a way we can provide some assistance or cover you in some way?"

"No good. If they spot anything out of the ordinary it may put Lori's life in jeopardy. From the sound of it, Malcolm hired the top gun in the terrorist field."

"What is his name?"

"According to Malcolm, he is just called 'Colonel K.'"

"Colonel K!" Alphonse exploded. "That man has been trained both as a terrorist and a terrorist fighter. He has been hired by a dozen different countries to do unspeakable things that they could never be publicly associated with."

"Alphonse, I don't have much time. I must try something, anything, to see if I can get Lori away from them. I have an idea, and I am going to need someone from your old Legionnaire's group. Someone fearless, small and a dead shot. Someone who could hide comfortably in the trunk of a limousine."

Alphonse thought for a moment. "Perhaps. He is not with my group at the IMF, but he is a special agent at the French Embassy and used to be in our old Algiers command group. I would have to call and see if he is available to do the job you have in mind and see if he is willing."

"Good, get on the horn and call him and call me right back with the answer. We've got exactly eight minutes before Malcolm has to initiate a call to them."

"*Oui, mon ami*. I will call you back as soon as I have contacted him. What is your number?"

John told him, hung up the phone and said, "You and I are going to see Lori together Malcolm. You are going to do and say exactly what I tell you to do and say. If there is one tiny slip up, if you use any kind of code word to tip them off, I am going to see that you are gut shot through the side, shoot your balls off and shoot off your kneecaps.

"Now you don't know what pain is 'til you experience dying a slow death in that manner. You're not just going to die, you're going to die a very painful death. Got it?"

Malcolm nodded his head and gently touched his throbbing nose.

The phone rang and John nodded to Malcolm to answer it while he listened. When he heard Alphonse's voice he took the phone and said, "It's me, Alphonse."

"My friend at the embassy just wants to know where to meet you."

"Good, tell him to meet us on the street behind the Mayflower Hotel a couple of hundred feet south of the parking-garage exit."

"Very good, he will be there in a few minutes."

John hung up and said, "Now for our next act, Mr. Malcolm. Be sure you get it right because your pain-free life may depend on it."

John asked Malcolm if he had a limousine in the hotel garage. Malcolm told him he did. John asked him if it had a car phone. Malcolm said it did. Then he told Malcolm exactly what to do and say.

Malcolm made the call with one and a half minutes to spare. He told Colonel K that Garland insisted on seeing Lori alive and well before he would initiate a shutdown of the Global network.

The man on the other end asked why they couldn't just grab Garland too, force him to make the call and then, eliminate them both.

"First of all you can't force this man to do anything, and second, he's not stupid. He set up a procedure long ago which

Page 278

requires his associates to see him free and clear of any force to verify that his order is of his own free will before they carry it out, even if it meant that he might be killed otherwise.

"My bodyguard, my chauffeur and I will bring John Garland to wherever you are holding Miss Young in my limo. Just tell me where you want us to meet you."

The voice at the other end of the line said, "You have a phone in your car?"

Malcolm looked at John who nodded. "Yes, of course I do," Malcolm said.

"What's the number?"

Malcolm gave him the number.

"Good, you, your body guard and Garland will get in your car, drive north on Connecticut Avenue 'til you intersect Military Drive. Turn right onto Military Drive and into Rock Creek Park. I'll call you thirty minutes from now somewhere along that route and tell you what to do from there."

Malcolm, arrogant to the end, said, "What's the matter, after I put up several million dollars to finance this operation, you don't trust me?"

The man answered, "You didn't trust me with all the money up front. Furthermore, the reason I'm still alive is I don't trust anyone," and hung up.

Taking a lock hold on Malcolm's wrist, John twisted until he had Malcolm walking on his toes and steered him out of the apartment to the private elevator.

When they got to the basement garage, he pushed Malcolm into a corner until he could see that no one but his crew was there. He then walked him out to the car where Swede, Johnny and the military driver were waiting.

"Where's your limo, Malcolm?" Malcolm pointed to a stall with his head. "Where's the key?"

"My chauffeur has it, but he is up in his room."

"What's his room number?" John asked.

"Room 327."

There was a house phone by the elevator and John walked

Malcolm over to it.

"Call him and tell him you're sending a special driver up to get a uniform from him and the keys and that he can take the rest of the night off."

Malcolm did as he was told. John motioned to Johnny Honey Umptewa. "Johnny, you're going to play chauffeur tonight. You've got five minutes to get upstairs to room 327, get into the chauffeur outfit, get the car keys and get back here." Johnny was on his way before John stopped talking.

John told the Army sergeant to get back to the base as fast as he could and tell the base commander that the kidnapped lady is the under secretary of Commerce. He was not to call any police agencies, but if he could put a couple of choppers in the air to circle the area around Rock Creek Park, John would call him from a car phone for backup when he was ready.

Then he asked the sergeant for the base commander's number and told him he would call the commander as soon as he was able to and tell him what backup or assistance was needed. The sergeant peeled out of the garage.

The elevator opened and Johnny ran out in a tight-fitting, but passable, chauffeur's uniform and cap, waving a set of keys as he ran for the limo to get it started.

John walked Malcolm to the car's rear door, shoved him inside and climbed in beside him. The Swede picked up their bags and threw all but one into the trunk of the car, slammed the lid and climbed in and sat sideways on a jump seat opposite John and facing Malcolm. The limo drove out of the garage and pulled up to the curb a couple of hundred feet past the exit.

A small, slight man with a limp came up to the car. John rolled the window down and identified himself. Lt. Chalfont introduced himself. John explained that he needed a secret backup to insure Malcolm would do his bidding without giving them away. If there was trouble, he then needed Chalfont to provide some surprise gunfire. It would require Lt. Chalfont to hide in the trunk of the car with a weapon pointed at Malcolm.

At the first sign of a double cross on Malcolm's part or on orders from John, Chalfont was to gut shoot Malcolm, shoot his balls off and then shoot off his knee caps. After that, they would be in a shooting war with whoever they were confronting. Did he think he could do that?

"In my sleep, *M'sieu,*" Lt. Chalfont answered. Johnny passed his knife back to John who quickly cut a nearly invisible air hole into the rear seat for Chalfont while Johnny opened the trunk of the car for him. There were two lap robes in the trunk which Chalfont used to make himself comfortable.

John showed Chalfont how he could use the sharp end of the tire iron to turn the spring-loaded trunk latch and open it from the inside.

Johnny Honey Umptewa removed two gallon-size plastic bags from the travel bags they had transferred from the Army vehicle's trunk to the trunk of the limo. He was stuffing them under the car's dashboard way above its steering column when John asked him what was in the bags and Johnny smiled as he replied, "Some of Swede's dynamite fuses and caps. A good scout always goes prepared."

John looked at his watch. They were fifteen minutes into the allotted contact time.

"Let's go, Johnny. I'll give you directions to Connecticut Avenue and to Rock Creek Park."

The big car slid smoothly from the curb.

John thought, *Now all we've got to hope for is that they didn't have anyone watching the back of the hotel and catch our action.*

As they drove, John outlined several possible plans of action based on what might be the case they were confronting.

"Mostly," John said, "we'll have to play it by ear. Johnny, if you use that dynamite, make sure you know how to fuse it."

"It's already fused. We figured that ten seconds would be the best time. It worked fine at Box Canyon, and I got the count down pretty good from Swede."

Page 281

"Good. If I'm out of the car and you're still behind the wheel, watch for my finger signal. If I give you two fingers down, it's dynamite time. Pick a target farthest from us. I'll concentrate on whoever is holding Lori. Swede, you're left-handed so you start taking them out from left to right. I'll start from right to left. If we're lucky enough to meet in the middle, we win."

"Gotcha boss. I got my automatic sawed-off shotgun in a coat sleeve holster. I can trigger off five shots before they hear the sound from the first one."

John noticed a car following them as they approached Military Road which cut across the park. When they turned onto Military Road, the car behind also turned and he could see four men in the car.

He said, "Don't turn around to look but there's a car behind us with four men in it, no doubt armed to the teeth."

Two minutes later, the car phone rang and John picked it up and held it so that Malcolm could answer while he listened.

"This is Malcolm."

"Colonel K. Mr. Malcolm, apparently you have Mr. Garland with you and it appears you are not being followed either on the ground or in the air. That's good."

"Yes, Colonel, he's riding in the back with me. My bodyguard is covering him."

"Fine, Mr. Malcolm. Now there is a car behind you, it's going to speed up and go around your car. You just follow it."

"I'll tell my chauffeur."

"Good. I'll call you back in a few minutes and give you further directions."

That time of night in the cold March weather, Rock Creek Park was all but deserted. The car that had been following them sped up and went around them to take the lead.

John was trying to analyze the mind of the man who had called on the phone. Obviously very clever and very survival oriented. Probably guerrilla or army training. He had every move mapped out and undoubtedly had drilled his men in sev-

Page 282

eral possible scenarios.

The park was a perfect setting because the Colonel could choose his vantage points giving him a perfect view of a large area. In the event of trouble, he would have plenty of time to take evasive or defensive action.

"I gather from the phone conversation that you still owe him a substantial amount of money for this job?"

"A million and a half."

John shook his head. "That's a lot of money."

"It was supposed to guarantee success for kidnapping someone almost as important as the President."

"When is he supposed to get the balance?"

"At the end of the week when Global's operation is shut down."

"And what was he going to do with Lori after you got me to shut down the operation?"

"The plan was to turn her over to you after the week was up."

"That's bull shit Malcolm and you know it. Lori could identify the man and he hasn't even allowed you to know what he looks like. You don't give a damn about anybody, do you?"

Malcolm flinched and put his hand up to protect his throbbing, sore nose.

The car had just crossed a bridge over Rock Creek and the lead car turned south onto a tree-lined dirt road. As they approached a clearing, the lead car stopped and Johnny smoothly stopped the limo to a halt thirty feet behind the lead car.

The phone rang again and John, having outlined what he wanted Malcolm to say, nodded to Malcolm to pick it up and answer it since they were now being watched from the lead car.

"Malcolm speaking."

"Malcolm, my men wish to shake down your people."

"You understand that my bodyguard carries a weapon and is going to keep it on him with which to control Garland."

"Yes, of course."

"Very well Colonel, send them over."

John quickly gave his gun to Swede, removed the clip from Malcolm's automatic and placed the gun under a short liqueur bottle in the car's bar while he shoved the clip through the air hole slit into the trunk of the car.

Johnny slid his knife into the springs under the front seat of the car without apparently moving a muscle.

Two men got out of the lead car and walked back to stand one on each side of the limo. They motioned to Johnny, "Please get out of the car."

Johnny opened the door and got out looking for all the world like a frightened, immigrant chauffeur holding his hands in the air.

The man on Johnny's side of the car expertly patted him down while the man on the other side opened the front door, checked the glove compartment, felt under the seat and over the visors and ran his hand along the underside of the dash board looking for a clip-on holster. Apparently the plastic bags of dynamite were out of his reach, and he signaled the other man that all was satisfactory. The other man then nodded to Johnny and said, "Get back in the car."

Then he walked to the back door on his side and opened the door revealing Swede's massive shoulders and back.

"Will you please step out, sir?"

Swede swiveled smoothly out of the jump seat and un-coiled to his full six foot, seven inches and held his arms out and said, "My gun's in a clip-on holster under my jacket."

Swede's sawed off shotgun was in his coat sleeve which was too high for the man to reach. He was satisfied by John's pistol, holstered and now clipped to Swede's belt."

"OK, big man, want to step to one side please." Then nodding to John, he said, "Your name?"

"John Garland."

"Want to step out please, Mr. Garland?"

John stepped out and raised his hands. The man shook him down quickly and then nodded to the other man who opened the door where Malcolm was sitting.

"You Mr. Malcolm?"

"Yes."

"No guns?"

"That's what I have that bodyguard for."

"Yes sir, mind if I just look inside a minute?"

Malcolm looked at John and could feel Chalfont's gun poking him in the back.

"Help yourself."

The man looked in, felt under the jump seat, the back seat and the side pockets on the doors. Then stood up and signaled the other man.

"OK."

"You can all get back in the car now."

John slid back in beside Malcolm and Swede slid back onto the jump seat as before. The two men walked silently back to the car and John could see one of them on a car phone, obviously reporting to the Colonel.

Moments later, the car phone in the limo beeped its signal. Malcolm picked it up. "Malcolm speaking."

"My men are satisfied. Please follow them again."

John had to admire the care with which Colonel K handled the operation.

The lead car started up and slowly drove on along the dirt road. Johnny started the limo and smoothly fell in behind them. The tension in the limousine could be felt by everyone.

CHAPTER FORTY-ONE
THE FAT LADY FINALLY SINGS

Rock Creek Park
March 7, 6:10 p.m.

The phone rang again and, after a signal from John, Malcolm answered, holding the phone so John could hear the conversation.

"Malcolm speaking."

"In a few moments you will come upon a parked van. Miss Young is in the van. She is tied to a seat in the back. There is no one in the van, but I am in the vicinity where I can observe you both and hear everything that takes place. My men will be beyond the van to observe your car and the other side of the van.

"Tell Mr. Garland the van is rigged with a powerful bomb and I have, in my hand, the triggering device. Any attempt by him to remove Miss Young will result in both of their deaths. Is that clear?"

Malcolm looked at John and John nodded. "Yes, Colonel, that is quite clear."

The Colonel continued, "Mr. Garland will leave the car by himself. After he is satisfied that she has not been harmed, he is to return to your car, get in and await my call. Is everything quite clear?"

John nodded his head and Malcolm answered. "Quite clear, Colonel."

"We will speak again later Mr. Malcolm," and the Colonel hung up. Malcolm cradled the car phone. His hands were sweaty.

The van suddenly loomed in the darkness parked at the edge of an open field area. The lead car slowly drove past it and made a U-turn so that its headlights were focused on the van and its open door.

John closed his eyes for a moment then reached for the

door handle and got out. Walking quickly to the van, he looked into the open side door and saw Lori bound hand and foot to a swiveling van chair.

She cried out when she saw John who quickly held his finger to his lips as surreptitiously as possible.

"Are you all right, Miss Young?"

She nodded her head and said, "Yes, Mr. Garland, I'm fine so far. Will I be getting out of here soon?"

"As quickly as possible. Please keep your spirits up and know that all those who love you will be working unceasingly for your release."

With that John quickly turned and strode back to Malcolm's limousine. His face set grimly as he got into the car.

"You dirty sonofabitch," he muttered under his breath to Malcolm.

The phone rang immediately and Malcolm, with a faint glimmer of hope, picked it up. "Malcolm speaking."

"Put Mr. Garland on, please."

Malcolm handed the phone to John without a word.

"This is Garland."

"Are you satisfied, Mr. Garland?"

"Yes, she's obviously alive and seems to be unharmed so far."

"According to Malcolm's information, this lady was supposed to mean more to you than just 'Miss Young.'"

John thought quickly before answering.

"Look, Colonel, I sense you are an intelligent, well-educated man, despite the business you're in."

"Go on," the Colonel said.

"Please correct me if I'm wrong, but this sort of thing is your business, is it not?"

"That is correct, Mr. Garland."

"I assume that you do not conduct this sort of business without being well paid for your services."

"You assume correctly," Colonel K answered.

John continued, "As I understand it, Colonel, Mr. Malcolm

still owes you $1.5 million for this particular service contract."

"Yes."

"I must presume from your modus operandi that you are a well-informed man and therefore you must also be aware that every country in the world worth living in, is teetering on the brink of economic disaster."

There was a long pause as the Colonel thought before answering.

"Yes, I must admit that is a reasonable analysis."

"Then, in order to have a pleasant environment in which to spend your fee there must be a place for you to go that has financial stability."

"Go on," the Colonel urged.

"The Global computerized monetary system is the only way for a financially stable, and therefore pleasant, country to come to pass at the moment. As you must know, most paper currency is now considered all but valueless."

The Colonel interrupted John. "What is it you are leading to, Mr. Garland?"

"Just this. If you finish this job and get paid in paper money, there is a good chance that it will be all but worthless within a few weeks or months. However, if you get paid in the new computer credits, credited to a legal account of your choice, be it a numbered Swiss bank account or any other account, a banker such as Malcolm is the only one who will be able to arrange such a transaction."

"Agreed," the Colonel answered cautiously.

John continued. "Now, if Malcolm were to suddenly die in the next few moments, you would never be able to collect that $1.5 million whether it was in valueless currency or spendable credits. You would have put your life and your efforts on the line for nothing."

"What is it you are proposing, Mr. Garland?"

"What I am proposing, Colonel, is a swap of Miss Young for David Malcolm."

Malcolm whimpered, "Oh no."

"I don't understand, Mr. Garland?"

"You will," John answered "when I tell you that I am not Malcolm's prisoner, he is my prisoner and the big man that is supposed to be his bodyguard is in fact, my man guarding Malcolm's body.

"If we should decide to dispose of Mr. Malcolm, all your work will have been in vain, regardless of what happens to Miss Young or myself."

There was a long pause before the Colonel answered.

"I must assume that what you have just told me is true or else I would have heard from Mr. Malcolm by now. Therefore, please continue."

"I have found, Colonel, that Mr. Malcolm cannot stand pain at all. Now if he were in your custody, I am quite certain that you would find a convenient way to assure your payment was made to an existing, legitimate account that had been transferred to the new computerized monetary system.

"If such is the case, then there would be absolutely no need to hold Miss Young since it is to your advantage to have the new system in operation. That is, if you want some pleasant, untroubled place such as the French Riviera in which to spend your fee."

"Ah yes, Mr. Garland, I see what you are driving at. You are a clever man my friend. You would have been great in my business. How do you propose that we make our, shall we say, 'swap'?"

"Call me back in ten minutes and I will have worked out something."

"Very well Mr. Garland, ten minutes it is," and he clicked off his phone.

Malcolm's face was shiny with sweat. "You're not going to swap me to that man? He'll kill me the moment he gets his money."

John looked at Malcolm. "It didn't seem to bother you that this is what he was going to do to Lori. Now shut up."

Turning to Swede and Johnny, John began to outline

Page 290

his plan.

"I'm sure that the Colonel must have a couple of other men with him, probably somewhere in the trees. I can tell that he's on the phone right now to the men in the car and I'm just as sure he isn't about to let us live after the swap.

Johnny, on my signal, I want you to turn the car around and drive back into the trees on the road we came in on and stop so that one side of the car is shielded from that field's view."

"Got it Big John."

"Now, once there, park your hat on the back of your seat so it looks like you're still sitting there. Take a bag of those short-fuse sticks from under the dash and slip out on the blind side into the trees. Reach under the dash and pull the door light fuse so it won't go on when you open the door. Now hand Swede that other bag of sticks.

Swede, you're going to be on the blind side too, but it wouldn't do for you not to make an appearance, so you get out of the car on that side and stand up where they can see you. By the way, hand me my gun."

The Swede complied and then slid his sawed-off shotgun out of his sleeve.

"Here you go, John."

"Chalfont, can you hear me?"

"Oui, M'sieu," the muffled voice in the trunk answered.

"When you hear Johnny get out of his door, pop the trunk lid very carefully, slip out and close it. It is so dark out there right now, I doubt they can see any of this, especially if you're screened by the car and the trees.

"Johnny and Chalfont, you two sneak into the trees and double around behind that hill at the far side of the field where the van is parked. I'm sure there are other people up there with heavy duty weapons who have orders to make sure we don't get out alive after the swap. We must get them before they have a chance to do anything. Swede and I will try to disable the car with the other four in it."

Page 291

"What about calling the watch commander at Edwards for those choppers to back us up?" Swede asked.

"No time for that. Besides, we don't dare tie up the phone or take a chance that the Colonel has equipment that lets him monitor calls we might try to make on it. When the fireworks start, those choppers will see it and head this way."

John pulled out his gun and clicked off the safety.

"Swede, do you have any electric caps in that powder bag?"

"No, only primacord, fuses and caps."

"OK, then I want you to wire together Malcolm's hands. Then wire two sticks around his chest so they can be seen on his chest when he walks. Don't put caps in 'em. This is strictly for show.

Now, when the call comes, and after the car is backed up to the tree line, I'll walk Malcolm over to a central point for the prisoner swap. Swede, you'll be out and behind the car. Get your short-fuse sticks out and get ready to make like a grenade launcher on my signal, or if that car starts to move towards us before my signal. Everybody ready?"

"Ready," Johnny said excitedly.

"Me too," the Swede chimed in.

"Vivre la France," came the muffled assent from Chalfont in the trunk.

"You can't do this to me," Malcolm was whined. "The man will just torture me and then kill me."

John looked at Malcolm.

"Don't worry, asshole. If we get the chance, we're gonna pull you out of the fire just so I can have the pleasure of seeing you go before a court of law."

Just then the phone rang. John picked it up.

"This is Garland."

The Colonel responded, "I presume you have decided on a method for handling this transfer?"

"Yes, and I presume you have a plan for seeing that you get what you want and we don't get away."

"Clever man, Mr. Garland."

"Clever enough to assure you that if we do not get a head start, my friend, Mr. Malcolm will not be alive for long."

"Oh, how so?"

"That is something you will learn should you attempt to double cross me, dear Colonel."

The Colonel sighed a tired sigh. "Very well, Mr. Garland, please describe your plan."

"I am going to have Malcolm's chauffeur turn the car around and drive back onto the road we came in on at the edge of this field. Then I will get out of the car with Malcolm acting as a shield and walk halfway to the van.

"You, or one of your men, will go to the van, untie Miss Young and bring her to the same halfway point. You will notice that Mr. Malcolm is wired with explosives so that any gunfire will cause a button to be depressed and Mr. Malcolm will disappear in a puff of smoke.

"The range of our radio-controlled firing mechanism is limited so that when you have Malcolm safely away and I have Miss Young safely in the car and underway, the triggering device will no longer be within radio range. Is everything clear?"

"Clear, Mr. Garland. You may begin when ready," and the Colonel hung up.

John nodded to Johnny Honey Umptewa to turn the big car around slowly and head back into the trees.

"Make sure you turn the car so that the trunk lid can't be seen from the clearing."

Johnny nodded and drove onto the road they had come in on until they were somewhat shielded by the trees. There he stopped the car.

"OK, Johnny and Chalfont, do your disappearing act. And Malcolm, if you hope to get out of this alive, you better not say one frigging word. Do you understand me?"

Malcolm nodded his head nervously as Johnny barely cracked open the car door, wriggled out onto the ground and disappeared. John could hear Chalfont click open the trunk lid slightly, slide out of the trunk and click the lid back.

"OK Swede, get out on that side and watch over the top of the car. Better do that from as far to the front as possible so you've got more of the car's sheet metal between you and any one that might be shooting at you."

Swede slid out of his side and allowed himself to be seen from the clearing.

"Now, big shot, your turn." John prodded Malcolm, who reluctantly opened the door and stepped out with John right behind him.

They slowly started walking toward the van. One of the men who had been in the other car walked over to the van, un-tied Lori and slowly began walking her towards John and Malcolm. The other three men were lined up behind the car they had arrived in.

John searched the woods behind the van but could see nothing. He heard the faint sound of choppers in the distance. Small comfort at this time. His ear was straining to gauge the distance of the approaching choppers when he heard a slight sound to the left of the hill, like a grunt.

He saw no one else reacting to the sound, but he was sure of what that sound meant. One of the Colonel's backup force was out of action.

They were five feet apart and John slowly pulled Malcolm's coat back so that the man bringing Lori could see the dynamite in the glare of the car's headlights. The man nodded, they continued and met.

The man shoved Lori toward John and he caught her arm as she stumbled. She was sobbing quietly and John whispered, "Don't react, sweetheart. Just walk towards the limo while I walk backward to keep them covered."

Then he heard the second sound, a thump and a clang, off to his right. *That would be Johnny,* he thought, and then he heard the Colonel's voice.

"Mark, are you OK?" John tried to pinpoint the source of the Colonel's voice halfway up the hill. Then he heard a grunt,

"Yeah," he recognized Johnny trying to disguise his voice.

The Colonel was obviously suspicious and called out again, "Barry, buzz my position."

"Time to go to war," John said to Lori as he ran diagonally towards the trees, slightly to the left of the limo, dragging her behind him.

"Swede, get away from the limo." He could see Swede heave a mighty. over-arm throw and a trail of sparks from a sputtering fuse just as John dove into the trees pulling Lori down with him.

There was a mighty double explosion as the Colonel's car erupted in a ball of flame, consuming the three body guards with it. Almost simultaneously, the van went up with a bang and Malcolm and his captor fell to the ground shielding their heads from falling debris.

The sound of the choppers was now very loud and John was sure they had seen the blasts. He grabbed Lori and ran in a crouched position to his left from where he had entered the trees and fell to the ground with her.

Rolling over and looking at the hill above the burning van John saw the muzzle flash of a weapon followed by a whistling sound and an explosion near where he and Lori had entered the stand of trees from the field.

He was straining to pinpoint the position of that muzzle flash when a second rocket's flash gave him a precise fix. A split second later the limo stood on its end and the gas tank exploded as the missile impacted.

"He must have night vision glasses on," John whispered to Lori. "Keep your beautiful, blond head down because he can see that color in an instant."

John raised his head to see if he could spot the Swede and what had happened to him, but the Swede was nowhere to be seen. Malcolm and his guard were still lying on the ground in the middle of the field shielding their heads.

John said, "Lori, you stay here and don't move. I'll be back in a couple of minutes." Lori nodded and made herself as small as possible.

John got up and quickly ran through the trees toward the limo and around the perimeter of the field. Darting across the fire glow, he ran into the stand of trees just beyond the limo and kept running.

Then he quickly changed his course. A rocket whistled over his head and hit the ground where he had been a moment earlier. Then he suddenly ran full tilt onto field, snapped a shot at the man with Malcolm, hitting him in the back, grabbed Malcolm and stood him up on his feet. Using him as a shield, John started to walk deliberately towards the last muzzle flash.

"Okay Colonel, this is your meal ticket, shoot if you don't expect to collect."

The sound of the choppers indicated they were closing in fast. Suddenly, John saw a man stand up on the hillside holding a shoulder-fired missile launcher. It had to be the Colonel.

"Mr. Garland, let us arrive at a quick agreement. I am throwing away my weapon. I still have a pistol, but I am only interested in Malcolm, my friend. You may keep a weapon aimed at him as insurance, but I'm coming down there on a motorcycle. As part of our bargain, I will pick him up and be on my way. Acceptable?"

"Come on, Colonel, he's all yours."

"You can't do this to me, Garland, *it's . . . it's unfair!*" Malcolm was frightened out of his wits.

One of the choppers was overhead now, trying to determine who the enemy was. On the hill across the clearing, Colonel K pulled a motorcycle upright from the bushes, cranked it twice. As it roared to life, he jumped on and careened down the hill towards John, with his hand wrapped around both a pistol and the handlebar. John held Malcolm upright by the scruff of the neck as he approached.

Out of the corner of his eye, John suddenly saw the Swede break out of the trees just to the left of the motorcycle and bring his shotgun to bear on the Colonel.

Three sharp blasts could be heard over the thumping sound

of the chopper blades and the motorcycle suddenly fell to the ground, the wheels still churning. The Colonel tried to drag himself away.

John could see the Colonel pull a grenade from his upper pocket. John dropped his hold on Malcolm, took deliberate aim and shot the top of the Colonel's head off. The Colonel slumped over the live grenade from which he had just pulled the pin. An explosion raised him off the ground in two pieces.

John yelled at the Swede to come and hold Malcolm. Then he turned and ran back to where he had left Lori.

She was lying on the ground with her face in the dead leaves sobbing loudly.

John knelt down beside her and lifted her up, cradling her to his chest and gently stroking her hair.

"It's all over, Lori. Everything is all right now. The fat lady just sang."

In spite of herself, Lori began to laugh through her tears. She sat up and threw her arms around John's neck.

"Oh, John, I knew you would come. I just knew you would come."

John helped Lori to her feet and slowly walked her toward the chopper. Shaking his head and looking down at her, he said, "Boy, I thought that fat lady was never gonna' sing."

CHAPTER FORTY-TWO
SOMETIMES THE END IS JUST THE BEGINNING

Lake Tahoe, Nevada
March 19, 6:20 p.m.

The television set was tuned to the ABC nightly news and the screen had just switched from the last of the commercials back to Peter Jennings.

"And tonight, for our 'Person of the Week' segment, we make a departure from our usual singular person to choose a group of Persons of the Week. It is a group of persons who displayed great imagination, dedication, and courage in what one might call actions 'above and beyond the call of duty.'

"Our Persons of the Week are responsible for creating and bringing about a new international monetary system which will do much for making this planet a better place to live.

"Therefore we choose as our Persons of the Week:

John Garland, the man who conceived the idea for a global electronic monetary system and had the tenacity and faith to invest his own resources and time, and who risked his life to help make it a reality.

"Charles Ross and Bob Trainer, two brilliant computer experts and all those who worked with them, dedicating their time and effort to develop the hardware and software and implement the concept.

"Lorelei Young, the under secretary of Commerce, who had been sent to analyze the system's potential and was responsible for convincing the President on the systems reliability. He was literally on the line when she was kidnapped and held hostage by hired terrorists.

"And finally, all the brave men and women of Delta Mining Company and Global Computer Trading Company who were involved in nurturing and protecting the system.

"The Persons of the Week are really too numerous to mention in the short time we have here but, suffice it to say their efforts will long be remembered by those who will benefit from the new monetary system.

"Just before air time, the ABC News research department sent me a list of the changes that the new system has already brought about. "Among other things, crimes for profit in New York City has decreased 45 percent. The sale of drugs has almost come to a standstill. Congress is considering a bill which will cut taxes by 10 percent across the board because of the new tax collection methods permitted under this system. And the list goes on and on.

"We salute our Persons of the Week for having helped to bring about something that will have a worldwide effect for the betterment of all mankind."

John reached over and turned off the set and turned on the tape deck playing soft music. "Embarrassing, isn't it?"

Lori had her feet curled under her beside John on the couch. She looked rested and showed no signs of her recent ordeal. Looking at John, she smiled.

"Oh I don't know, I could add a few things about how you bribed the President and my boss to accept my resignation so we could be together. You sneaky old man."

He laughed as he glanced at her and said, "You must admit it was for a good cause."

Lori suddenly put her hand to the side of her face, "Oh my God."

John looked at her with alarm. "What, Lori? What is it?"

Lori shook her head, holding her hands to her face. "In all the excitement, I completely fortgot about Martine. What happened to that wonderful old legionnnaire who said he would die before he let anything happen to me?"

John laughed with relief and reached over and gently caressed her face. "He's fine, Lori. He's nursing a bump on his hard legionnaire head and a badly bruised ego, but he's fine. They found him in a utlity room down the hall from your office—tied up and unconscious—but all in one piece."

Lori gave a sigh of relief. "Thank God. Oh, John, I've got

to call him and tell him how much I appreciate what he went through on my account."

John smiled at Lori softly, and said, "I don't suppose you could wait until tomorrow?"

Lori took a deep breath as she relaxed and smiled coyly. "I suppose so. But first thing tomorrow I'm going to call Martine."

John nodded and pulled Lori to him. "You never did tell me what you thought about the 'cause.'"

Lori got up from the couch and walked around it to stand behind John. She reached her arms around him from behind and nuzzled his neck. "I love you so much, John. Yes, it was for a good cause. 'Cause I desperately want to be with you. Howzat for a cause?" and she kissed him on the ear.

"Seems like we had somewhat similar feelings at a little farmhouse somewhere in Maryland."

She looked dreamily out of the window at the scenery before she answered. "That was a lifetime ago."

"Yes, it was a lifetime ago. Now we have a brand new life ahead of us and it's going to begin here in the most beautiful, restful country you ever saw. No phones, no people except us. Front row seats to the most incredible sunsets you've ever experienced. The only sounds are the birds and ducks in the morning, the nightingales at night."

"And what else, Mr. John?"

"Lots of huggin', lots of kissin', lots of lovin'. "

She leaned over and nuzzled his ear again and whispered, "Can we start now?"

He glanced up at her and said, "Keep your bloomers on lady, the sun hasn't even set yet."

"And what, pray tell," she whispered, "has the setting of the sun got to with anything?"

Reaching up behind him, John pulled Lori over the back of the couch until she was lying across his lap on the couch with her head and shoulders in his arms.

"By golly," he said in mock amazement, "you're right, the

sun has nothing to do with this." And he kissed her as she slid her arms around his neck and kissed him back with a responding warmth and passion.

. . . And when one thinks about it, if the sun did have anything to do with it, it might have blushed and had the decency to sink quickly below the horizon.

The End and Perhaps a New Beginning